NEW YORK REVIEW BOOKS
CLASSICS

THE SLAVES OF SOLITUDE

PATRICK HAMILTON (1904–1962) was born in West Sussex, England. His father was a bullying alcoholic comedian and historical novelist; his mother, a sometime singer. After his mother withdrew him from Westminster School at the age of fifteen, Hamilton worked in the theater and then took up writing, publishing his first novel when he was nineteen and rapidly making a name for himself as an up-and-coming author. In 1927 Hamilton fell unhappily in love with a prostitute—an experience which was to inspire one of his masterpieces, the trilogy *Twenty Thousand Streets Under the Sky* (forthcoming from NYRB Classics). In 1932, he was badly injured and permanently disfigured after being hit by a car. Hamilton's finest works include *Hangover Square*, a Depression-era psychological thriller about intoxication, infatuation, and murder, and *The Slaves of Solitude*, a remarkable comedy about life behind the lines during World War II. Both books are marked by a mixture of black humor and, in the words of his London *Times* obituary, a sensitivity to "the loneliness, purposelessness and frustration of contemporary urban life." Hamilton also enjoyed a flourishing career as a writer of plays, several of which were made into successful movies, most notably Alfred Hitchcock's adaptation of *Rope*, starring Jimmy Stewart, and George Cukor's of *Gaslight*, which won Ingrid Bergman an Oscar. Hamilton died of cirrhosis of the liver and kidney failure after a lifetime of heavy drinking.

DAVID LODGE is a novelist and critic and Emeritus Professor of English Literature at the University of Birmingham, England. His novels include *Changing Places, Small World, Nice Work*, and *Author, Author*. His most recent works of criticism are *Consciousness and the Novel* and *The Year of Henry James*.

THE SLAVES OF SOLITUDE

PATRICK HAMILTON

Introduction by

DAVID LODGE

NEW YORK REVIEW BOOKS

New York

THIS IS A NEW YORK REVIEW BOOK
PUBLISHED BY THE NEW YORK REVIEW OF BOOKS
1755 Broadway, New York, NY 10019
www.nyrb.com

Library of Congress Cataloging-in-Publication Data
Hamilton, Patrick, 1904 Mar. 17–1962.
The slaves of solitude / by Patrick Hamilton ; introduction by David Lodge.
p. cm. — (New York Review Books classics)
ISBN-13: 978-1-59017-220-9 (alk. paper)
ISBN-10: 1-59017-220-5 (alk. paper)
1. Soldiers—United States—Fiction. 2. Middle-aged women—Fiction.
3. Single women—Fiction. 4. World War, 1939–1945—England—Fiction.
5. Boardinghouses—Fiction. 6. Great Britain—Social conditions—
20th century—Fiction. I. Title.
PR6015.A4644S57 2006
823'.912—dc22
[B]

2006034781

ISBN: 978-1-59017-220-9

Printed in the United States of America on acid-free paper.
10 9 8 7 6 5 4 3 2 1

INTRODUCTION

PATRICK Hamilton was born in 1904 into a troubled middle-class family of a kind which generates much unhappiness for its members but excellent material for fiction. In the words of his biographer, Nigel Jones, "Patrick's father was a widowed, womanizing alcoholic and a bullying, absentee patriarch. His mother Nellie was a divorced, possessive, unhappy snob and a suicide." Because of the father's feckless behavior the family were often hard up and lived for long periods in boarding houses. Patrick was taken away from Westminster School when he was only fifteen and completed his education in much-inferior institutions. He did not go to university, but had a brief career as an actor before making a promising and precocious debut as a novelist with *Monday Morning* (1925). His theatrical experience helped him write the extremely successful stage plays *Rope* (1929) and *Gas Light* (1938), which made him financially independent. But at the peak of his early celebrity he was run over by a recklessly driven car, badly injured, and facially disfigured. This misfortune accelerated an inherited tendency to alcoholism, which eventually caused his death in 1962, at the age of fifty-eight. In *Hangover Square* (1941) he wrote a powerful fictional study of this destructive addiction, set against the gathering storm clouds of World War II. Politically, Hamilton was a typical English literary Marxist of his generation, who combined an idealized view of Soviet Russia with a comfortable middle-class lifestyle and a slightly snobbish disdain for the British Labour Party. The exposure of Stalinist tyranny in the cold war period intensified his melancholy without fundamentally changing his views. He was married twice but the biographical facts indicate an unhappy sexual life and conflicted attitudes toward women, which are reflected in his fiction, especially *Hangover Square* and his trilogy, *Twenty Thousand Streets Under the Sky* (1935)—though not in *The Slaves of Solitude,* a novel notable for its empathy with the central female character.

When *The Slaves of Solitude* was published in 1947, the poet John Betjeman wrote: "I think Mr Hamilton is one of the best living novelists, and that this is the best book he has yet written." Both parts of this opinion were widely shared in the English literary world at the time. But in the 1950s, when I was a student of English literature and an aspiring novelist, I picked up no suggestions that Patrick Hamilton was a writer I should read, and by the 1960s he was completely in eclipse. This often happens to writers after their deaths, especially if their later work was generally found disappointing even by their admirers, which was Hamilton's fate (his *Gorse Trilogy*, published in the 1950s, was not well received.) In recent decades devotees of his fiction have made efforts to revive interest in it, and his reputation now stands somewhere between assured canonical status and the obscurity of the unread. *The Slaves of Solitude* was reissued as a "Twentieth Century Classic" by Oxford University Press in 1982, and similarly by Penguin in 1999, but these editions did not remain in print, and the latter, with an eloquent introduction by Michael Holroyd, is quite a rare book.

Why should this be? Perhaps Hamilton's oeuvre, considered as a whole, is not as impressive as the work of other writers of the same generation who are still widely read, like Evelyn Waugh and Graham Greene—or Henry Green, whose reputation suffered similarly after his death, but has been more successfully rehabilitated since. It seems to me, however, that there is another explanation. In our culture "classic" status is chiefly conferred by academic endorsement, and Hamilton's work does not fit easily into the categories of academic literary criticism and literary history. It was neither modernist nor consciously antimodernist, and it contained no anticipations of postmodernism. *The Slaves of Solitude* is an original, satisfying, enormously enjoyable novel, but it is hard to situate it in any particular literary style or movement. For this reason it is unlikely to appear as a "set text" in university courses on the modern British novel or attract the attention of theory-driven critics.

Hamilton is a realistic novelist, with obvious roots in the English tradition and an eclectic technique. He is sometimes compared to Dickens, whom he read with enthusiasm from an early age, and there is certainly a Dickensian quality in his comic characterization and occasional passages of heightened rhetorical prose. But there is also an affinity with Jane Austen, especially evident in *The Slaves of Solitude*, in the minute analysis of manners in a small closed community—manners in the old-fashioned sense that also includes "morals." The analysis is rendered primarily through the consciousness of the central character, but Hamilton shifts the narrative point of view to other characters, or interpolates an authorial comment, whenever it suits his purpose, disregarding the Jamesian principle that intensity and beauty of effect in fiction require the consistent adoption of a limited point of view. This description makes *The Slaves of Solitude* sound like a rather naively or clumsily written book, yet it is quite the reverse: it is subtle, surprising, and perfectly formed for its artistic purposes.

The Slaves of Solitude is a novel about the Second World War—indeed it is one of the very best English novels written about that war—yet it contains no descriptions of combat or death and destruction caused by warfare. The soldiers who appear in it are always seen off duty. The heroine, Miss Roach, is an unexceptional single woman aged thirty-nine who works in a humble capacity for a publishing firm in London, commuting from a boarding house in Thames Lockdon, a small riverside town at a safe distance from the capital. Most of the action takes place in this boarding house, still incongruously known by its pre-war name, the Rosamund Tea Rooms, and in the pubs round about. (The contrast between the repressiveness of boarding-house life and the spurious, alcohol-fueled bonhomie of pub culture is a key structural component of the novel: Hamilton was a consummate observer of both institutions.) The story begins in the winter of 1943. There is a lull in the bombing of London; the tide of war is turning against Nazi Germany, especially in the east, and Thames Lockdon, like the rest of the country, is full of American soldiers preparing for the opening of a Second Front. But for Miss Roach and the other principal characters, mostly lonely aging genteel men and women of limited means, the war in Europe, with all its epic carnage and horror and suffering, could be happening on another planet: it is known to them only through rumor and speculation and the partial reporting of newspapers and newsreels. Their war consists of the blackout, shortages, ration books, and a thousand petty restrictions and inconveniences, of which, for Miss Roach, who was "bombed out" of her London flat, the most burdensome is having to live in the boarding house, occupying a dreary bedroom lit by a feeble bulb with a stained-oak bed and a "pink bedspread which shone and slithered and fell off... and the stained-oak chest of drawers with its mirror held precariously at a suitable angle with a squashed match-box," and having to eat her meals in the common dining room, sharing a table with the unbearable Mr. Thwaites.

Mr. Thwaites is a great comic creation, who has the tireless malice and negative energy of Dickens's villains—Quilp, Fagin, Squeers, Bounderby, Pecksniff. Not that Thwaites commits any crime, or inflicts any physical pain on his victim, Miss Roach. He tortures her purely through language, through the manipulation and exploitation of the conventions of polite conversation which apply to middle-class communal eating. Hamilton is a master of what linguists call "pragmatics" and philosophers call "speech act theory" and theatrical directors call "actions," all based on the principle that every utterance, however trivial, is not only saying something, but *doing* something to the addressee, by tone, by implication, by allusion, or by some other means. What Mr. Thwaites is invariably doing to Miss Roach is bullying her; by, for example, forcing her to deny things which she has never affirmed in order to extricate herself from false imputations. By this means he exerts control over her. Thus the first remark he addresses to her at table in the novel is:

"'*Your* friends seem to be mightily distinguishing themselves as usual,' and oh God, thought Miss Roach, not that again, not that again." This remark is Mr. Thwaites's way of referring to Russian victories on the Eastern Front. He himself was an admirer of Hitler before the war, and is rabidly opposed to communism; the success of the Russian armies in the Allied cause is therefore a source of displeasure to him, though he dare not admit as much, so he seeks to dissociate himself from it by gratuitously associating the Russians with Miss Roach, while at the same time devaluing it by the dismissive phrase "as usual." Miss Roach attempts to counter this move, which she understands very well, by remaining silent, but Mr. Thwaites insists on repeating it, so the code of polite conversation forces her to reply, first by pretending not to understand: "Who're *my* friends?" "Your *Russian* friends," says Thwaites. "They're not *my* friends," says Miss Roach "any more than anybody else." And when Mrs. Barratt, who shares the table, comes to her support by saying, "You must admit they're putting up a wonderful fight, Mr. Thwaites," he replies, "Oh yes... They're putting up a fight all right." His omission of Mrs. Barratt's epithet, "wonderful," is full of implication: "the savage and sombre way in which he said this suggested that they were not putting up a fight as other and decent people would, or that they were only doing so because they jolly well had to, or that their motives were of a kind which he did not care to make public." Then, as he usually does when his argumentative strategy is blocked, Mr. Thwaites proceeds to torture his victims indirectly by torturing the English language, making remarks in a ghastly idiolect full of phoney archaism, stage dialect, threadbare cliché, and proverbial bromides: "I Keeps my Counsel, like the

Wise Old Bird . . . I Hay ma Doots . . . as the Scotchman said—of Yore." It is equally impossible to reply to these remarks either in their own style or in normal English, so the listeners are obliged to endure them in silence as long as the meal lasts, and at every meal. "Now, after more than a year of it, Mr. Thwaites was president in hell."

Hamilton is taking a risk with this hyperbolic metaphor, which is repeated more than once. It invites the reflection that in 1943 there was a real hell elsewhere, in Auschwitz, in Stalingrad, in a thousand places—so why bother with these trivial boarding-house conflicts? But Hamilton is making the valid point that all suffering is relative. We feel most keenly what most immediately affects us, and although we may be cognitively aware of much greater and more terrible suffering than our own (as Miss Roach shows herself to be on several occasions) it can never engage our thoughts and emotions with the same intensity. Furthermore there is a kind of equivalence between the struggles in the great theater of war and in the boarding house; in both good is pitted against evil, decency against devilry, and the fact that this opening exchange in the Rosamund Tea Rooms actually refers to the real war underlines the connection between microcosm and macrocosm. It is a connection which is maintained throughout the novel as it follows Miss Roach's fortunes. (At this point the first-time reader may prefer to put aside this introduction and return to it after reading the novel, since what follows reveals a good deal of the plot.)

"Miss Roach." I cannot think of another English novel whose heroine and principal "center of consciousness" is referred to in such a formal style. (Muriel Spark's Miss Brodie is presented only through the eyes and thoughts of her "girls.") About halfway into the book the narrator reveals that Miss Roach has "the unfortunate Christian name of Enid," but she is addressed by it only once, to her displeasure, in the diminutive form of "Eeny." She is "Miss Roach," naturally, to the other inhabitants of the boarding house and its proprietor, but it is strange that she should be "Miss Roach" to the narrator of a novel which gives us access to her most intimate thoughts and emotions. It is what stylisticians call a foregrounded phrase: what would be automatic and insignificant in its familiar context becomes highly expressive when used in another context. In this novelistic context "Miss Roach" establishes a cool distance between narrator and character: Hamilton observes his heroine with respect and sympathy but not without irony—this is not a sentimental novel of special pleading.

"Miss Roach" also emphasizes the heroine's celibate spinsterhood, the "solitude" of the title. At the outset of the story she is resigned to this fate, but the circumstances of war put her in the path of a genial American, Lieutenant Pike, who seems to offer her the prospect of "love" and "marriage" (ideas so unlikely that she can only contemplate them in quotes). He takes her to pubs, plies her with drink, gives her respite from Mr. Thwaites by buying her dinners, and kisses her enthusiastically on park benches in the blackout dark. ("On the whole she disliked this at first, but after a while she found that she disliked it a great deal less.") His appearances are separated by long unexplained absences, but just when she decides that his "almost explicit offers" of marriage after the war are all moonshine, he turns up again, eager to lure her out of the boarding house and into a pub. On one such occasion when she objects to his calling her "Eeny" he says, "Well, what am I to call you? . . . I can't very well call you Roach." She replies, "Well—I'd rather that than Eeny," and being drunk he says: "All right, then. I'll call you Roach. How are you, Roach?" But in all their other conversations he never addresses her by name at all, thus ensuring that the character of the heroine remains, for the reader, inseparable from "Miss Roach." The title slightly softens the ugly sound and unpleasant associations of the surname, about which Miss Roach has been teased in her schoolmistress past.

The next disturbance of the repressed but relatively calm tenor of her customary life is provoked by Vicki Kugelmann, a single woman of about Miss Roach's age, of German extraction though a British citizen since childhood. They became acquainted when Miss Roach defended her in public against anti-German prejudice, but when Vicki moves into the boarding house she shows herself to be as much of a monster as Mr. Thwaites. Like Thwaites she has her own ghastly idiolect, composed of slightly out-of-date and mildly suggestive slang expressions, and like Thwaites she takes a sadistic delight in teasing and taunting Miss Roach with this language, and by flirting with Lieutenant Pike. She also has an intensely irritating habit of walking uninvited into Miss Roach's room, picking up her comb, and combing her own hair with it, a double violation of privacy. When she does this one night, after returning from a drunken and dissipated expedition to a roadhouse (a wonderfully orchestrated episode), and defends her behavior by saying "You are not sporty. You must learn to be sporty, Miss Prude," Miss Roach "knew she hated Vicki Kugelmann as she had never hated any woman in her life." In the course of a sleepless night she goes over Vicki's sayings in her throbbing head, drawing out their spiteful implications, and gradually demonizing her into a crypto-Nazi and possible German spy. But she is recalled to reality by the sound of bombers overhead "coming back from burning and burying and exploding German Vickis, German small children, German charwomen and others . . . It was all very confusing, and she fumbled in the purring dark for another aspirin with her next sip of water."

Miss Roach's struggle to retain her sanity and sense of proportion under extreme provocation is one of the most sympathetic traits of her character. But it is "war to the death" between herself and Vicki. Perceiving this, Mr. Thwaites, who himself becomes grotesquely infatuated with Vicki, stirs up the animosity between the two women, and their table is charged with tension at every meal. Of the regular boarders, only Mr. Prest, an out-of-work actor, perceives with sympathy for Miss Roach that "something pretty nasty was going on between those three, one way and another," but he leaves the boarding house as the atmosphere worsens with the approach of Christmas. "Ah—that Christmas!—that Christmas of hatred, fear, pain, terror, and disgrace!"

The absence of any hint of religious transcendence in the celebration of Christmas at the Rosamund Tea Rooms—not even a single carol is sung or heard—intensifies its hellishness. But the action reaches its climax on one of the hungover days following Christmas, when "deathly dullness and boredom gripped the house, whose guests looked at the end of the year, and the beginning of the next, with misery and stupefaction." Like so many passages in the novel this scene is all about the interpretation of speech acts—but with a difference. Goaded beyond endurance, Miss Roach finally abandons the code of polite conversation and demands that Vicki and Mr. Thwaites declare what they have so far merely insinuated—Vicki in her pious hopes for peace with "understanding" for Germany, and Thwaites in his oblique sneers about Miss Roach's person and personality. Pursuing Thwaites up the stairs with her interrogation ("*Will you tell me what you're talking about, Mr. Thwaites?*"), she finally provokes him into an explicit insult, upon which she furiously pushes him in the chest. The surprised old tyrant falls down.

That night Mr. Thwaites is taken ill, and within two days he is dead, from peritonitis, his last delirious words being "Dame Roach." Even when she is assured by a doctor that her push was not contributory, she feels she is in disgrace and prepares to move back to London, though in fact it is Vicki who is asked to leave by the landlady—sweet revenge for Miss Roach. New developments and revelations come thick and fast. She receives news of a modest legacy, which is particularly welcome since the only temporary accommodation she can get in London is at one of its classiest hotels, Claridge's—the very antithesis of the Rosamund Tea Rooms. Mr. Prest the actor informs her that Lieutenant Pike has been going about the country proposing marriage to scores of women ("so this was the final touch to her 'romance'") and invites her to come and see him in a pantomime at the Theatre Royal, Wimbledon. In a subtle way the conventional triumph of good over evil in the pantomime echoes and confirms the redemption of Miss Roach from the hell of the boarding house. She finds Mr. Prest transformed by his success with the largely juvenile audience in the role of the wicked but comic uncle (a benign version of Thwaites, one might say), and for the first time in the novel a note of spiritual transcendence is sounded. "There was an extraordinary look of purification about the man—a suggestion of reciprocal purification—as if he had just at that moment with his humour purified the excited children, and they, all as one, had purified him . . . And, observing the purification of Mr. Prest, Miss Roach herself felt purified."

Miss Roach's story has a kind of "happy ending," but it is not a sentimental one. There is no hint of anything more than friendship with Mr. Prest. Her employer is kind to her and gives her dinner at Claridge's, but goes off afterwards to another assignation. Miss Roach enjoys a long hot bath, knowing nothing, the narrator observes, "of the February blitz shortly to descend on London, knowing nothing of flying bombs, knowing nothing of rockets, of Normandy, of Arnhem, of the Ardennes bulge, of Berlin, of the Atom Bomb." Who can tell if she will survive the February blitz to live through the other events? Meanwhile she is still the "slave of her task-master, solitude." Although she enjoys the unwonted luxury of her spacious bedroom, "the presence of the other bed made her feel that she was sleeping with the unhappy ghost of herself . . . And then she decided that she felt like sleeping, and would probably have a good night and so everything was all right, in fact very nice." The novel ends, surprisingly, but perfectly, with a prayer: "at last she put out the light, turned over, and adjusted the pillow, and hopefully composed her mind for sleep—God help us, God help all of us, every one, all of us."

—David Lodge

THE SLAVES OF SOLITUDE

AUTHOR'S NOTE

In *The Slaves of Solitude*, whose characters are entirely fictitious, Thames Lockdon bears a rough geographical and external resemblance to Henley-on-Thames. The Rosamund Tea Rooms, however, resembles no boarding-house in this town or in any other, though it is hoped that it resembles in some features every small establishment of this sort all over the country.

CHAPTER ONE

I

LONDON, the crouching monster, like every other monster has to breathe, and breathe it does in its own obscure, malignant way. Its vital oxygen is composed of suburban working men and women of all kinds, who every morning are sucked up through an infinitely complicated respiratory apparatus of trains and termini into the mighty congested lungs, held there for a number of hours, and then, in the evening, exhaled violently through the same channels.

The men and women imagine they are going into London and coming out again more or less of their own free will, but the crouching monster sees all and knows better.

The area affected by this filthy inhalation actually extends beyond what we ordinarily think of as the suburbs—to towns, villages, and districts as far as, or further than, twenty-five miles from the capital. Amongst these was Thames Lockdon, which lay on the river some miles beyond Maidenhead on the Maidenhead line.

The conditions were those of intense war, intense winter, and intensest black-out in the month of December. The engine carrying the 6.3 from Paddington steamed into Thames Lockdon station at about a quarter past seven. It arrived up against buffers, for Thames Lockdon was a terminus, and it hissed furiously. That hiss, in the blackness of the station, might have been the sound of the crouching monster's last, exhausted, people-expelling breath in this riverside outpost of its daily influence and domain. Or it might, tonight, merely have been the engine hissing through its teeth against the cold.

One waiting at the barrier to meet a friend could see compartment doors being flung open rapidly everywhere (as though some sort of panic had occurred within the train), and the next in the middle of the room and which was shaded by pink parchment. She saw the pink artificial-silk bedspread covering the light single bed built of stained-oak—the pink bedspread which shone and slithered and fell off, the light bedstead which slid along the wooden floor if you bumped into it. She saw the red chequered cotton curtains (this side of the black-out material) which were hung on a brass rail and never quite met in the middle, or, if forced to meet in a moment of impatience, came flying away from the sides; she saw the stained-oak chest of drawers with its mirror held precariously at a suitable angle with a squashed match-box. She saw the wicker table by the bed, on which lay her leather illuminated clock, but no lamp, for Mrs. Payne was not a believer in reading in bed. She saw the gas-fire, with its asbestos columns yellow and crumbling, and its gas-ring. She saw the small porcelain wash-basin with Running H. and C. (the H. impetuously H. at certain dramatic moments, but frequently not Running but feebly dribbling—the C. bitterly C. yet steadfastly Running). She saw the pink wall-paper, which bore the mottled pattern of a disease of the flesh; and in one corner were piled her "books", treasures which she had saved from the bombing in London, but for which she had not yet obtained a shelf.

Such was Miss Roach's pink boudoir in Thames Lockdon before dinner at night. Before washing she looked at what she could see of herself in the mirror—at the thin, bird-like nose and face, and the healthy complexion—too healthy for beauty—the open-air, sun-and-wind complexion of a uniform red-brick colour, of a texture and colour to which it would be impossible or absurd to apply make-up of any sort. She had, she knew, the complexion of a farmer's wife and the face of a bird. Her eyes, too, were bird-like—blackly brown, liquid, loving, appealing, confused. Her hair was of a nondescript brown colour, and she parted it in the middle. She was only thirty-nine, but she might have been taken for forty-five. She had given up "hope" years ago. She had never actually had any "hope".

Like so many of her kind—the hopeless—she was too amiable and tried too hard in company and conversation, and so sometimes gave an air, untrue to her character, of being genteel.

Oddly enough, though "hopeless", she had only recently had an offer of marriage—this from an elderly accountant in the publisher's firm in which she worked—a mean, impossible man who had somehow perceived her possibilities. As she sensitively and kindly rejected him in the taxi that night, with "No—it's impossible—I'm very sorry, but I'm afraid it's *impossible*!", her liquid, loving eyes, looking shyly out of the taxi window, were probably less those of one sympathising with the man she was rejecting (though they were this, too) than of one contemplating, with pensive resigned sadness, the joy which would have been hers had she now been receiving, or had ever in her life received, an offer which she could reasonably accept.

She had a slim, straight figure, but she was slightly flat-chested. She was the daughter of a dentist. She had two brothers, one of whom, the youngest of the family, had recently been killed in the air. The other, older than she and from whom she heard about once every two years, was in Brazil. Both her parents were dead. She had matriculated, and had at one time been a schoolmistress in a boys' preparatory school at Hove.

When she had been bombed out of her room in Kensington, escaping with her life (for she was in the West End at the time) but with only a few of her small possessions, she had come down to Thames Lockdon and the Rosamund Tea Rooms at the invitation of her aunt, who had let her sleep in her room. Since then her aunt had moved on to Guildford to friends, and she had been given this room of her own at the top.

Thames Lockdon had been "heaven", then, with its dark, still nights, over which the sirens occasionally came yelling triumphantly forth, only to be gradually snubbed by the profound silence of the firmament, undisturbed even by the distant sound of guns and bombs, which followed. And she had been made a fuss of, then, a sort of heroine indeed, and given a fortnight's holiday. And the town was "pretty", and the food "very good", and the people "very nice"—even Mr. Thwaites had seemed "very nice".

But now, after more than a year of it, Mr. Thwaites was president in hell.

She would have gone back to London if she had known where to go, or if she had not still feared guns and bombs at night, or if she could have summoned up enough initiative at any given moment.

When she had washed she heard the tinny Oriental gong being hit pettishly by Mrs. Payne. Before going down to dinner, however, she paused in her room, listening at her door for Mr. Thwaites' voice as he came out of the Lounge on his way down to the dining-room on the ground floor. Although she had to have dinner at the same table with him, her feelings towards Mr. Thwaites were of such a nature that she desired to put off the evil moment, to spare herself even the risk of an encounter with him outside the Lounge door, and the consequent necessity of walking down the stairs with him to eat. This morbid conduct she called to herself "letting him get down first".

3

About the dining-room there was something peculiarly and gratuitously hellish. For this quite small room, with its bow-window jutting out on to the street, had once been the famous Tea Room itself!—the room into which, long ago, the seeker after tea in the street had hastily glimpsed, or perhaps rudely stared, rapidly absorbing through his pores the quality of the cakes, the class and quantity of the customers, the size of the room, the cleanliness of the cloths, and the comfort of the chairs, before making his decision to enter or go elsewhere! . . . And since those days hardly anything had been changed: all that had happened, practically, was that all the Tea Room now belonged to all the boarders at all the meal-times. (Mrs. Payne spoke with complacency of "Separate Tables" on her printed leaflet.) There was the same slippery oilcloth of parquet pattern: there were the same tables covered with red chequered cloth: the same cheap black wooden chairs with rush seats: the same red chequered curtains (this side, never let it be forgotten, of the black-out material): the same passepartouted etchings of country cottages on the wall. . . . Ghosts of hot riverside trippers still haunted this room—ghosts of exhausted families, of sweating fathers shyly rebuking their children, of young men with open collars and a look of sunburned eczema, of timid husbands and wives exchanging no word with each other in corners, of cyclists with packs, and all the rest. . . . And it was this distant yet indelible air of populous summer which brought home to the heart, so gloomily, the present cold and bleakness of the boarding-house in winter and war and black-out.

The red chequered tables were, of course, fewer in number than in those days, and what remained were huddled in relation to the gas-fire in the middle of the wall opposite the window. The room was lit by two electric bulbs hanging from the ceiling —these bulbs being as weak in spirit as the one in Miss Roach's bedroom, and shaded by the same pink parchment.

The table for four, at which Mr. Thwaites sat, occupied the best situation in regard to the fire, and Miss Roach and Mrs. Barratt sat at this table. The other guests sat at tables for two, either in couples or by themselves.

This system of separate tables, well meant as it may have been, added yet another hellish touch to the hellish melancholy prevailing. For, in the small space of the room, a word could not be uttered, a little cough could not be made, a hairpin could not be dropped at one table without being heard at all the others; and the general self-consciousness which this caused smote the room with a silence, a conversational torpor, and finally a complete apathy from which it could not stir itself. No one, it seemed, dared to speak above the level of a murmur, and two people, sitting at the same table and desiring to talk to each other, in order not to call attention to themselves, to enable the whole room to enter into the question and reply of their conversation, were compelled to employ that adenoidal, furtive, semi-audible tone such as is used by two lovers about to kiss each other.

Sometimes an attempt at a conversational jailbreak was made, and there would be some unnecessarily loud and cheerful exchanges between table and table: but this never had any hope of success. As the maid handed round the vegetables one voice dropped down after another: the prisoners were back in their cells more subdued than ever.

Mrs. Payne would, of course, have done better to have reverted to the practice of her boarding-house forebears, and have put back—in place of this uncanny segregation in the midst of propinquity—the long table with herself at the top dominating a free, frank intercourse in which all would be obliged to join as at a party. But no such step backwards had entered her mind, and, in the existing state of affairs, she made no attempt to assist her guests in their predicament, for she was careful never to appear at meals.

It was in this respect that Mr. Thwaites yielded, unwittingly, a certain measure of relief. For long periods the self-conscious guests gave up any attempt at talking, and listened to Mr. Thwaites, who was not self-conscious.

4

"*Oh, how the lodgers yell*
When they hear the dinner bell! . . ."

went the old parody of the hymn. But all that exuberance has gone into the distant past. They enter now, not yelling, but slinking, murmuring, in a desultory manner, often three or four minutes late.

When Miss Roach came in they were all in their places and no one was speaking.

Mr. Prest was at his separate table, and Miss Steele was at hers. The two new war-time guests—the two shy American "Lootenants" who had only arrived yesterday—were at their table for two in a corner by themselves. Mr. Thwaites and Mrs. Barratt were at the table at which she had to sit.

How she had originally got "put" at this table Miss Roach could not remember, but there was nothing to be done about it now. Nothing, that is, apart from asking to be put at a separate table, which, in a room and atmosphere of this sort, would bring about a sensation such as she was incapable of causing.

"Ah—good evening, Miss Roach," said Mr. Thwaites, and she saw his moustached, elderly face giving her a funny, slightly nasty look. It was a look (or so it seemed to her acutely sensitive imagination) which seemed to be conscious of her having dodged him on the journey downstairs from the Lounge and of his having lost thereby a moment or so of good torturing-time, and for this reason it was a faintly rebuking, menacing look. At the same time this look bore traces of gratification at having got her safely now, of relief at the fact that she was back and was going to be present at dinner to be tortured—after all, she might have somehow managed to have got a meal with a friend outside. Mr. Thwaites was certainly on Miss Roach's "nerves".

"Good evening, Mr. Thwaites," she said. "Good evening, Mrs. Barratt. . . ." And she smiled feebly at both as she sat down.

This Thwaites was a big, tall man, anything between sixty and seventy. He had a fresh complexion, and was, for his years, and for one who took practically no exercise, unusually healthy and virile. He resounded, nasally and indefatigably, with a steady health and virility. He was, above all, a steady man in all his ways. In his large, flat, moustached face (with its slightly flattened nose, as though someone in the past had punched it), in his lethargic yet watchful brown eyes, in his way of walking and his way of talking, there could be discerned the steady, self-absorbed, dreamy, almost somnambulistic quality of the lifelong trampler through the emotions of others, of what Miss Roach would call the "bully". That steady look with which as a child he would have torn off a butterfly's wing, with which as a boy he would have twisted another boy's wrist, with which as a man he would have humiliated a servant or inferior, was upon him as he now looked at Miss Roach; it never entirely left him. He had money of his own and he had lived, resounded through boarding-houses and private hotels all his life. Such places, with the timid old women they contained, were hunting-grounds for his temperament—wonderfully suited and stimulating to his peculiar brand of loquacity and malevolence. He was as unfamiliar with toil as he was with exercise. He had at one time had a family connection with a firm of solicitors in London; but here he had never worked seriously, save at the task of torturing clerks and typists. "Ah—I Knows the Law", or "Ah—I Happens to Know the Law" were favourite expressions of his. He was particularly fond of this facetious substitution of the third in place of the first person in the verb.

He had further narrowed his mind by a considerable amount of travel abroad, where he had again always made his way to the small hotels. He was noticeably clean in his person, and wore high white collars and old-fashioned ties with a tiepin. He wore suits of durable material, coats with high lapels, trousers which did not turn up at the bottom, and elastic-sided boots.

He could make himself agreeable when he wished, and had frequently been known to charm old ladies in the early stages of his acquaintanceship with them, going out of his way to do small services for them. Behind their backs, however, he would speak of them, to fellow-guests or servants, as "old frumps", "desiccated spinsters", and so forth.

Having said "Good evening" and looked at Miss Roach, Mr. Thwaites had nothing more to say at the moment, and no one else in the room spoke as Sheila, the Irish maid-of-all-work, now working as a waitress and dressed as such, hurried about putting plates of soup on the table.

This soup, like the rest of the food, came up on a small service lift hidden behind a screen in a corner of the room. The lift-shaft communicated directly with the kitchen underneath, and conversations frequently took place through this medium between whoever was serving the guests above and whoever was serving the lift below—enquiries, comments, and sometimes remarks of a censorious nature being hurled down from above in the hearing of the guests, and appropriate rejoinders from below feebly making their way to the surface amidst the rumbling of the lift. In the long pauses, when no one was talking, the guests listened, in a hypnotised way, to these back-stage noises and manœuvres.

Soon after Mr. Thwaites had started upon his soup—which he always sprinkled, first of all with lumps of bread, and then with pepper, with a vigour and single-mindedness which displeased Miss Roach—he opened the conversation.

"Well," he said. "*Your* friends seem to be mightily distinguishing themselves as usual," and oh God, thought Miss Roach, not that again, not that again.

5

Miss Roach's "friends"—according to Mr. Thwaites—were the Russian people, and Mr. Thwaites did not like or approve of these people at all. Indeed, it would not be exaggerating to say that the resistance and victories of the Russian people in the last year had practically ruined this man's peace of mind—a state of affairs which was aggravated bitterly by the fact that he was unable fully to vent his mind upon the matter in public.

Mr. Thwaites had since 1939 slowly learned to swallow the disgrace of Hitler, of whom he had been from the beginning, and still secretly remained, a hot disciple. He could now even force himself to speak disparagingly of Hitler: but to speak well of the Russians was too much for him. He could not mention them save gloweringly, defensively, almost savagely. He had also undergone the misfortune of capturing Moscow and Leningrad within three weeks of the outbreak of the war, and so his boarding-house sagacity had been struck at along with his personal feelings.

Actually the Russians were not in any very particular sense Miss Roach's "friends". Miss Roach was too completely bewildered, stunned, and unhappy in regard to all that was happening in the world around her for this to be so. But Miss Roach sometimes brought back literary political weeklies from London, and had been foolish enough to leave them about in the Lounge, and this, in the eyes of Mr. Thwaites, was in itself a diseased and obscurely Russian thing to do. He had therefore come practically to identify Russia with Miss Roach; and in the same way as Russia gnawed at him, he gnawed at Miss Roach.

Miss Roach now tried to dodge his fury, to apologise, in so far as it was possible, for the present state of affairs on the Eastern Front, by smiling, making a vaguely assenting and agreeable noise in her throat, and looking hard and giddily at her soup. But Mr. Thwaites was not the sort of man who would permit you to look at your soup when he was anxious to talk about the Russians.

"I said," he said, looking at her, "*your* friends seem to be mightily distinguishing themselves, as usual."

"Who're *my* friends?" murmured Miss Roach, and she was, of course, aware that the rest of the room was listening intently. Sitting at the same table with Mr. Thwaites, and having him talk at you directly, was very much like being called out in front of class at school.

"Your *Russian* friends," said Mr. Thwaites, who was never afraid of coming to the point. There was a pause.

"They're not *my* friends . . ." said Miss Roach, wrigglingly, intending to convey that although she was friendly enough to the Russians, she was not more friendly than anybody else, and could not therefore be expected to take all the blame in the

Rosamund Tea Rooms for their recent victories. But this was too subtle for Mr. Thwaites.

"What do you mean," he said, "they're not your friends?"

"Well," said Miss Roach, "they're not my friends any more than anybody else." And here Mrs. Barratt came to her rescue, as she often did.

"Well," said Mrs. Barratt. "You must admit they're putting up a wonderful fight, Mr. Thwaites."

Mrs. Barratt was a grey-haired, stoutish, pince-nezed, slow-moving woman of about sixty-five, with an unhappy and pallid appearance which probably derived from the preoccupation which secretly dominated her life—a preoccupation in pills, medicines and remedies for minor internal complaints—for indigestion, constipation, acidity, liver, rheumatism—as advertised in the daily newspapers and elsewhere. An elderly believer in magic, with passion yet patience she sought and sought for ideal remedies, without ever finding what she sought, but without ever a thought of abandoning her quest. Mrs Barratt's eyes, behind her enlarging pince-nez, bore, if one could but see it, the wan, indefatigable, midnight-oil look of one who yet had faith in the Philosopher's Stone of the sedentary sufferer inside. She gave her mind over to research, and her body over to endless experiment upon herself. No new advertisement in the paper, with a fresh angle, approach, or appeal, ever escaped her close inspection, nor did any article "By a Doctor" or "By a Harley Street Specialist". She grew iller and iller—an ageing, eerie product of the marriage between modern commercial methods and modern medicine. Her outward behaviour was, however, entirely normal, and the Rosamund Tea Rooms had no knowledge of the influences which in fact dominated her life, though it noticed the many different pills and patent foods which appeared from time to time upon her table. She had a kind heart and now came to the rescue of Miss Roach.

"Oh yes," said Mr. Thwaites. "They're putting up a fight all right."

And the savage and sombre way in which he said this suggested that they were not putting up a fight as other and decent people would, or that they were only doing so because they jolly well had to, or that their motives were of a kind which he did not care to make public.

"You know," said Mrs. Barratt, "I don't think you really like the Russians, Mr. Thwaites. I don't think you realise what they're doing for us."

"No," said Miss Roach, taking heart, "I don't believe he does."

Mr. Thwaites was momentarily taken aback by this unexpected resistance, and there was a pause in which his eyes went glassy.

"Ah," he said at last. "Don't I? . . . Don't I? . . . Well, perhaps I don't. . . . Maybe I thinks more than I says. Maybe I has my private views. . . ."

Oh God, thought Miss Roach, now he was beginning his ghastly I-with-the-third-person business. As if bracing herself for a blow (as she looked at the tablecloth), she waited for more, and more came.

"I Keeps my Counsel," said Mr. Thwaites, in his slow treacly voice. "Like the Wise Old Owl, I Sits and Keeps my Counsel."

Miss Roach, shuddering under this agonisingly Thwaitesian remark—Thwaitesian in the highest and richest tradition—knew well enough that there was more to follow. For it was a further defect of Mr. Thwaites that when he had made a remark which he thought good, which he himself subtly realised as being Thwaitesian, he was unable to resist repeating it, either in an inverted or a slightly altered form. He did not fail to do so on this occasion.

"Yes," he said, "I Keeps my Counsel, like the Wise Old Bird. . . . I Happens to keep my Counsel. . . . I Happens to be like the Wise Old Bird. . . ."

And in the silence that followed, broken only by the scraping of soup-spoons on plates, the whole room, with all its occupants, seemed to have to tremble in hushed reverence before the totally unforeseen and awful Bird which had materialised in its midst—its wisdom and unearthly reticence. . . . Miss Roach guessed that honour was now satisfied, and that this would be enough. It was not, however, enough. With Mr. Thwaites nothing was ever enough.

"I Hay ma Doots, that's all . . ." said Mr. Thwaites. "I Hay ma Doots . . ."

(He is *not*, thought Miss Roach, going to add "as the Scotchman said," is he? *Surely* he is not going to add "as the Scotchman said"?)

"As the Scotchman said," said Mr. Thwaites. "Yes . . . I Hay ma Doots, as the Scotchman said—of Yore. . . ."

(Only Mr. Thwaites, Miss Roach realised, could, as it were, have out-Thwaited Thwaites and brought "of Yore" from the bag like that.)

The room, which had by this time finished its soup, maintained its stupefied silence—a silence permeated and oppressed, of course, by the knowledge that Mr. Thwaites, in regard to the Russians, kept his counsel like the wise old bird, and hayed his doots as the Scotchman said of yore. If he had nothing else, Mr. Thwaites had personality in a dining-room. The maid went round quietly removing the soup-plates . . .

"Ah, Wheel . . ." said Mr. Thwaites, philosophically, and by some curious process of association identifying himself with the Scotchman of yore whom he had quoted. "Ah, Wheel . . ."

And again, as the maid replaced the soup-plates with the plates of warm spam and mashed potatoes, the room seemed to have to echo reverently Mr. Thwaites' "Ah, Wheel", and to be bathing in the infinite Scottish acumen with which it had been uttered.

"Oh, well," said Mr. Thwaites a little later, briskly returning to his own race and language, and with a note of challenge, "we'll all be equal soon, no doubt."

This, clearly, was another stab at the Russians. The Russians, in Mr. Thwaites' embittered vision, were undoubtedly perceived as being "all equal", and so if the Germans went on retreating westward (and if Miss Roach went on approving of it and doing nothing about it) before long we should, all of us, be "all equal".

"My Lady's Maid," continued Mr. Thwaites, "will soon be giving orders to My Lady. And Milord will be Polishing the Pot-boy's boots."

Failing to see that he had already over-reached himself in anticipating very far from equal conditions, Mr. Thwaites went on.

"The Cabby," he said, resignedly, "will take it unto himself to give the orders, I suppose—and the pantry-boy tell us how to proceed on our ways."

Still no one had anything to say, and Mr. Thwaites, now carried away both by his own vision and his own style, went on to portray a state of society such as might have recommended itself to the art of the surrealist, or appeared in the dreams of an opium-smoker.

"The Coalman, no doubt, will see fit to give commands to the King," he said, "and the Navvy lord it gaily o'er the man of wealth. The Banker will bow the knee to the Crossing-Sweeper, I expect, and the millionaire take his wages from the passing Tramp."

And there was yet another silence as Mr. Thwaites gazed into the distance seeking further luxuriant images. He had, however, now exhausted himself on this head, and for half a minute one could hear only the clatter of knives and forks upon plates. . . .

"The Lord Forefend," said Mr. Thwaites, at last. "The Lord, in His grace, Forefend. . . ."

And Miss Roach had a fleeting hope in her heart that, with this little prayer, the discussion, or rather monologue, might be terminated. But Mr. Thwaites, suddenly aware of the quietness which had for so long surrounded him, and sensing, perhaps, that it was a little too heavy to be wholly applauding, looked around him and did not hesitate to throw down the gauntlet.

"At least," he said, looking straight at Miss Roach, "that's what *you* want, isn't it?"

Miss Roach, putting food into her mouth, now gave as clever an imitation as she was able of one who was not being looked at at all, but knew how futile such an endeavour was.

"I gather that's what *you* want," said Mr. Thwaites, "isn't it?"

This was the whole trouble. It was always *she* who had to bear the brunt, *she* who had to be made the whipping-boy in public for his private furies and chagrins.

"No," she said, her voice insecure with humiliation and anger, "it's not what *I* want, Mr. Thwaites."

"Oh," said Mr. Thwaites, "isn't it? That's funny. I thought it was."

Here Miss Steele, who sat at a table by herself, behind Miss Roach but in view of Mr. Thwaites, took a turn at helping her out.

Miss Steele was a thin, quiet woman of about sixty, who used rouge and powder somewhat heavily, whose white, frizzy, well-kept hair had the appearance of being, without being, a wig, and whose whole manner gave the impression of her having had, without her having had, a past. Miss Steele affected infinite shrewd worldly wisdom acquired in this imaginary past, reticence in conversation (she prided herself that she "never opened her mouth unless she had something to say"), and the spirit of modernity generally. She was careful to avow at all times her predilection for "fun", for "cocktails", for "broadmindedness", for those who in common with her were "cursed" with a sense of humour, and for the company of young people as opposed to "old fogies" like herself. But she had, in fact, little fun, no cocktails, and no company younger than that furnished by the Rosamund Tea Rooms. She was also advanced in the matter of culture, for she had "no time for modern novels". Instead she read endless Boots' biographies of historical characters, and was, in fact, a historian. This came in handy, for if you "happened to know a little something about History", you were able to compare present events with those in the past, and roughly see how things would be going in the future. All this, of course, made Mr. Thwaites furious, and he would have used her as the Rosamund Tea Rooms whipping-boy had he not been a little afraid of her and had he not already fixed upon Miss Roach. Behind her not unpitiful and not uncourageous little shams, Miss Steele had, like Mrs. Barratt, a kind and sensible heart.

"Well," said Miss Steele, "there's a lot to be said on both sides, really, isn't there, Mr. Thwaites?"

"What?" said Mr. Thwaites, and was so surprised by this second attack from outside that for the moment he could say nothing. Then he added: "Oh yes, there is. On *all* sides."

"After all," said Miss Steele, "it's the younger generation that's got to decide, isn't it? It always was that way, and it always will be, won't it?"

Thus, with a clever mixture of the spirit of modernity and the wisdom of history, Miss Steele brought down two birds with one stone, and Mr. Thwaites was practically knocked out.

"Ah well, we shall see," was all he could manage.

But Miss Roach again guessed that he had not done yet, and she was again right.

All at once she saw his eyes shoot over to the other side of the room in the direction of the two American Lieutenants, who had so far been too shy to speak a word, even to each other.

"I wonder," he said, "what our Friends across the Water think about it all. What?"

And he fixed them with a horrible sort of ogling and encouraging eye.

This was too hideous—Miss Roach felt she would rather be attacked herself. Not content with disgracing the Rosamund Tea Rooms, he was now going to disgrace his country as well.

"I wonder," said Mr. Thwaites, having had no answer, "what our Democratic friends from across the Atlantic think about it all—our redoubtable friends from across the Pond—the Lil Ole Pond—eh?"

There was yet another ghastly pause—the ghastliest yet. Always, with Mr. Thwaites, the pauses got ghastlier and ghastlier. Then one of the Americans, the bigger of the two, could just be heard murmuring that he reckoned he agreed with the lady, there was a whole lot to be said both ways. . . .

"What?" said Mr. Thwaites, who had not heard what was said. But the big American would not repeat himself.

"The Whale of a Problem," said Mr. Thwaites, considerately assuming what he assumed to be the idiom of those to whom he was addressing himself. "What?"

But the American still would not speak, and at this point things were made easier by Sheila beginning to remove the empty plates of spam and mashed potatoes, and replacing them with plates of steamed pudding and custard.

He will certainly, in a moment, say "Say, Bo" or "Waal, Bo", thought Miss Roach, for he hardly ever failed to do this when imitating American speech, or talking about Americans. But this time he did not do exactly what she feared. Instead, he paused a long while, and then came out with something which even she could not have foreseen.

"*The Almighty Dollar*," said Mr. Thwaites, weightily, out of the blue, and in a measured tone. . . . That, and nothing else.

It was not easy to see exactly what Mr. Thwaites intended to establish by this—not easy, that is to say, for one who was not acquainted with the workings of his wild and circuitous mentality. To one so acquainted, however, his meaning was fairly clear. He meant Americans in general. He had been put into the presence of Americans: it therefore seemed to him his business, as master and spokesman of the boarding-house, to sum up and characterise America, and in this way he summed it up and characterised it.

And here it seemed that he was conscious of having found perfect expression for the perfect thought, for he said no more.

And because Mr. Thwaites said no more, the atmosphere in which pins could be heard dropping returned to the room, and no one else dared to say any more. Ruminatively, dully, around the heavy thoughts set in motion by Mr. Thwaites, the heavy steamed pudding was eaten.

Miss Steele was the first to rise and leave, stealing from the room with her *Life of Katherine Parr* under her arm.

Coffee was served in the Lounge upstairs. The others followed Miss Steele one by one, their chairs squeaking on the parquet oilcloth as they rose, and squeaking again as they were self-consciously replaced under the tables.

6

She couldn't stand it, she decided on the stairs. Tonight she simply couldn't and wouldn't stand it any more. All the same she would go into the Lounge for coffee. Why should she be done out of her coffee? She wondered whether the Americans, whom she had left behind in the dining-room, would be coming up into the Lounge. She could talk about America. She knew quite a lot about America, from what she had read, and from what her brother had told her. Perhaps, if she talked to them, she could eradicate or compensate for the stupidity and rudeness of Mr. Thwaites. Perhaps they were lonely in a foreign country, as lonely as she was in her own.

The Lounge was the same shape and size as the dining-room, but here Mrs. Payne, abandoning pink, had struck out whole-heartedly into brown, and made something of a hit. The wall-paper was of mottled brown, with a frieze of autumn leaves above the picture-rail: the carpet was brown: the lamps were shaded with mottled parchment of a brown tinge: and the large settee and two large armchairs were upholstered in brown leather. Cunningly slung over the arms of the armchairs were ash-trays attached to brown leather straps fringed at the ends. The room was heated by a big, bright, hot gas-fire.

Here, for two hours or more every evening, the guests of the Rosamund Tea Rooms sat in each other's company until they were giddy—giddy with the heat, the stillness, the desultory conversation, the silent noises—the rattling of re-read newspapers, the page-turning of the book-reader, the clicking of the knitter, the puffing of the pipe-smoker, the indefatigable scratching of the letter-writer, the sounds of breathing, of restless shifting, of yawning—as the chromium-plated clock ticked out the tardy minutes. Finally they went to their bedrooms in a state of almost complete stupefaction, of gas-fire drunkenness—reeling, as it were, after an orgy of *ennui*.

Mr. Thwaites was, of course, noisy to begin with, but in due course the atmosphere went even to his head, and silenced his tongue.

As Miss Roach came in he was settling down in his armchair with a book and taking out his reading-spectacles from a case. Mrs. Barratt, getting her knitting ready, asked him what he was reading.

"This?" said Mr. Thwaites in a slightly shamefaced way. "Oh—only something I picked up at the library. What is known, in vulgar parlance, as a 'thriller' or 'blood-curdler', I believe. It serves pour passer le temps."

Miss Roach went over to warm herself at the fire, and Mr. Thwaites went on.

"It may not be Dickens or Thackeray," said Mr. Thwaites, puffing at his spectacles and wiping them with his silk handkerchief, "mais il serve pour passer le temps." (Mr. Thwaites frequently adopted, among his many other roles, that of the linguist.)

Sheila now entered with the coffee-tray, but there was no sign of the Americans. Mr. Thwaites took it through again.

"I'm not going to say it's Dickens," said Mr. Thwaites, "and I'm not going to say it's Thackeray. I'm not even going to say it's Sir Walter Scott. But we've got to pass the time somehow."

The Americans clearly were not coming up, and tonight she couldn't stand it another minute. She left the room, strolling out with the casual air of one who leaves it for a moment.

Mr. Thwaites glanced at her suspiciously, but had no idea what she was doing. She ran upstairs to her room, hastily put on her hat and coat, grabbed her torch, and came down the stairs again to the front door and went out into the black Thames Lockdon.

7

But what did she think she was doing and where did she think she was going now?

The black street resounded with the gloomy, scraping tramp of the boots of conscripted British soldiers far from their homes. There were some Americans about, too, further still from their homes. At this time of the evening they passed through Church Street on their way towards or returning from the public-houses over the bridge. Sometimes they shouted or sang, but for the most part they said nothing, giving expression to their slow sorrow and helplessness in their boots.

Where did she think she was going, amidst all these boots? She found herself in the narrow High Street, walking in the direction of the Station.

She had better walk as far as the Station, and then walk back and go in again. She had better try to look upon herself as one who had come out in a sane way for a short walk, not as what she really was, one who had rushed out on to the black streets of a small riverside town in a sort of panic.

Two Americans, lurking at a corner, spoke out to her invitingly, calling her "sister". She walked on, conscious of having let them off—of having spared them the chill embarrassment which would have fallen upon them had they realised their ambition to talk to her and see her—conscious, therefore, of a blackness within the blackness of this fleeting street episode of which they, in common with other soldiers who accosted her under similar conditions, remained unaware.

Blackness. Cockroaches were black. "Miss Roach." "Old

Cockroach." As the schoolmistress at Hove that had been her nickname—she had heard them using it more than once—so little fear did they have of her that they had almost used it to her face. She could never even keep proper discipline in class. And she had set out with such ideas, such enthusiasm, such grave, exhilarating theories in regard to "youth" and "modern education". She had thought she had found her gift and place in life. They had "liked" her, however, though she couldn't even keep proper discipline, and had abandoned her exhilarating theories within three weeks.

She passed the Station and went on towards the river-front. She was now moving back towards the Rosamund Tea Rooms by the route she had used earlier in the evening.

Mr. Thwaites would be missing her by now, wondering what she was up to. Though he didn't do much talking and bullying after dinner, he liked you to be there. He didn't like anyone to be out. It filled him with angry curiosity and jealousy. He was never out, off duty, himself. He looked upon the Rosamund Tea Rooms as a sort of compulsory indoor game, in which he perpetually held the bank and dealt the cards.

She turned into Church Street again, and was again amongst the boots. What now? Go in and submit to Mr. Thwaites after all? Never. Or go to her room and try somehow to read and go to bed? No, no. Or stay out amongst the boots? Or go by herself to the Cinema? She had no desire to do so—in fact she hated the idea—but it was either that or the boots on the dark streets, and she had better go round and see if she could get in.

8

The quite recently built Odeon Cinema was in the narrow High Street. She pushed back the heavy door, and was dazzled by the light in the foyer, and smitten suddenly by the air of tension pervading the house—a tension which comes into being in the foyer of a crowded theatre anywhere, which centres around the inimical box-office, which repels the newcomer, and gives rise to a feeling of awe, of having to lower one's voice and walk practically on tiptoe in deference to what is taking place inside.

She could only get the most expensive sort of seat—three and sixpence upstairs—and she was lucky to get this. That was the war. In the old days you could have strolled in at any time of the evening for ninepence. In the war everywhere was crowded all the time. The war seemed to have conjured into being, from nowhere, magically, a huge population of its own—one which flowed into and filled every channel and crevice of the country—the towns, the villages, the streets, the trains, the buses, the shops, the hotels, the inns, the restaurants, the movies.

She was given a seat in the gangway, and was no longer awed, because she was now herself taking part in the rites which had seemed so momentous from the foyer. The "News" was on—war pictures, naturally—war, war, war. . . . The war shone on to the lurid, packed, smoke-hazed, rustling audience, the greater part of which was dressed for war. The familiar, steady voice of the announcer threaded its way through the pictures—a curiously menacing voice, threatening to the enemy, yet admonitory to the patriot, and on one tireless note. Through pictures of aeroplanes falling, guns firing, ships sinking, bombs exploding, this voice maintained its polite but hollow and forbidding character.

One studying Miss Roach's face in the white darkness would soon have become aware that she had not given up her three shillings and sixpence for that for which most of those surrounding her had given up their money—that is, for entertainment. Such a student might well, indeed, have been at a loss to read correctly the feelings betrayed by her expression. From its tenseness, its unhappy and half-frowning absorption he might have guessed bewilderment, sorrow, commiseration for others, loneliness—and he would have been right in suspecting the presence, in some degree, of all these. But the emotion he would primarily have been watching was, in fact, nothing more complicated than the simple emotion of fear. Miss Roach stared at the screen with plain fear on her face—fear of life, of herself, of Mr. Thwaites, of the times and things into which she had been born, and which boomed about her and encircled her everywhere.

CHAPTER TWO

I

IT was a quarter past five in the afternoon, and she sat in the white darkness of the Odeon Cinema at Thames Lockdon.

It was Saturday. Three weeks had passed since she had rushed out from Mr. Thwaites and hidden herself in here, and this afternoon there was no expression of fear upon her face. She was still, however, looking at the screen without seeing what she was looking at. Beside her the American—"her" American—Lieutenant Dayton Pike—sat silently.

"Her" American? . . . Yes, she believed she could, in an obscure way, claim him as "hers". In the last astonishing three weeks it seemed that she had actually acquired her own American—just as every shop-girl, girl-typist, girl-clerk, girl-assistant, girl-anything in fact, in the town, had acquired her own.

The Americans had stormed the town. Those two shy Lieutenants who had been in to dinner that night at the Rosamund Tea Rooms had been two mere timid scouts sent on ahead of the reverberating, twanging, banging invasion. Of those two Lieutenant Dayton Pike had been one, and he was no longer timid. He was, indeed, very far from being timid.

"Her" American, then . . . But to what extent hers? And in what exact meaning of the word? That remained an enigma. Lieutenant Dayton Pike remained an enigma. He had begun as such, and he remained so.

She had soon learned that he was not as shy as he had appeared that night in the dining-room with his friend.

The next night she had caught an early train from London and had entered the Rosamund Tea Rooms at about six o'clock. He was coming down the stairs. "Good evening," he said, and grinned at her in the dim light of the hall. She smiled back, and said "Good evening," and went on up the stairs. But he called her back.

"Say," he said, speaking in a low voice (the dimness of the light somehow caused one to speak in a low voice). "Are you coming round the corner?"

She did not get his meaning. "Corner?" she said. "What corner?"

"The Sun?" he said. "Or whatever it's called? They open up at six, don't they?"

She now saw that he was inviting her to go with him to the public-house—the River Sun. She was taken aback, and said "Well, I don't know . . . I was going upstairs to tidy up."

"Aw," he said. "Come on. You can tidy up round there—can't you?"

"Well . . ." she said, and "Aw," he said. "Come on." And a moment later she was out in the blackness with him.

He guessed it was "kind of a dark night", and he took her arm in the most natural way as they crossed the road. With equal naturalness he failed to relinquish her arm as they walked along on the other side. He asked her if she worked in London and she said that she did. She was completely bewildered and taken aback. She was too stunned to react to the situation or the man in any way, favourably or unfavourably. She was conscious, however, of a slight feeling of pleasure, pleasure at having the monotony of her evening blown to smithereens in this way, and at the thought of the minor tumult which this would cause in the boarding-house when it got to hear of it—the tumult, in particular, in the breast of Mr. Thwaites, who was no doubt at this moment complacently awaiting her return and booming away in the Lounge. She was also pleasantly conscious of the bigness of the man who held her arm in the dark. Finally she was conscious that the man, without being drunk, had been drinking during the afternoon.

They went into the bright Saloon Lounge of the River Sun and took a seat at a table in a corner near the fire. She asked for a small gin and french, and he went to the bar. He returned with a large gin and french and a large whisky and soda for himself. She now had a chance to look at him. He was big and broad in his uniform, and wore large spectacles. He had a fresh brown complexion, and at moments she thought that he was under forty and at moments she thought that he was over this age. His complexion, like her own, was at the moment glowing with the cold weather. His eyes were slightly bloodshot, and at moments she thought that this was due to the cold, and at moments she thought that this was due to his drinking alcohol regularly and heavily. He had gorgeous American teeth in a warm, broad American grin. He talked nineteen to the dozen.

Soon enough her heart, in occult collusion with the gin and french inside her, began to warm towards him, and she was aware of relaxing and enjoying herself whole-heartedly. The Rosamund Tea Rooms were mentioned, and he asked what the hell sort of a joint that was anyway? He just couldn't get the hang of it. This attitude delighted her. She said that if it came to that, she couldn't get the hang of it either, though she had been there more than a year. She explained that she had been bombed out of London, and that that was why she was living down here. He said he guessed that must have been pretty tough, and he looked at her with considerable awe and naïvety. She felt a sudden, delightful, modest, gin and french pride in her experience as a 1940 Londoner. He said that he and his friend were billeted next door to the Rosamund Tea Rooms, and that they had come to an arrangement with Mrs. Payne to use the Lounge and have their evening meal there. They had thought it would be convenient, being next door, but they weren't so sold on the idea now. He asked who was this Thwaites guy? He talked enough for five or six, didn't he? She said he did, indeed.

He asked her if she was going to have the same again, and she said she really didn't think she ought to have any more—that had been a big one. He told her not to start that sort of thing, and she said well then, she would, but a small one this time. As he went to the bar she found herself glowing through and through. Very little alcoholic spirit was required to cause Miss Roach to glow through and through.

He returned with a large gin and french and a large whisky and soda for himself. They continued to discuss the Rosamund Tea Rooms. She enlarged upon its many obscure evils, glooms, oddities, and inconveniences, and glowed more and more. He asked her questions and listened sympathetically and agreed. It was as though they had then and there resolved to found an anti-Rosamund Tea Rooms society, and were exhilaratedly rushing through its first rebellious motions.

She was now hardly capable of glowing more brightly within, but something he said made her do so. He said that, in spite of his dislike of the place, he had "spotted her first thing" and that he had "made up his mind to meet up with her". She was to think about this for many days to come. Indeed she was, really, to think about little else.

Then, all at once, everything went bad. His friend, Lieutenant Lummis, entered with two girls, and the tête-à-tête was transformed into an awkward yet noisy party of five. Miss Roach knew the two girls well by sight in the town: they worked in shops, and were not, as one's mother would have said, "in her class", and the meeting was therefore, from this point of view, "embarrassing". Moreover, Lieutenant Lummis was drunk, and insisted upon buying her another large gin and french. This she hated, for she was already feeling giddy, hungry, and unhappy, but courtesy enforced her to drink it—

courtesy, along with a deep-seated hatred of waste of money which Miss Roach's simple upbringing and lack of experience completely disabled her from overcoming. Also the two girls, conscious of the conventions which would have existed for Miss Roach's mother, were on the defensive, and would not talk to her, or even look at her, properly. They were voluble enough with the two Americans, however, and if Lieutenant Pike talked nineteen, Lieutenant Lummis talked ninety-nine to the dozen.

She was, in fact, almost completely left out of it, and her sole desire was to go home. Like a child anguishing to get down from table, she remained silent amidst the noise, and watched their faces, seeking an excuse to depart, and a moment to make her excuse. "Well, I must be off," she tried, but no one heard her, and three or four minutes passed before she had an opportunity of trying again. . . . "Well, I really must be off," she said, and touched Lieutenant Pike's arm. "Aw—don't be silly," he said, without looking at her. "What're you all having?" "No—this is me," said Lieutenant Lummis, rising insecurely. "What's it to be, folks?"

But the idea of being made to drink any more now put her into a kind of panic, and this brought her to her feet. "No—I really must go," she said. "I'm awfully sorry—I must go." The two men jeered at her, and Lieutenant Pike tried physically to force her down into her seat. But, while hiding her hideous embarrassment and feigning to be amused, she managed to remain standing, saying "No . . . no! . . . I really must go. I'm awfully sorry. I must go. Really! . . ."

Then there was an awkward, one might almost say a nasty, silence—the panic in her breast having been made manifest to the company. She saw the two girls staring at her, crudely and with a sour expressionlessness. Lieutenant Pike had the grace to rise and say "Well—if you must . . ." "Yes, I really must," she said. "Thank you so much. Good night! And thanks so much!"

The two men said "Good night" cordially enough. The

two girls said nothing. She was out in the street, stumbling along in the blackness back to the Rosamund Tea Rooms. She was aware of an involuntary swaying in her walk, and in front of her eyes was a vision of Lieutenant Pike's face as he had said "Good night"—his look of disappointment, of embarrassment, and, almost certainly, of contempt. All the sudden delight and triumph had gone out of the evening, and she was more alone than ever. She had thought to score off the Rosamund Tea Rooms, but the Rosamund Tea Rooms had scored off her. She had to go back to the boarding-house now with her tail between her legs. She knew that those four back there were at this moment talking about her adversely or scornfully. She had no place in either environment, and she was alone in the world. She was, in fact, completely upset, and she fervently wished the thing had never happened. She was resentful towards the man for having upset her like this, and for having made her drink too much.

By the way she *had* drunk too much, too, and she had better look out. She was late for dinner as well—ten minutes late. Did she dare go in, ten minutes late and having drunk too much?

She washed hurriedly in her dim pink bedroom, and decided she was able to brazen it out. No sooner had she entered the dining-room, and taken her seat at the table, than she decided that she had made a mistake. She said "Good evening" to a floating Mrs. Barratt and Mr. Thwaites, and she heard them say "Good evening" back. She saw that they were well into the middle of the main dish, which was fish, and Sheila at once put some tepid soup in front of her. She stared at her soup as she ate it, and no one spoke. She waited for someone to speak, but still no one did so. Why? What was the matter? Was it because they knew she was drunk, because they were too appalled by her behaviour to speak? When Sheila replaced her soup with the fish, she looked up to see if they were looking at her. They were not. They were looking at nothing and not speaking.

Not a word was uttered throughout the meal. If Mr. Thwaites was not in a talking mood, such a thing was by no means unknown at the Rosamund Tea Rooms at dinner, but nothing could convince her that there was not some graver meaning behind the silence of the dining-room tonight. At last Miss Steele stole from the room with her *Life of Katherine Parr*. The others followed her one by one. Sheila put some jam tart in front of her and she was left alone, and as it were in disgrace, to eat it.

She went straight up to her room. Then she went to the bathroom and turned on a bath. She began to feel better, and stayed a long while in the hot water.

2

She slept well, but awoke at six, and could not go to sleep again. She reviewed the evening before dispassionately. She saw it in hues less black than those in which it had been steeped last night, but she still thought ill of it, and still had a feeling of having been, in a rather unfair way, upset.

She surprised herself saying to herself, with an air of resignation, that "that was the end of that, anyway", and she asked herself what she meant by this. What was the end of what? Had anything begun, which had now ended?

She sought carefully for a solution to this problem, and found it in his remark that he had "spotted her first thing and made up his mind to meet up with her". Most odd. Well, he would certainly have no further ambition to meet up with her now. Because of her general maladroitness, of her inability to drink, and of the arrival on the scene of those two girls, the whole thing had been bungled and was at an end.

The day was Saturday, and she did not have to go to London. In the morning she did some shopping in the town and succeeded, for the most part, in putting yesterday evening from her mind. She did, however, occasionally wonder what kind of night Lieutenant Pike had had after she had left him, and at what hour and in what place it had ended.

In the afternoon, coming in late to tea in the Lounge, she found Lieutenant Pike seated on the settee and in conversation with Mr. Thwaites. Mrs. Barratt and Miss Steele were also present. He rose as she entered, cup in hand, and smiled at her. Then he sat down and went on talking to Mr. Thwaites.

American and British institutions and customs were being compared and contrasted, and Lieutenant Pike, in the matter of words per minute, was more than holding his own with the tyrant. This pleased her a good deal. She realised that they were both, in their different ways, insurmountable talkers, but the Lieutenant, in a combat of this sort, had the power of youth, together with the gift and tradition in loquacity peculiar to his nation, on his side.

They talked until a quarter to six, and then Mr. Thwaites left the room in a sardonic temper and disliking the United States of America more than usual. By this time Mrs. Barratt and Miss Steele had also gone, and she was left alone in the Lounge with Lieutenant Pike. "Well," he said, rising and smiling at her again, "it's just about time you and I went for a walk, isn't it?"

She had no difficulty in seeing that by this he meant that it was just about time that the public-houses were opening their doors, and although she was not certain that she was going to accept his invitation, she felt a lift of pleasure and relief. So it was not "all over", after all!

"Is it?" she said, and a few minutes later he was holding her arm as they steered a course along the black street in the direction of the River Sun.

3

She begged him to make her gin and french a small one, and this time he did as she wished. This improved her opinion of him. She noticed that he was faithful to a large whisky and soda for himself. She asked him how they had all got on last night, and he groaned deeply and raised his eyes to heaven—thus indicating that he had drunk to excess and now bitterly repented it. She asked him about the two girls, and he said, casually, oh, they had faded out soon after her. At once her heart, in the same occult collusion with the gin and french as had come into being the night before, began to glow. He was now definitely on her side against yesterday evening, as yesterday evening he had been on her side against the Rosamund Tea Rooms, and the same warm, exhilarating atmosphere began to prevail.

The Saturday-night place became very crowded, but they had a comfortable corner to themselves. Every now and again he went to the bar to refill their glasses. She felt the drink affecting her potently, but this time the result was not one of making her unhappy, of setting her on edge, but of composing her beautifully, of balancing and refreshing her.

She dreaded the renewed appearance of Lieutenant Lummis and the two girls, but this did not happen. Soon enough she noticed that it was six and twenty minutes past seven, which meant that she had four minutes in which to return to the Rosamund Tea Rooms for dinner. She mentioned the time of the evening to Lieutenant Pike, but it did not seem to impress him. A little later she mentioned it again, and he explained that they were going to eat upstairs at the River Sun. Though she had been prepared for this, she was filled with joy and terror. She said, if that was the case, she must "let them know". He said why let them know, it was a free country, wasn't it? She said they would "worry". He said let them worry. Pressed on the point, he agreed that it might be wise to telephone, and said he would do so himself in the near future. Pressed to do so at once, he got up and did so. When he returned she eagerly asked to whom he had spoken, and what had been "said". But he gave her no satisfactory information: he said no more than that it was "all O.K.": he was uncommunicative and inconsequent.

It was, actually, at this moment that there first dawned upon her a realisation of the quality which mainly characterised the Lieutenant—his inconsequence. He was not only inconsequent, as most human beings are, in drink: he was chronically and inveterately inconsequent. His sudden suggestion, the night before in the hall of the Rosamund Tea Rooms, that she should join him in a drink, had been inconsequent. His remark that he had spotted her first thing and had made up his mind to meet up with her had, she believed, been inconsequent. His prompt and easy relinquishing of her when his friend and the two girls had joined them had been inconsequent. Now he had on the spur of the moment decided to give her dinner, adopting an inconsequent attitude in regard to the Rosamund Tea Rooms and any social consequences whatsoever.

She was far from being in a mood to criticise this characteristic trait tonight, however. On the contrary, in her escape from the long inhibitions enclosing her at the Rosamund Tea Rooms, she was disposed to regard it as a merit, and to remind herself that she herself would be improved by a more inconsequent attitude generally. Bearing this in mind, she did not think it fitting to refuse his next offer of a drink, nor yet another offer which came a little later.

They were not up in the dining-room until half-past eight, did not begin to eat until ten to nine, and had not finished until a quarter to ten. After this he was anxious to add a final polish to his evening's drinking with further whiskies downstairs, but the bars below were now so packed with noisy civilians and his compatriot soldiers that he allowed her to prevail upon him to abandon the project and leave the place—not, however, before he had fought his way to the bar and obtained a half-bottle of whisky for his pocket in the way of insurance. She observed that he was now drunk, but not as yet dangerously so, and she herself had enough drink inside her to fear no evil results.

Walking along arm-in-arm in the direction of the Rosamund Tea Rooms she asked him where they were going, and he said he didn't have any notion, where were they? Then he said,

"Let's go and see the folks." She asked him what folks, and he said "The folks. The old guy. Let's go and see 'em." At this she realised that the old guy was Mr. Thwaites and that he proposed to burst in upon the sacred after-dinner stillness of the boarding-house Lounge. Her spirits being as high and bold as they were, she was for a moment tempted to support this plan, but was wise enough to see its folly in time, and to attempt to dissuade him. He asked where in hell could they go, anyway, and she said she personally would like to go to bed. There followed an argument about this, which continued until they reached the steps of the Rosamund Tea Rooms, where it had to be continued in lowered voices. She was now hardened in her resolution to go to bed, and all at once and again inconsequently—he consented. He himself would go into the Lounge for a bit, and then he also would go to bed.

She did not like the idea of his going into the Lounge, but it was not her responsibility or business. Also he seemed suddenly more sober, and she thought this would be the best compromise. In the hall, as he took off his overcoat, she thanked him, in whispers, for the evening, and on the stairs going up he said good-night, he'd be seeing her. She went on up to her room. She heard him entering the Lounge.

She decided to wash some stockings before going to bed. For this reason, when, a quarter of an hour later, she heard a soft knocking on the door, she was not undressed. She opened the door and found Lieutenant Pike standing in the doorway with a half-bottle of whisky in his hand. He explained that he had come up for one for the road, and had she got a glass and some water or something? She whispered he mustn't, he must go away, he *mustn't*! He said Come on, just one for the road, and she could have one too. She noticed that he was now drunk again, drunker than he had been throughout the entire evening. He was a very baffling man. She let him in and said he must be quiet, he must go and he must be quiet.

She went out on to the landing to see if anyone was about.

She heard nothing, and concluding that her fellow-lodgers were all as yet in the Lounge, guessed that the situation might be retrieved if she got rid of him at once.

She came back, not knowing whether to shut the door so that nothing was heard, or to leave it open so as to defeat the charge of clandestinity. She compromised by leaving it two inches open. He had already poured a large amount of whisky into her tooth-glass and filled up with water from her tap. He said God Almighty they were a stuffy bunch down there. She said he must be quiet. He must be quiet and *go*! Didn't he *understand*?

He was quiet. He nodded with the air of a man who had cottoned on to a clever idea. He was quiet with a mad, infinitely portentous quietude. This caused him, as it were, to go to sleep on his feet as he gazed at her, glass in hand, and to sway faintly from side to side. He took another swill at his drink, and was as quiet as a contemplating Buddha. She saw that he was willing to go on standing there being quiet in this way all night.

She went out on to the landing again. She returned and said "Go on. Drink it up. You must go!" He drank it up. She stuffed the bottle of whisky into his pocket and manœuvred him towards the door. He said "Well—good night," and looked at her. She said "Good night," and smiled. He paused, and put his arms around her, in order to kiss her. She offered him her cheek to be kissed. He kissed her cheek, and then kissed her neck. Then he kissed her mouth. She said "Good night." He said "Good night" and disappeared.

She closed the door and went on washing her stockings. She undressed and smoked a cigarette in bed. She was not nauseated or shocked by what had just happened. She was curiously pleased and cheerful. She had enjoyed her evening to the full. She wondered what he meant by it all, and she did not much care. She hoped he had not made a fool of himself in the Lounge, but she did not much care about that, either.

It was not her business. In a curious way she felt a new woman. She put out her light and slept profoundly.

4

No arrangement had been made between them to meet again, but she had a feeling, the next morning, that she would see him at tea-time. She appeared ten minutes late for tea, half expecting to find him there; but he was not. Nor did he appear at all for tea, though she waited in the room an hour and a half. Nor did he appear anywhere during the evening.

On Monday evening, returning from her work, she again imagined she would see him, if not by himself, at any rate in the dining-room with his friend. But she was again disappointed. On Tuesday she heard accidentally, through Mrs. Payne, that he and his friend had three days' leave which they were spending in London.

She did not see or hear from him again until Thursday evening. Then, as she was dressing for dinner in her room, Sheila came rushing up the stairs to announce that she was wanted on the telephone. The telephone being in Mrs. Payne's private room on the ground floor, this was a boarding-house sensation. The residents of the Rosamund Tea Rooms were not telephoning-using animals. Mrs. Payne was in the room, and did not see any reason to leave it.

He asked her how she was, and said that he had been in London for three days and that he was now at the River Sun. She was to come round at once to have a drink. She explained that she was just about to have dinner, and he said she needn't bother about dinner, there was plenty of that round where he was. He sounded in extremely high spirits, and if only in order to cut the conversation short, she agreed to do as he said. She rang off, and thanked Mrs. Payne for the use of the telephone. Mrs. Payne replied affably, but not ostentatiously so. Miss

Roach had a remarkable feeling that Mrs. Payne was the headmistress of an academy from which, if she went on like this, she was likely to be expelled at an early date.

She did not know exactly how much Mrs. Payne had heard, and she did not have the courage to tell her she would not be in to dinner. Instead, as she went out, she caught Sheila in the dining-room, and quietly broke the news to her.

She was a little dubious as to the condition she was going to find him in, and was relieved to see that his high spirits seemed to be due to nothing in addition to high spirits. A small gin and french was awaiting her on the table in their corner of the Lounge, along with his large whisky and soda, and they began at once busily and cheerfully to talk. He described his trip to London, and had many questions to ask about the town, questions which she was able to answer with the same modest Londoner's pride as he had evoked in her the first evening they had met.

They were in the dining-room by half-past eight, and had finished eating by nine.

After dinner he did not seem to want to go on drinking, but suggested that they should take a walk along the river. It was a mild night, and not so completely black as usual because of a little diffused light from an invisible moon. It was still very black, however. She suggested that they should cross the bridge and walk along on the far side of the river, but it seemed that he preferred to walk through the little Thames Lockdon park on the near side. The thought flitted across her mind that on this near side there were seats upon which one could sit in comfort and look at the river: on the far side there was nothing of this kind. It also flitted across her mind that the same thought had flitted across his. She rebuked her mind for these hyper-imaginative flittings.

They walked slowly for twenty minutes in the darkness by the side of the river, and then turned round and walked back. On again reaching the little park he suggested that they should sit down on one of the seats. They did so, and soon he put his arm around her and began, as in her bedroom earlier in the week, to kiss her with unabashed enthusiasm and thoroughness. On the whole she disliked this at first, but after a while she found that she disliked it a good deal less. After half an hour, in which they scarcely spoke, they rose and moved into Thames Lockdon again.

He said he could do with a drink, and she also welcomed the idea. They returned to the brightly lit Lounge of the River Sun. He prevailed upon her to have one of his large whiskies and soda. They sat in their usual corner, and as the placed filled up in preparation for the final din and panic of closing-time, they talked with renewed freshness and eagerness.

The Lieutenant did most of the talking, and for the first time furnished some details of his personal background—of his life "back home" and of his "folks". He came from Wilkes Barre in Pennsylvania: his folks were in the catering business, and he was now attached, on the catering side, to a medical unit stationed three or four miles outside Thames Lockdon. They were building a camp out there. Though his folks were in the catering business, his personal ambitions, beliefs, and hopes for the future lay in the way of the laundry business. He descanted upon the laundry business at some length, speaking of the connections he had already established with it, and making it clear that on his return home after the war the laundry business was as eager to embrace him as he was eager to embrace the laundry business.

Though she did not exactly know why, she found his enthusiasm for the laundry business faintly disheartening. Perhaps it was because the cold thoughts set in motion by the laundry business assorted so quaintly with the warm thoughts recently set in motion on the seat in the park—because of the crude contrast, in fact, between kisses in the darkness by the river and washing other people's clothes in America.

5

He had in all four large whiskies before closing-time, and prevailed upon her to have two. It was not until he had his last whisky in front of him, and she had reason to believe that he was drunk again, that he exploded his next bombshell. The talk had still been running upon himself and his future, and somehow or other the question of his getting married and settling down had arisen, and somehow or other she had asked him who, or what sort of person, he would like to marry.

"Why—who do you suppose," he said, "after all that?"

"All what?" she said, too stunned to get his meaning, or at any rate to believe that his meaning was what she thought it might be.

"All that out there," he said.

"Out where?" she said.

"Oh—along by the river," he said, and he looked at her. She looked quickly away at her glass, and there was a silence. Then he changed the subject, and she volubly assisted him to do so. This was simply too much even to think about at the moment: she must put it away and take it out later, when she was alone.

Soon after this the River Sun closed down and they walked back to the Rosamund Tea Rooms. Outside the front door he embraced and kissed her again, and this lasted for two or three minutes. Then they said good-night and she went up to her room.

The next day was Friday, and she spent a large part of her spare time, in the office in London and in the train going up and down, in puzzling out his meaning. The more she thought about it the less she could recall the exact form the conversation had taken, and the mood in which it had taken place. Had she asked him what sort of person he *wanted* to marry, or what sort of person he was *going* to marry. Or had she gone further and asked him *who* he wanted to marry, or even who he was going to marry? The significance of his reply "Who do you suppose, after all that?" (or was it "*What* do you suppose, after all that?") depended, of course, entirely upon the way in which she had framed the question. And then, even if he had, as she certainly had believed he had at the time, as good as said that it was she herself, or that she was the type, that he desired, or hoped, or was determined to marry, what value was to be attached to the statement? Was he drunk at the time, and if he was not drunk was it not all in keeping with his total inconsequence? Or was it a joke—a sort of leg-pull? Or again, had she completely misheard or misunderstood what he had said?

She decided at last that it was probably something between all these things, and she decided to put it out of her mind. But this she was unable to do successfully, and on returning to Thames Lockdon that night she definitely hoped that she would meet him, and that he would take her out again—that he would, even, give her drinks and dinner, and say something else or further which would in some way clarify the problem. But he did not put in an appearance and did not telephone.

On the next day, Saturday, he came in late to tea, and surreptitiously invited her to have a quick one at the River Sun. They had, he said, to hurry it up because he was going on to meet his friend Lieutenant Lummis at seven o'clock—he did not say where. He proceeded inconsequently but imperturbably to stay with her until twenty minutes past seven, and he then left in such a rush that no appointment was made for a future meeting.

During the next fortnight, without previous arrangement, he invited her two or three times to drink with him at the River Sun, but on only one occasion did he give her dinner afterwards. Then he took her for the same walk by the river as before, this ending up in the same way upon the seat in the park. But on none of these occasions did he explode any further bombshells, or make any attempt to adjust the psychological confusion created by the one he had already thrown.

Finally he had invited her to go to the movies with him on this Saturday afternoon, and she sat beside him in the white darkness looking at the screen without seeing what she was looking at and wondering in what sense she might be permitted to call Lieutenant Pike "her" American.

CHAPTER THREE

I

LOOKING at the clock glowing above the Exit sign to the right of the screen she saw that it was nearly half-past five.

"Isn't it time you were going?" she said.

On meeting her this afternoon he had told her that he had to catch a train into Maidenhead at a quarter to six. There he had an appointment to meet his friend Lummis—they were going, he said, to some sort of joint, Bindles or Spindles or what the hell it ever was. She had told him that he meant Skindles, and had mutely wondered who had introduced Lieutenant Lummis to Skindles, and who else would form part of the company when the two friends got there. She even had a faint feeling of displeasure, perhaps jealousy, at the thought of this meeting, and at the way in which Lieutenant Lummis had at such an early date found his feet and learned to get about generally. Nor was it quite the first time that she had felt faint internal intimations of this ungenerous feeling. It was, perhaps, because it was always Lieutenant Lummis with whom Lieutenant Pike had the appointment to which he was going when leaving her; and because no information had ever been forthcoming as to what took place at these meetings. Not that she had ever asked, or that any sort of pressure or curiosity under the sun would ever induce her to contemplate asking.

His eyes were glued upon the screen and he did not answer her.

"It's about time you were going," she tried again, "isn't it?"

In answer to this he kept his eyes fixed on the screen, but, to show that he had heard her, he put out his hand and held hers.

What a man this was! And what perfect inconsequence again! What did he mean to convey now? "Be quiet—I want to look at the picture"? Or "Never mind—I've plenty of time to catch the train"? Or "Bother the train—I'll catch the next one"? Her knowledge of his character informed her that the answer might lie in any or all of these.

She sat in silence, and he held her hand. And this hand-holding, in the darkness, with its quiet possessiveness and informality, seemed all at once to convince her finally that she was at any rate in a position to regard him, without any sort of presumption, as "her" American in Thames Lockdon.

But what if someone else could claim him as "*their*" American in another locality? At Skindles tonight, for instance? What if he went out and behaved in the same way with other girls (or rather with girls, for she was not a girl)?

And what, again, if he did nothing of the sort? What if, as was extremely likely, he was exclusively and faithfully her American? What if, as she still in her heart honestly believed, he had as good as told her that it was she herself whom he desired or intended to marry?

What then? What about "love"? What about the Laundry business? What if he "loved" her, and she "loved", or came to "love", him, and they were one day "married"? So unreal and outlandish was the whole hypothesis that she was compelled at present mentally to put these words in inverted commas: all the same, she had to put the hypothesis in front of her. What if her present existence as a toiler in London and boarding-house solitary in Thames Lockdon were to be exchanged for one as the inspirer, mistress, and power behind the throne of a Laundry business in America—a Laundry queen?

What was there so peculiarly droll about the thought of the Laundry business, which always brought her back to earth when she indulged in these flights of fancy? Wherein did it differ from the car business, say, or the building business, or the legal business, or the book business? What, also, was there so faintly yet persistently chilling to her heart about the Laundry business when thought of as a steadfast flame of ambition burning in the breast of her companion?

"Come on, then," he said suddenly. "Let's get going." He removed his hand from hers, and they rose, and went down and out into the street, upon which the black-out blackness of night had already fallen.

She said that he would have to hurry to catch his train, and he said that he would not have to do this, and told her that she was to come round with him to see if he got it. On their arrival arm-in-arm at the station he was proved right: he had six minutes in hand. This was not to be wasted: he rushed her over to the public-house immediately opposite. She would drink nothing, for any time before six o'clock she regarded instinct-ively as tea-time, and her whole chemical and spiritual being forbade her to drink alcohol during such a well-defined phase of the evening: instead she watched him drink, with some haste and difficulty, a large whisky and soda. As he drank he asked her what she was doing with her evening. She said she was meeting Vicki. He asked her who was Vicki, and she said the German girl, she had told him about her. He said he remem-bered, and he was surprised at her going out with Germans, and she told him not to be so silly.

All at once he banged down his drink and made her escort him over to the station and on to the platform. He found an empty compartment, pulled down the window, leaned out, and made her wait till the train moved off. When she heard whistling noises she was about to go, but he called her back. This was so that he might kiss her. She was not used to being kissed by him at this time of the evening—did not, indeed, remotely associate such a time of the evening with kissing—and as the train pulled out she walked down the platform in the state of confusion and bewilderment he only too often evoked in her, but not displeased.

2

She had arranged to meet her German friend at half-past six at the River Sun.

It was not, as might be thought, the Lieutenant who had introduced Miss Roach to the River Sun or to the habit of meeting and drinking in bars. The blitz in London, with its attendant misery, peril, chaos and informality, had already introduced Miss Roach to this habit. She had no longer any fear of entering public-houses, and would, if necessary, and provided she was known in the place, enter one unaccompanied. Here again the war, the sombre begetter of crowds everywhere, had succeeded in conjuring into being yet another small population entirely of its own to help fill and afflict the public places—a population of which Miss Roach was a member—of respectable middle-class girls and women, normally timid, home-going and home-staying, who had come to learn of the potency of this brief means of escape in the evening from war-thought and war-endeavour. Without any taste for drink, and originally half-scandalised by the notion of drinking in public or of drinking at all, these women would at first imagine that the pleasure they obtained from the new habit lay in the company, the lights, the conversation, the novelty or humour of the experience: then, gradually, they would perceive that there was something further than this, that the longer they stayed and the more they drank the more their pleasure in this pastime was augmented, reaching, at moments, a point, almost, of ecstasy. Finally would come the realisation that the drink itself was not only intimately associated with, but was almost certainly the immediate cause of their sensations, and the bolder spirits among them would come to profess this openly, going so far as to make jokes about it, urging their friends, with naïve abandonment, to "have another", speaking of having "had too much", finally of being "drunk" or of the danger of getting "drunk". Actually very few of these women were constitutionally capable of getting drunk—but only of getting swimming sensations in their heads and wanting to go home and eat or go to bed.

Miss Roach, then, had had no hesitation in arranging to meet her friend at the River Sun—she had, in fact, met her there two or three times before. Then again, the River Sun had a reputation in Thames Lockdon which rendered it something slightly different from an ordinary public-house. Well known to those who knew the river well, and, owing to its position or some obscure tradition, singled out as the rendezvous of the well-to-do in the town itself, it had a style of its own, and to be heard of drinking in there was not altogether the same thing as to be heard of drinking elsewhere. In almost every country town nowadays there is a house, or more than one house, of this sort.

If Miss Roach had had any apprehensions this evening, they would have arisen, rather, from the nationality and reputation of the woman with whom she was to be seen in public—the fact that she was "going out with a German", as the Lieutenant had put it. But this did not disturb Miss Roach either. On the contrary, she took a certain defiant and perhaps slightly childish pleasure in her enlightenment in regard to this matter—an attitude which probably had in fact assisted in bringing about the friendship. Certain self-indulgent shopping and shopkeeping members of the Thames Lockdon public, on the outbreak of hostilities with Germany in 1939, having stampeded themselves into the exhilarating assumption that a German spy was flaunting herself in their midst, Vicki Kugelmann had to some extent been victimised. Miss Roach had, in fact, first met her in a greengrocery, where she was being singled out for public humiliation by disregard on the part of the assistants, and she had gone out of her way to talk to her and help her get what she wanted. After that they had spoken to each other, from time to time, on the street, and one morning had had a coffee together at a confectioner's. From this had arisen a habit of having coffee together on Saturday mornings, a visit or two to the pictures, and, lastly, an occasional meeting at the River Sun for a drink.

Mr. Thwaites getting to hear of this, innuendo at table was at once begun, astutely detached mention being made of "our German friends in the town" and certain people who "seemed to like them", thus, according to Mr. Thwaites, encouraging the ineptitude of the authorities, who, instead of locking up, hanging, or shooting them, caused them to multiply and flourish. For although Mr. Thwaites in his heart profoundly respected the German people for their political wisdom, he was not the sort of man who could refrain from participation in any sort of popular chase when one appeared on his doorstep. A supreme and overpowering master in the craft of eating his cake and having it too, he was often led into such contradictions. His remarks, however, only served to harden and fortify Miss Roach in her pursuit of the friendship.

Vicki Kugelmann, who was about the same age as herself, and who worked as assistant to a local vet, seemed to Miss Roach to be quiet, cultivated, and intelligent, and because isolated in the town (for different reasons but in much the same way as herself) admirably cut out as a friend. Apart from one or two joking references, made by Vicki herself, to her own reputation as a spy, and apart from one allusion made to the Hitler regime ("Ah—I do not know what has happened to my country," she had said, and shuddered, or rather imitated a shudder, and looked into the distance), no mention ever arose between them of her race, and for this she seemed modestly grateful. Miss Roach began to look forward to these meetings, and to exchange confidences. The German girl was unhappy in her rooms, where her landlady, it seemed, was privately taking financial and other advantage of public prejudice, and Miss Roach had even gone so far as to speak of approaching Mrs. Payne and trying to get her into the Rosamund Tea Rooms—not in the house, of course, which was full, but in a room near by, whence she could come over to meals and take advantage of the Lounge. In the excitement of the last few weeks, however, and in the feeling of marked trepidation towards Mrs. Payne brought into being by certain telephoning incidents resulting from this excitement, she had neglected to do this.

Miss Roach arrived promptly on time at the River Sun, and her friend was not there. She went to the bar, obtained a gin and french, and took it over to the corner in which she usually sat with the Lieutenant. She had been careful to take with her, as a sort of escort, a newspaper, which she could read while she waited. There were very few people in the bar, however, none of whom were interested in her, and she sat looking about her, studying the people and the room. This, about five years ago, had been redecorated by a new proprietor, and in such a startling manner as to give the impression of having been redecorated only yesterday—in fact, it would probably, as numerous saloon lounges all over the country do, bear permanently the stamp of redecoration. The house being Elizabethan in origin, a curious aim at an Elizabethan manner had been made in the way of black beams, wooden panelling, uncomfortable black chairs and tables, odd pieces of armour, suspended swords, and almost indecipherable Gothic lettering over the doors. But upon this a Scottish atmosphere had been imposed—samples of Scottish tartans having been inserted into the upper panels, and pictures having been put up which dealt exclusively with Scottish Highlands and other Scottish matters. Also framed Scottish proverbs had been hung on either side of the red Devonshire fireplace, in which an electrical apparatus, set in an external semblance of burning coal, revolved incessantly. To add to the confusion, and in destruction of the other illusions, there were two electric ball-machines (one representing, when lit and clicking, an imitation of the sport of racing-motoring, and the other of the sport of ski-ing); a glass-enclosed machine with a chromium-plated crane which was by natural law capable of extracting cameras, watches, and wallets, but which in historical practice brought force nothing save one or two hard, pea-like sweets to console the operator; several green-leather chromium-plated high stools along the bar, and a modern green carpet with whorls which put one in mind of sea-sickness.

Nearly a quarter of an hour passed without Miss Roach's friend appearing, and she was just about to fear that "something had happened", when the door opened and she came in, looking about her. Spotting Miss Roach, she came over and sat beside her, smiling and saying "Ah—here you are!" It struck Miss Roach that she made no mention of being late; in fact she gave out an atmosphere as if Miss Roach herself were a little late, and Miss Roach guessed that she might have made a mistake about the time, and said nothing. Miss Roach asking her what she was drinking, the other said, "No—what are *you* drinking?", to which Miss Roach replied, "No—what are *you* drinking?"; and there began a rapid fire of protestations, all beginning with the word No, in regard to whose turn it was, who was "in the chair", who had arrived first and who had invited whom—Miss Roach finally going to the bar and getting two gin and french.

"And did you enjoy your visit to the pictures this afternoon?" said the German girl, when they were settled again and were lighting cigarettes. She said this with a certain arch, suggestive, and old-fashioned air which was characteristic of her.

Thirty-eight years of age, with blonde hair, a fair complexion, a reasonably good figure, and a face which, with its large blue eyes, pinched nose, and fullish mouth, would not be noticed in the street as attractive or otherwise, or as indicating any age more or less than her own, Vicki Kugelmann gave forth a faintly old-fashioned, or rather out-of-date, atmosphere, which Miss Roach had never been able fully to analyse. It might have been caused by her hair, which was actually "shingled" in the manner of 1925: it might have been her clothes, which, though neat and becoming enough, had an off-fashionable and rather second-hand air: it might have been her manner, her quick facial expressions, the too industrious use of her eyes and mouth to express surprise, sympathy, or resignation—her habit of making *moues*. It might have been her way of powdering her nose in a hand-mirror or smoking a cigarette with a cigarette-holder, both of which she would do with more fuss, precision, and ceremony than was usual, as if these things were novelties to which she had been lately introduced and by which she was still fascinated. In all these ways she impressed Miss Roach as being slightly, and somewhat naïvely, behind the times; though Miss Roach often thought that it might be less that she was behind the times than that she was behind the customs and idiom of the country in which she was residing, that these mannerisms arose from the fact that she was to a certain extent a fish out of water—in a word, a "foreigner".

"And how did you know I was at the pictures?" asked Miss Roach.

"Ah. I know. I know everything," said Vicki, in the same mocking and suggestive way, and taking a puff at her cigarette she threw her head back and puffed the smoke out in a thin, premeditated stream, as though aiming at some precise target in the air. She then neatly tapped at her cigarette over an ash-tray —doing this simply for the sake of neatly doing so, for there was as yet hardly any ash upon her cigarette.

Her English accent was curiously in keeping with her cigarette smoking—a little too excellently polished, a little too much at ease, and conscious of being so. Her skill here, however, was remarkable, and could only have been acquired by one who had spent, as she had, the greater part of her adult years in England. It was, when first meeting her, only in the consciousness that she was speaking English extraordinarily well that the listener realised that she was not English.

"No—how *did* you know?" asked Miss Roach, genuinely puzzled and interested, for she had not as yet said a word to the German girl about the Lieutenant, and could not conceive how this last meeting with him had become public property already.

"Ah—I have my spies," said Vicki, and then added, "As a matter of fact, I was the other side of the street and saw you going in."

"Oh—really?" said Miss Roach. "I didn't see you."

"No—I know you didn't. But I saw you." And at this Vicki again needlessly tapped at her cigarette over the ash-tray, and then looked at her cigarette in an amused and mysterious way.

It was now quite clear to Miss Roach that Vicki was deliberately making a "thing" of her visit to the pictures with an American, and she thought this rather absurd and characteristic of the other's slightly old-fashioned, "foreign" psychology. On the other hand, was she not in reality fully justified? Was there not, if all was told, a very positive and mature "thing" already in being? But how could Vicki know this?

"As a matter of fact," Vicki went on, "I have seen you with him before. I have seen you sitting in here."

This was a double surprise to Miss Roach; firstly because, quite unknown to herself, she had been seen in here with the Lieutenant by someone who knew her; and secondly because of the rather strange item of news accidentally furnished, that the German girl had been in here apart from her. She would hardly have come in here alone, so who had brought her in? A man? It flashed across Miss Roach's mind that she had, conceivably, created a false mental picture of her new friend, that the lonely "German spy" she had taken under her protection might, conceivably, lead a life of her own, with other protectors. But the thought passed, and she said, "Oh—so you've seen me in here, have you?"

"Oh yes," said Vicki, "I have seen you in here. It seems you have adopted your pet American already, my dear. . . . No?"

Again Miss Roach was slightly taken aback—partly because Vicki had unexpectedly called her "my dear" for the first time in their acquaintanceship, and partly because of the boldness and outspokenness of the remark itself—her direct allusion to a sexual aspect of life, and her jaunty assumption of its normality, not only for men and women in general, but for Miss Roach in particular. Hitherto Vicki had never opened her mouth with her save shyly and reticently to speak of purely impersonal or sorrowful matters.

"Well," she said, not quite knowing what to say, "I don't know about *adopted* . . ."

"Kidnapped, then, perhaps?" said Vicki. "You are a fast worker, my dear."

This time Miss Roach could hardly believe her ears. To be called, at her age, with her physical equipment, in Thames Lockdon of all places, and by Vicki Kugelmann of all people, a "fast worker"! As if she were a young, attractive girl, who went about with and was neither incapable nor guiltless of enticing men! And that "my dear" again. And "kidnapped"—what an extraordinary expression! This indeed was a new Vicki Kugelmann. She also realised that Vicki was deliberately airing her fearfully outmoded idiomatic virtuosity. "Kidnapped", and "fast worker", along with "my dear", all bore that faintly grotesque stamp of 1925 which she had so often observed in her.

She was not quite sure whether she altogether liked and approved of this new Vicki Kugelmann, or whether she did not. It then occurred to her that Vicki's sole object in all this was that of pleasing, encouraging, and flattering her friend, and that she was partially succeeding in her object, inasmuch as she (Miss Roach) was already, and in spite of a warning voice inside telling her to do otherwise, feeling slightly pleased, encouraged, and flattered.

"Well, as a matter of fact," she said, "he's just staying in the same boarding-house, that's all. Or rather, he comes in for meals."

"Oh well," said Vicki, "one has to meet a person somewhere, doesn't one?"

Finding Vicki thus relentless in attack, Miss Roach now decided to counter-attack.

"And who were *you* in here with," she said, her tone and looks adding a sort of humorous "pray" to her words, "when you saw me?"

Thus, in addition to going over to the attack, she was able directly to seek the answer to a question which actually filled her with some curiosity.

"Me? . . ." said Vicki. "Oh—only Mr. Jordan. . . ."

And by the use of the word "only", it seemed to Miss Roach that Vicki intended to convey that Mr. Jordan—being the middle-aged vet in the town by whom she was employed—was not by any means an American, or anything like one, was not really, in the strict sense of the word, a "man" at all.

At this, a slightly disturbing thing happened to Miss Roach: she experienced a definite sense of relief and pleasure. She was disturbed because of the apparent implications of this feeling. Was it within the bounds of possibility that she was jealous—that she was pleased because Vicki did not, like herself, have an American, did not, after all, come in here with "men"? For the moment she could think of no other explanation. Then she realised that this was not jealousy of the common sort: that it arose only from the thought that her budding friendship with Vicki might go awry or not materialise as she had hoped. It was not that she grudged, or could in her nature ever grudge, anyone having men friends: it was simply that if Vicki was the sort of person who attracted and whose secret main interest in life was men, then there would not be, after all, any basis for a genuine companionship with Miss Roach, whose main interest it was not and could not, for obvious reasons, ever be. It was not a question of envy: it was a question of fear of having been mistaken in a specific type of person.

Miss Roach, glad thus to have explained this feeling to her entire satisfaction, was destined, however, to receive something of a shock in Vicki's next remark.

"At least," said Vicki, "I *think* it was Mr. Jordan . . . the time I saw you."

Which quite clearly meant, of course, that instead of having come in here on one occasion only, and on that occasion with her employer, she had come in here several times, presumably with several people, for she could not remember the individual she had been with when she had seen Miss Roach. Something slightly mischievous in her tone struck Miss Roach, also, that she was deliberately trying to convey this impression, and desired to be further questioned. It looked, indeed, almost as if she were fishing for some sort of return of the subtle flattery she had been dispensing to Miss Roach. Though she was not really enjoying this conversation, and would have preferred to lead it into other channels, she could not but oblige.

"Oh," she said. "So you've been in here with a lot of people, have you?"

"Oh—I don't know about a lot," said Vicki. "A few. . . ."

And again her tone and faintly smiling look suggested that she would not object to having further secrets extracted from her.

"You know," said Miss Roach, "I've got an idea that it's probably you who're the fast worker—not me."

There was a slight pause before Vicki answered.

"Me? A fast worker?" she then said, twirling the stem of her glass in her hand, and looking amusedly at it. "Oh no. . . . Not fast. . . . Slow but sure. . . . That is your Vicki. . . . Slow but sure."

If one multiplied her immediate reaction to this remark a hundred times or so, one might say that Miss Roach's hair stood on end. Her feeling was one of shame as much as shock—shame at the awful complacency of the "Slow but sure" and at the atrocious narcissistic use of "your Vicki".

What, in the name of heaven, did this mean? She had been prepared to visualise and accept Vicki as one in whom certain men might well be or become interested—but what was this? She was, it seemed, setting herself up as a sort of seductress. Miss Roach looked at her. Was she, perhaps, a seductress? She might be, but for the life of her Miss Roach couldn't see it. She saw nothing but an ordinary, rather badly dressed, foreign-looking woman in her late thirties, with rather nice blue eyes, and a pinched nose, and rather nice-coloured hair—the sort of woman who might, indeed, seduce some odd, elderly man who knew her (in rather the same way as Miss Roach had seduced the accountant in her firm), but whose immediate impact upon anyone, man or woman, seeing her in public or meeting her in private, would amount to zero. And now this *femme fatale* had appeared upon the scene, whose self-confessed deadly methods were slow but sure! The thought occurred to Miss Roach that she was, perhaps, a little sex-mad. Or had she been drinking before she came in here, and was she slightly drunk? She had arrived unaccountably (and unapologetically) late, and this might well be the explanation.

Whatever the answer, Miss Roach now had a definite feeling that this new Vicki Kugelmann was not quite the one she had bargained for, and that the friendship was not likely to develop on quite the lines she had hoped. In fact, she was not quite sure, if conversations of this sort were going to be the order of the day, that she would be absolutely happy in having Miss Kugelmann staying in the same boarding-house with her. This, in its turn, reminded her that she had promised to speak to Mrs. Payne about this very matter. She had failed to do so, and sooner or later she had to make some excuse for her failure. She decided that there was no time like the present, and that this would also serve to change the subject.

"Oh—by the way," she said, "you know I was going to talk to Mrs. Payne—round at my place. . . ."

"Ah yes? Mrs. Payne?" said Vicki, suddenly sitting up, and looking at Miss Roach with the utmost interest.

"Well, I was going—"

"No. Don't go on. I have a surprise!" Vicki put forth an admonishing finger with one hand, and finished off her drink with the other. "I have a surprise! . . . Now. What are you going to have? The same again?"

"A surprise? . . . What?" said Miss Roach. "Go on. Tell me."

"No," said Vicki gleefully, as she rose and collected the glasses. "First we have a drink and then I tell you. A great surprise, but first we have a drink. The same?"

Miss Roach said she would have the same, and Vicki went to the bar. Miss Roach wondered what was coming, and guessed that, as is so often the case on these occasions between friends, the person surprised was not going to take anything like the same amount of pleasure in the surprise as the surpriser. Trying to anticipate this one, she had a feeling that Vicki was engaged to be married, and was either going to leave the town altogether, or was going to settle down in it comfortably elsewhere. She did not know why she had this feeling, but it somehow fitted in with Vicki's conversation and manner in the last five minutes.

Vicki returned with the drinks, sat down, said, "Well—here's to you," and drank.

"Well. Go on," said Miss Roach, masking a faint feeling of exhaustion behind a show of delighted interest. "Tell me. What is it?"

"Your Mrs. Payne . . ." said Vicki, and took another sip.

"Yes?"

"I have seen your Mrs. Payne," said Vicki. "I have had a long talk with her! . . ."

"No! . . . Really? . . ."

"Uh-huh. . . ." (Vicki had a rather irritating habit, which Miss Roach had noticed before, of saying "Uh-huh" instead of "Yes".) "And what do you think?"

"What?"

"I am coming to stay with you, my dear. You have a new lodger at the Rosamund Tea Rooms!"

"*No!*"

"Yes indeed. It is all fixed up. What do you think of that?

"But, my dear, this is *marvellous*!" said Miss Roach, that slight film coming over her eyes which comes over the eyes of those who, while proclaiming intense pleasure, are actually thinking fast.

"Yes. It is marvellous, isn't it?" said Vicki. "Now we shall be together."

"But you don't mean," said Miss Roach, finally managing completely to dispel the slight film, "staying in the *house*? It's full up in the house, isn't it?"

"Yes. In the house. Your Mrs.—what is her name—Bart?"

"Barratt?"

"Yes. Mrs. Barratt. She is not sleeping well because of the noise of the traffic in front of the house, so she is moving over to a quiet room over the way, and I am coming into hers."

"What—next door to me?"

"Yes. That's what Mrs. Payne said. Next door to you. What do you think of that?"

"But this is marvellous!" said Miss Roach. "What made you go and see her?"

"Oh—I don't know. You told me she might do something, so I plucked up my courage and went round and saw her yesterday. She knows Mr. Jordan too. I'm coming in the week after next."

"Well," said Miss Roach, "I think that's marvellous!" And as further details were given her, she kept on saying well, and kept on saying that it was marvellous. But her heart, instead of fully seconding what she was saying, was feeling, for some reason, slightly hurt, and her brain was busily looking into the future to see what cause there was, if any, for misgiving.

She could not fully explain to herself this slightly hurt feeling. Snubbed was the word, perhaps, rather than hurt. She felt snubbed because it was she who, as the fairy-godmother of the lonely German girl in the town, had originated what had at the time seemed the audacious and adventurous suggestion of Vicki coming to stay at the Rosamund Tea Rooms—and now it had all happened without any bother, had been coolly and calmly fixed up, apart from her. You might almost say it had happened behind her back! The worst part about this feeling was that she not only had to grin and bear it: she had to grin and make a pretence of absolutely adoring it!

"Well," she said, a little later, "I think this calls for another drink." And she went to the bar with the empty glasses.

No sooner had Miss Roach got to the bar, which was now crowded, and at which she had to wait some time to get served, than she saw how peculiarly vile, petty, and absurd she was being all along the line. What was the matter with her? What business was it all of hers? Why shouldn't the wretched woman act upon a recommendation of a friend and make arrangements on her own behalf to enter a boarding-house? And why shouldn't she be attractive to men (if she was)? And why shouldn't men take her out (if they did)? And why shouldn't she talk in a rather absurd, old-fashioned, "foreign", kittenish way about men? Was she (Miss Roach) becoming spinsterish, possessive, jealous, jaundiced, or what? She must really take herself in hand.

Feeling the force of all these arguments in a sudden wave, the hurt feeling in her heart was as suddenly dispelled, and she returned in an entirely different mood to the table with the drinks.

They talked cheerfully for about ten minutes, then went out into the darkness, walked a little way together, and parted at a corner.

"We will be going the same way home soon!" said Vicki.

"Yes. Rather!" said Miss Roach, and noticed that this time her heart was responding to her voice, and that she was completely restored to a state of tranquillity and happiness over the whole matter.

She then wondered whether this feeling of tranquillity and

happiness was wholly dependent upon her new attitude, or partially dependent upon the three drinks inside her.

The thought of these three drinks, as she let herself into the Rosamund Tea Rooms, accidentally brought to her mind another thought—the thought that whereas she had paid for two out of these three drinks, Vicki had only paid for one, and that this unequal division of payment had taken place, actually, on three other occasions. She rebuked herself for this thought.

She was, she saw, always having thoughts for which she rebuked herself. It then flashed across her mind that the thoughts for which she rebuked herself seldom turned out to be other than shrewd and fruitful thoughts: and she rebuked herself for this as well.

CHAPTER FOUR

I

DAWN, slowing filling Church Street with grey light, disclosed another day of war.

Because it did this, this dawn bore no more resemblance to a peace-time dawn than the aspect of nature on a Sunday bears a resemblance to the aspect of nature on a weekday. Thus it seemed that dawn itself had been grimly harnessed to the war effort, made to alter its normal mode of existence, had been Bevin-conscripted.

As the weak, winter light grew, however, a charming thing happened: the time of day permitted the withdrawal of black-out curtains, and a few lights shone from the windows of early risers. These remained on for ten minutes or so, and in this period there was a Christmas-card effect, a brief resumption, or rather imitation, of the happy and unstrenuous lighting arrangements of the days before the war.

Much the same sort of thing would happen in the evening, when other social benefactors would keep on their lights unscreened until the last moment allowed by the regulations. But these evening lights gave forth, of course, quite a different atmosphere from those of the morning. At the end of the day such lights spoke soothingly of ease, recreation, repose: in the morning they burned intently and dramatically, speaking of renewed tension, of the battle of life, of the arduous endeavour and agitation of the day ahead.

Awareness of what went on outside penetrated hardly at all into the consciousness of those who lay on in bed within the walls of the Rosamund Tea Rooms. To these people, this part of the day in Church Street remained a pallid secret, which was either never disclosed to them at all, or was only disclosed when one of them, for some strange and forceful reason or other, got up to catch the early train to London. Then this adventurer would be delighted and impressed by the freshness, novelty, and quietness of what he saw: would be aware of being let into a secret: but the next day, sleeping on, he would become totally oblivious of its existence once again.

Certain sounds from the street did, indeed, float up into the stuffy, curtained bedrooms—an occasional lorry crashing through, the desultory disturbance of the quiet caused by the milkman and by the street-sweeper, the footsteps of the few people hurrying to the early train, the conversation of girls going to their war-work on bicycles—but the day did not begin at the Rosamund Tea Rooms until Sheila began to bounce about and knock on doors.

Even then the guests did not wake into full life. Instead, there was a dazed period in which each guest, turning in bed, renewed his acquaintanceship with his own problems and the fact that a war was being waged all over the world, and, finally rising and flinging back the curtains, contemplated the awful scene of wreckage caused by his sleep. The feeling of the morning after the night before is not a sensation endured by the dissolute only: every morning, for every human being, is in some sort a morning after the night before: the dissolute merely experience it in a more intense degree. There is an air of debauch about tossed bed-clothes, stale air, cold hot-water bottles, and last night's cast-off clothing, from which even the primmest of maiden ladies cannot hope to escape. Sleep is gross, a form of abandonment, and it is impossible for anyone to awake and observe its sordid consequences save with a faint sense of recent dissipation, of minute personal disquiet and remorse.

This perception, on the part of the guest, of his animal self, was made even more dreary by certain impressions which were now wafted towards him of the coarser bedroom selves of his fellow-guests. These impressions were conveyed to him in partially ghostly and mysterious ways—in the uncanny gurgling and throbbing of unlocated water-pipes, which seemed softly and eerily to answer each other all over the house: in the sound of unidentified windows shrieking open or being slammed shut: in sudden furious rushes of water from taps into basins: in the sound of bumps, and of thuds: of tooth-glasses being rattled with tooth-brushes, and of expectorations: of coughs, and stupendous throat-clearings: of noses being blown: even of actual groans. To listen carefully to these noises was to sense a peculiar intensity in the bedroom life of the boarders: it was as if they were taking advantage of their brief privacy to serve too eagerly the physical compulsions of life.

Mrs. Payne, pettishly hitting at her gong below, announced the proper commencement of day, and the end of privacy.

2

Mr. Thwaites made a habit of being the first in the dining-room for breakfast. No one had ever been known to beat him to it. Five, or even ten minutes before the time, he would be found sitting in his place at the table for four in the corner. It was as though he were fretful for the day to start, to be in his presidential position and to take charge of the day from the beginning. However early they appeared, those who entered after him, saying "Good morning, Mr. Thwaites" and catching his eye, had a distant feeling of being on the mat for being late. Miss Roach did, at any rate.

This morning, the Saturday following the one on which she had had drinks with Vicki Kugelmann at the River Sun, Miss Roach was in the room while the gong was still being hit, and took her place at the table with Mr. Thwaites.

"Good morning," said Mr. Thwaites. "You're very early, aren't you?" But this was not intended as a compliment: it still meant that she was late. It implied merely that a chronically late Miss Roach had appeared relatively early upon the scene.

"Yes," said Miss Roach, "I suppose I am."

Mr. Thwaites, fingering his knife, now quietly stared at Miss Roach. When alone with her he frequently stared at her like this, quite unconscious of her embarrassment and even of the fact that he was doing it. It was the preoccupied stare of one who sought to discover some fresh detail in her appearance or demeanour about which he could say or think something nasty. Prepared for this stare, she had come armed with her newspaper, which she now took up, looking at the headlines. She was defiantly conscious of her paper being the *News Chronicle*, which was, strictly speaking, banned by Mr. Thwaites. All newspapers, with the exception of the *Daily Mail*, which he himself took, were strictly speaking banned by Mr. Thwaites. But the fires of personal liberty are unextinguishable, even in so unlikely a precinct for their survival as the Rosamund Tea Rooms, and Miss Roach was not actually alone in her defiance. Miss Steele took *The Times* and Mr. Prest the *Daily Mirror*.

Miss Steele now came in, followed by Mrs. Barratt and, a little later, by Mr. Prest. Plates of porridge and racks of toast were handed round by Sheila, and breakfast began. The sky had cleared outside, and the sun, low in the sky, now shone into the room with the peculiar yellow brilliance which only a winter sun can achieve. In this hard and revealing light Mr. Thwaites succeeded in looking more immaculately clean and radiantly healthy than ever. There was not even any hope for Miss Roach that Mr. Thwaites would ever die.

As with his soup, Mr. Thwaites had a vigorous and single-minded technique with his porridge, and nothing was said for a minute or so, during which period there was a good deal of movement and adjustment of crockery and utensils upon the table. Even here the war had risen to the occasion and achieved its characteristic crowding effect, each guest having been supplied with a separate dish for butter and a separate bowl for sugar. This, in addition to its inconvenience, created a disagreeable atmosphere of niggardliness and caution, and caused Miss Roach further self-consciousness and difficulty. For Mr. Thwaites, she was fully aware, had his eye upon every cut she made at her butter and every spoonful she took of her sugar, mutely accusing her, if she took too much too early in the week, of greed or prodigality, or of parsimoniousness and tenacity if she saved either up for the end of the week and perpetrated the atrocious impropriety of having some left when all his had gone and consuming it in front of him. There was no pleasing this man.

"Nice to see the sun again," said Mrs. Barratt. "It looks as though it might be a nice day."

Mr. Thwaites, taking this remark, as he took all remarks made in this room, as being addressed to himself, looked over towards the window.

"Yes," he said. "A fine morning, in Troth.... In veritable Troth—a Beauteous Morning...." And he went on with his porridge.

When Mr. Thwaites started this Troth language it generally meant that he was in a good temper. If only as a symptom of this Miss Roach hoped that it might continue, and it did.

"And dost thou go forth this bonny morn," he said, addressing Mrs. Barratt, "into the highways and byways, to pay thy due respects to Good King Sol?"

Mrs. Barratt, familiar, as all in the Rosamund Tea Rooms were, with the Troth language, was able quickly to translate this, and see that Mr. Thwaites was asking her if she was going out for a walk. As she went for a walk every morning, and as Mr. Thwaites knew this perfectly well, the question was totally meaningless, and was put to Mrs. Barratt solely in order that Mr. Thwaites might exercise his eccentric and exuberant prose.

"Well," said Mrs. Barratt, "as a matter of fact I've got to go round and see my doctor at twelve."

There was a pause as Mr. Thwaites worked out what he could do with this.

"Ah," he said. "So at the Hour of Noon thou visiteth the Man of Many Medicines—dost thou?"

"Yes," said Mrs. Barratt. "That's right."

"Issuing therefrom, I take it," said Mr. Thwaites, "with diverse pills and potions, to heal thine ills?"

Mrs. Barratt did not reply to this.

"As for me," said Mr. Thwaites, "I betake myself unto the House of a Thousand Volumes—there to acquire a novel, detective, or of other vulgar sort, to beguile the passing hour."

"Yes," said Mrs. Barratt, "I want to change my book, too."

"And what of my Lady of the Roach?" asked Mr. Thwaites. "How doth *she* disport herself this morning?"

"I haven't really made up my mind," said Miss Roach, as agreeably as she was able.

"She goeth, perchance, unto the coffee-house," said Mr. Thwaites, "there to partake of the noxious brown fluid with her continental friends?"

Ah—here we were, thought Miss Roach. He had to get nasty sooner or later. This was a reference to Vicki Kugelmann, and her habit of having a cup of coffee with her on a Saturday morning.

"How do you mean?" she said, "my continental friends?"

"Why," said Mr. Thwaites, "dost thou not forgather, of a Saturday morning, with a certain dame of Teutonic origin?"

"Oh," said Miss Roach, "you mean Vicki Kugelmann. Yes—I do have coffee with her."

"Is that her name?" said Mr. Thwaites, and here Miss Steele, at her table alone, cut in.

"Yes. I've seen you with her," she said. "Is it true that she's coming here?"

"*What?*" said Mr. Thwaites, his amazement knocking him back into plain English. "Did I hear you say coming here?"

Miss Roach had for some time been wondering when this news was going to break. She herself had had a word about the matter with Mrs. Payne, but had not, for some reason, quite had the courage to mention it to anyone else. Though actually the whole thing had been arranged independently of her by Vicki Kugelmann and Mrs. Payne, she still felt that, because she was known in the boarding-house as the friend of the German girl in the town, she was in fact responsible and would have to bear the brunt of any shocked or resentful sentiment amongst the guests which the news might possibly cause.

Now, bracing herself to face this alone, she found succour from an unexpected source.

"Yes," said Mrs. Barratt, in the most matter-of-fact way. "She's coming in next Wednesday."

"*What?*" said Mr. Thwaites. "Coming in *here*—coming into the house?"

"Yes—that's right," said Mrs. Barratt. "I know, because she's coming into my room. I'm going over the way to a room at the back—away from the noise."

"Well," said Mr. Thwaites, after a pause, and staring at Miss Roach, "this is pretty good. I must say this is pretty good."

"What's pretty good?" Miss Roach was suddenly defiant. "How do you mean, Mr. Thwaites?"

"Well, *I* should say it is. I should say it's just about as good as it could be."

"Yes, it is good," said Miss Steele, sternly, from her table. "I think it'll be very nice to have her."

"Oh, so you think it will be nice to have her? What do you think, Mrs. Barratt?"

"Yes, I think it'll be nice, too," said Mrs. Barratt. "I hear she's very nice."

"Well, it's good to hear your opinions," said Mr. Thwaites. "Personally, it makes me wonder what we're fighting for, that's all."

"Well," said Miss Steele, who was evidently in a combatant mood, and looked as though she might use some History upon Mr. Thwaites at any moment, "we're not fighting against individuals, are we? We're fighting against Fascism, aren't we?"

"I don't know about Fascism—" began Mr. Thwaites, but Miss Steele went on.

"It's not as though she's not lived here the greater part of her life. And if she's adopted our ways and our country, it's up to us to give her our protection, isn't it?"

"I don't know about protection—" began Mr. Thwaites, but Miss Steele went on.

"That's what democracy is, isn't it?" she said. "It doesn't mean anything if it doesn't mean that, does it?"

"Yes, I quite agree," said Mrs. Barratt. "She *has* lived here nearly all her life, hasn't she, Miss Roach?"

"Oh yes," said Miss Roach, "she has."

And at this there was a silence as Sheila replaced the plates of porridge with plates which contained a small rasher of bacon set upon a generous pile of watery scrambled American dehydrated egg.

"Well, it's not what *I'm* fighting for, anyway," said Mr. Thwaites, at last, giving the impression that his principles had caused him to enter upon the second world war of his own accord, and that he was a formidable and tireless battler therein.

"Where's she going to sit, may I ask?" he asked a little later, again looking at Miss Roach. "Is she going to have a table with you?"

Miss Roach was seeking an answer to this when Mrs. Barratt answered instead.

"I hope not," she said. "I hope she's going to come and sit with us. There's plenty of room for another."

"Yes. I hope so, too," said Miss Steele.

This was slightly absurd of Miss Steele, as the table at which Mr. Thwaites, Mrs. Barratt, and Miss Roach sat was not, strictly speaking, Miss Steele's business at all. It was Miss Steele's only way, however, of supporting Miss Roach and again establishing her sentiments on this matter.

It was now clear to Miss Roach that the Rosamund Tea Rooms as a whole, so far from manifesting any symptoms of revulsion against the notion of a German girl appearing in its midst, was willing to throw out a warm and active welcome—so that Vicki Kugelmann was, in fact, to be treated with less fear and suspicion than any newcomer of the ordinary sort would have had to face, and was starting from something a good deal better than scratch.

"Oh—so she's sitting here, is she?" said Mr. Thwaites, and no one answered him. . . .

"Well—we shall see," said Mr. Thwaites. "Sometimes it happens that *two* people can play at that sort of game."

And on this mystifying yet menacing note he was silent for the rest of the meal.

As usual, Mr. Thwaites being silent, all the rest were silent. Knives and forks clattered on plates. Cups were raised to mouths and were heard being put back gently on to saucers. Chairs creaked.

3

After breakfast it was Mr. Thwaites' habit to go up into the Lounge. Here he sat in his chair, put on his spectacles, opened his newspaper, and, if anyone else was present, intermittently Saw things about what he called his "friends"—saw, for example, that our friends the Russians had retreated in a certain sector, that our friends the Italians were undergoing bombardment, that

Friend Rommel had done this, and that Friend Montgomery had done that, that Friend Churchill was to broadcast next week, that Friend Woolton was further tampering with "the nation's larder", that Friend Bevin had issued a fresh decree in regard to man-power, and so on and so forth.

After this, which took about twenty minutes, he left the Lounge and went into his bedroom, in which he was heard walking savagely about for at least half an hour—or at any rate what seemed at least half an hour to his fellow-boarders. What was he *doing* in there? This mystery, repeated relentlessly each morning, but never clarified, hung like a sullen cloud over the Rosamund Tea Rooms at this time of day.

When he at last came out the other elderly guests were already setting about their business—the business, that is to say, of those who in fact had no business on this earth save that of cautiously steering their respective failing bodies along paths free from discomfort and illness in the direction of the final illness which would exterminate them.

4

The relatively active Miss Steele was usually the first off the mark, and after her came Mrs. Barratt.

Miss Steele, who was fond of talking at length to her acquaintances on street corners, in whom street corners actually stimulated loquacity, invariably engineered excuses to go shopping in the town: while Mrs. Barratt, who disliked shopping and talking, went for a "walk" as an end in itself.

If Mrs. Barratt was not feeling up to the mark she satisfied honour with a short journey which included a stroll in the cemetery behind the neighbouring church: if she was well enough, however, and if it was warm enough, she made herself take a walk and sit down in Thames Lockdon Park.

Gloomy as both these enforced excursions were, Mrs. Barratt's soul was saddened less by the cemetery than by the Park. The

Park, in fact, was the cemetery—the burial-ground, to those elderly ones who came slowly limping along its asphalt paths to sit down and stare, of hope, vivacity, enthusiasm, animation—of life, in the positive sense of the word, itself. Where the cemetery spoke greenly and gracefully of death and antiquity, the Park spoke leaflessly and hideously of life-in-death, or death-in-life, amidst immature municipal surroundings. Though of small, almost miniature dimensions, and bearing the singular characteristic of running by the side of a river, Thames Lockdon Park closely resembled other parks of its kind all over the country. Dominated by a small red-brick building, which was seemingly deserted all the year save by the gardener, and devoid of all furniture save the gardener's brooms, machines, and tools, Thames Lockdon Park, within its small acreage, contained and enclosed with neat hedges a green bowling-green, a green putting-green, a brown hard tennis-court, a sandy enclosure with swings for children, and a small recreation-ground for games of all sorts.

Threaded through these were the asphalt paths, bordered in places with grass verges and flower-beds, and ornamented here and there with brand-new trees about ten feet in height. Though much was thus offered to the public, little, even in the summer, was taken advantage of, and more was forbidden—Cycling, Spitting, walking on the grass, picking flowers, defacing the Corporation's property, removing its chairs, using the bowling-green, putting-green, or tennis-court without asking its permission, etc., etc.—these ordinances being proclaimed in white lettering on green boards here, there, and everywhere, and a reward of forty shillings being in some cases offered to amateur detectives of culprits.

Backed and tolerably comfortable seats, each accommodating five or six persons, were placed at intervals facing the river, and to these Mrs. Barratt—oblivious of putting, bowls, and tennis, or of the temptation to Cycle, remove or deface—went to sit. Nor was Mrs. Barratt, this morning, alone in the pursuit of this object, the unexpectedly fine and warm day having brought out several other people of a similar mind, age, and constitution from the boarding-houses of Thames Lockdon, of which there were many.

Nor was this weak, semi-tottering parade of death-in-life in the winter sun taking place in Thames Lockdon alone. Though happening so quietly, and as it were clandestinely: though utterly unknown to and unsuspected by the busy world of train-takers, office-goers, and workers, it was as much a feature of the English social scene generally as train-taking, office-going, and working. At eleven o'clock each morning, far and wide over the land—in Parks, in Gardens, on Sea-fronts—in shelters, on seats, in crazy-paved nooks; beneath walls, behind hedges, facing flower-beds, these inert and silent sessions were in progress, out of the wind and forgotten by the world.

For the most part without books, newspapers, or knitting; with only the river and those who passed by to watch; in behaviour curiously shy and curiously bold (shy in that they seldom spoke to each other, bold in that they would not hesitate to squeeze into a vacant place among strangers on a bench), these people would sit together for as much as two hours at a stretch, depart without a word, and obey, in general, their own peculiar precedents. Certain seats and positions grew, in the course of time, under the sphere of influence of certain individuals or groups, and such rights, once established, were hardly ever infringed save by newcomers or casuals. In fact, each real veteran had in due course acquired his own place on a particular seat to which it was practically his privilege to go—this privilege turning into an obligation, of course, when the wind was blowing in an adverse direction.

Amongst such regulars the ice would at last be broken: conversations would be started: and from these there would gradually and timidly arise bench-companionships of the extremest pathos. Two old ladies, beginning by talking about the weather, would go on to compare their respective boarding-houses, the times of meals, the amenities, the food, the quiet. From this they would proceed, from day to day, to disclose their motives in living in what way and where they did, their former manner of life, the doings of their near relations, what they considered their real background as opposed to the illusory and temporary background of their present abode. Soon, with a feeling of having found a detached and intelligent listener, met under novel circumstances totally different from those in which they would converse with anyone in the boarding-house from which they came—with a feeling of being out of school, as it were, or of playing truant with someone from another school —they would begin to look forward to these apparently casual meetings, would at last come shyly to a tacit acknowledgment that they met regularly, would be found in their places on time, speaking of being "early", or "late", even gleefully and conspiratorially of "keeping", with a bag or newspaper, each other's "seats".

Or again, two old men, at first hostile and suspicious, would learn to tolerate each other—in retrospective travel pursuing each other, if necessary through the medium of distant family connections, to the ends of the earth—in the matter of past institutions, personalities, directorships, or sporting events and techniques, sticking at each other's throats with unwearied resource—but at last hammering out a gruff mutual respect tempering dislike. Or, yet again, an old lady might enter into the same sort of relationship with an old man—an ex-military man from India perhaps—to whom she would listen, Desdemona-like, charmed and impressed, at last walking back with him in the direction of the town and parting from him with an almost emotional feeling of having conversed with a "gentleman", and being gratified by this fact both for its own sake and because she, unlike anyone in the establishment where lunch awaited her, was able to understand and meet such an individual on an equal footing. For nearly all who lived in the boarding-houses of Thames Lockdon were conscious of having descended in the world, of having arrived where they were by a pure freak of fate, and of courteously but condescendingly acting a part in front of their fellow-boarders.

Just as the great world was oblivious of what went on in Thames Lockdon Park at this time of day, so were these old people oblivious of what went on in the great world—oblivious, in particular, of what took place, and had taken place only the night before, on the actual seats, and hallowed corners of seats, in which they now sat in so demure a way. Though distantly appraised of the scandalous behaviour of the American soldiers with the shop-girls of the town, which was indeed a matter of common gossip, such was their blindness, or rather psychological remoteness from such things, that the thought never flashed across their minds that each morning they were entering, and complacently occupying, the front stalls of the very theatre of these misdemeanours. Had such a vision of the truth and the night before ever entered their heads, and had the full story been revealed in detail, they would have shunned in horror and disgust a locality which in fact they regarded as belonging solely to themselves and bearing a peculiar respectability owing to their morning visitations. The Americans and shop-girls were similarly in the dark as to what went on in the day, but were on their part devoid of scruples: and the river flowed on by night and day indiscriminately.

This morning Mrs. Barratt, walking a little further than usual, unwittingly sat down on the same corner of the actual seat always instinctively chosen by the Lieutenant when disposed to kiss Miss Roach fervently and at length.

With Miss Steele and Mrs. Barratt respectively in the town and the Park, with Miss Roach avoiding him like the plague, and Mr. Prest about his business, Mr. Thwaites had on fine mornings no one to boom at in the Rosamund Tea Rooms, and spent much of the time writing embittered letters in the Lounge. These, after he had put on his overcoat and cap, he took round to the Post Office and posted in the most acid way. He passed pillar-boxes on the way, but did not trust them, as not going to the root of the matter.

After this he would return to the Rosamund Tea Rooms, where he would prowl restlessly, and whence he would, perhaps, make one or two rapid, tigerish excursions into the town, to make an enquiry, to buy something, or to change a book—invariably tying the assistants into knots, and, in the ironical pose of a stupid man, saying he was *so* sorry, no doubt it was *his* fault, entirely.

By a quarter to one he was back in the Lounge, impatient, after so long an interval, to wield again the boarding-house rod, and hopeful of the return of Mrs. Barratt, Miss Steele, or Miss Roach, but not of Mr. Prest, who never appeared in the Lounge before meals, and who was nearly always the last to sit down in the dining-room.

Mr. Prest was, in fact, the black sheep of the boarding-house, and this not only in Mr. Thwaites' estimation.

CHAPTER FIVE

I

THOUGH speaking, when he did speak, with a "common" accent, and dressing in a "common" way, Mr. Prest seemed to have no ambition to force his company upon the others, and kept himself very much to himself. This curious contradiction, combined with the fact that he was known to indulge in the totally alien and eerie practice of drinking beer locally, had earned him the reputation of being "funny", "strange", "odd", "queer". Though too quiet in his manners, and too seemly in his comings and goings, to give offence, he was yet regarded as being somehow beyond the pale. A silence fell as he entered the dining-room, and people found themselves staring at him, seeking to discover his secret.

A big man, nearing sixty years of age, Mr. Prest had a resonant and beery voice, and a face of that pugilistic cast which is acquired by certain music-hall comedians as well as pugilists: it is almost as though they bear the marks of eggs, vegetables, and dead cats thrown at them on Saturday nights in their strenuous past. In Mr. Prest's face, in fact, was to be found his secret: as "Archie Prest" he had long ago topped bills in provincial pantomimes and been featured with some distinction in London and provincial Variety.

The Rosamund Tea Rooms knew nothing of this precisely, though it was rumoured amongst them that he had at one time been on, or connected with, "the stage"—a rumour which only added to their fear and displeasure. Mr. Thwaites, for a long while unable even to pass the time of day with him on a staircase with civility, had finally sent him to Coventry absolutely, and the other guests, though without active malice, would have seemed to have taken their cue from Mr. Thwaites.

The Rosamund Tea Rooms, thus almost unanimous in its attitude of superiority towards Mr. Prest, was incapable even of the conjecture that Mr. Prest, on his part, had any attitude other than a humble and negative one towards the Rosamund Tea Rooms. But this, in fact, he had, looking, as he did, upon the Rosamund Tea Rooms with the supreme, leisured, and assured contempt of a cultivated man for Philistines of the most fearful type—with the disdain of an original and educated person who had seen life for small-town ignoramuses too confined and paltry in their outlook to take seriously for a moment—and regarding the Rosamund Tea Rooms, indeed, as a sort of zoo, containing easily recognised types of freak animals, into which an ironical fate had brought him.

Mr. Prest was too polite, and indeed too innately modest and tolerant, to let this be seen; and so this curious turning of the tables, whereby the Rosamund Tea Rooms was in reality being sent to Coventry by Mr. Prest, remained unsuspected.

The mistake arose, of course, from the inability of the Rosamund Tea Rooms to perceive that all it looked upon as being symptomatic of Mr Prest's "commonness", Mr. Prest himself looked upon as the very backbone of his culture: that his own upbringing and manner of life, his music-hall history, his achievements, his traditions, his friends, the fact that he had been associated with and could still call by their Christian names many well-known stars both of the past and present, speaking, if he went to town, their liberal and racy language in public-houses, and understanding their professional jokes—that all these things were to Mr. Prest reasons, not for faint opprobrium, but for complacence and pride.

Mr. Prest was, however, conscious of never having fully succeeded in life, of now belonging to the past, of being in more or less enforced retirement, and of being utterly unknown as a personality outside a circle of acquaintances in London which diminished year by year. He was, therefore, a miserable man—his sense of failure and futility showing in his demeanour. He had, in fact, something of the character and manner, as well as the external semblance, of a certain sort of ex-pugilist—an air of having been battered silly by life, of submissiveness to events, of gentleness, of willingness to please, of dog like gloom and absent-mindedness as he floated through the day.

Two or three times each month Mr. Prest was missing at his place in the dining-room for lunch and dinner, and was not seen till the next day. The guests would be silently forewarned of these absences by a complete change in the aspect and carriage of the solitary man at breakfast—by the smart lounge suit which replaced the plus-fours or loose tweeds which he normally wore, by the stiff white collar and glistening tie—an air of freshness and rejuvenation. Mr. Prest was going to town, and could be seen, soon after breakfast, on his way to the station, wearing a tight-fitting overcoat with heavily padded shoulders, a bowler hat and leather gloves, and looking, on the whole, rather more than less "common" than usual.

The Rosamund Tea Rooms had no idea of what Mr. Prest

did in London: nor did he have any specific business or know exactly himself how he was going to spend the day, which would actually be devoted to nothing apart from the pursuit of fraternal companionship in the atmosphere of the past.

With this object in mind he would invariably be found, at about twelve o'clock, in some bar off Leicester Square, Charing Cross Road, or St. Martin's Lane, sipping at his beer and hoping for the best. With people of his profession, he knew well enough, there were fashions and crazes for certain public-houses—which gained or lost popularity either mysteriously or according to the movements of the premises of certain theatrical agents, managers, or shows in their vicinity—and with these migrations and fashions he found it hard, in his retirement and comparative isolation, to keep up. For this reason he would sometimes be lucky, but at other times very much otherwise, going with high spirits and confidence into a bar which a month or so ago had been filled with a delightful assembly of old friends and the cream of his one-time profession, only to find the place forlorn and all but empty, doing a feeble trade with alien customers. Then, thinking that perhaps he had arrived too early, he would wait patiently, and order another beer, finally, with feigned detachment, asking the barmaid whether so-and-so was "coming in" or was "about these days", or whether someone else had "been in lately"—the barmaid answering him indifferently and with total lack of comprehension of his spiritual needs.

At other times, when he expected least, most would come his way. At the moment of entering he would be hailed by a friend, or swept into a circle of familiars amongst whom he took his turn, with mounting gaiety, in buying rounds of drinks. On these occasions one thing would lead to another, one public-house would lead to another, movements would be made from place to place where the "crowd" was known or reputed to be, introductions would be made, friendships would revive, or blossom, and Mr. Prest, in his old element, now completely elated rather than dejected by his own yesterdays, meeting on an equal footing and talking of professional matters with famous men of the immediate moment, with people of the same stature as a Trinder, an Askey, or a Fields, would go from strength to strength. Lunch would be taken late and noisily upstairs in some public-house known to the crowd he was with: in the afternoon he would go to a show, or to the pictures, or to tea in the dressing-room of a friend in work: and in the evening he would be once again in the bars, taking up assignations he had made at lunch. The last train brought him in at about ten-thirty to Thames Lockdon Station, whence he would emerge into the blackness, full of drink, certainly, but fuller still of the day behind him, of the friends and celebrities he had met—the "grand scouts" as he called them—of the humour, humanity, spaciousness, and grandeur of that manner of life as opposed to the inhibited and petty provinciality of the riverside town. At such moments he held Thames Lockdon and the Rosamund Tea Rooms in more profound and philosophic scorn than ever. If he staggered occasionally, or even tripped, as he walked back from the station by the same way taken each evening by Miss Roach, it might well have been due to the black-out, and in any case he always pulled himself together in time to make a noiseless and dignified entrance into the Rosamund Tea Rooms, whose guests remained in complete ignorance of his condition and sentiments in regard to themselves.

2

For Mr. Prest there were other days in London when, though alighting upon the right bar in the West End at the right time, something would go wrong. His friends would be there, but busy in discussion, or not to be greeted in the usual way because talking to strangers, or with their backs to him, or inaccessible owing to the crowd, or, if at last encountered squarely, compelled to drink up their drinks and go off elsewhere. The stars, also, would be present, but keeping, today, in their own orbits, far away at the other end of the bar, surrounded by possibly hateful or contemptible satellites.

On such unfortunate days, standing alone at the bar sipping his self-bought beer, furtively watching all that was taking place, silent, embarrassed, self-conscious, compelled in the last resort to read a newspaper, or even take a letter out of his pocket and pretend to be reconsidering its contents, Mr. Prest would suffer a far keener sense of disappointment than on the days when the members of his circle failed to put in an appearance at all. Nor did he have the character to remedy this state of affairs. Too proud to "butt in" anywhere, because obsessed, in secret, by an ever-present fear of being "out of it" and "not wanted" nowadays, he stood there miserably, unable fully to believe that his solitude in the crowd was an entirely fortuitous matter, though in fact for the most part it was. Sometimes, after hanging on for an hour or more in this way, he would drink up his beer and go out into the street without a word to anyone, lunch by himself, and, after a visit to the pictures, take a train home early in the evening, occasionally catching the same train and sitting in the same compartment as Miss Roach, who would observe him curiously, as he sat opposite reading his newspaper or looking out of the window, and sense something of his sadness and disappointment, in his smart lounge suit and overcoat.

But on such evenings he would never dine at the Rosamund Tea Rooms: that, crowning his failure during the day to enjoy himself as he had hoped, would have been asking him to bear too much. Instead he went the round of his favourite locals, had a sandwich at a bar, and went to bed early.

3

The next day the ex-comedian would be in his tweed suit at breakfast, and his normal life would be resumed.

This varied hardly at all. After a short walk round the town to buy a newspaper, or to see the times of showing at the local cinema, he would go to a garage in Church Street, where he kept a bicycle, and cycle to the local golf-course about three-quarters of a mile away. Here he played golf for two hours by himself, carefully avoiding all other players, of whom there were practically none at this time of year, going to the loneliest part of the course, playing with several balls and giving the impression, to the club secretary, the club professional, and the greenkeeper, of being slightly off his head. In fact, his sanity on this matter would not be too demonstrably easy to defend. Having, in the past, played games of golf on non-matinée days with his associates on provincial golf-courses all over the country, and having acquired then the naïve and dangerous belief that he required only continuous practice to become a good player, he had resolved to devote the leisure of his retirement to the pursuit of this end, and later to astonish his opponents. Now, after seven years of intense mental labour and daily concentration, his opponents would have remained unastonished.

Though obscurely aware of this, his naïvety and freshness of belief remained unabated. Also, having the treacherous faculty, at certain intervals, of being able to hit the ball squarely off the middle of the club-head four or five times in succession, Mr. Prest would exhibit the curious caution (the caution of a madman) of packing up his clubs and going home only when such an interval had just occurred and remained unmarred by disaster, and thus enable himself during the rest of the day to embrace the pleasant belief that he had at last alighted upon the simple explanation of golf which had by the merest chance eluded him for so many years.

Alone in the distance, lost in the wind, this obsessed figure, requiring, really, the pen of a Wordsworth to suggest the quality of its mystery and solitude, could be seen on the course each morning, hitting ball after ball, keeping its head down, examining its own methods, observing its own swing half-way through, and watching results with misery or triumph, until about a quarter past twelve.

Then Mr. Prest, having again at the last moment snatched light and faith from chaos and gloom by a process of mental self-deception which a child would scorn to use, would return with his clubs to the professional's shop and cycle home.

Having washed and changed his shoes at the Rosamund Tea Rooms, Mr. Prest would now go out and drink beer, come in as much as ten minutes late for lunch, after which, still avoiding the Lounge and the company of others, he would go to his bedroom, fail to appear for tea, and not be seen again until dinner-time.

The guests, haunted and faintly depressed, in spite of themselves, by this odd and independent personality, often wondered what he did in his bedroom during the long afternoon. Actually, having locked the door, he promptly removed his coat and trousers, lit the gas-fire, got into bed, read a Western story (a form of literature in which he was erudite), and went to sleep.

Sometimes, when he heard the gong for tea being hit below, he would get up and go out and have tea at a neighbouring confectioner's: but usually he would miss tea altogether, preferring to lie on in bed, dozing, or (as darkness gathered outside, and the gas-fire, slowly making its presence and individuality felt, lit with a red and dramatic light the walls and ceiling) with open eyes thinking gloomy thoughts.

At one minute to six, six being the hour at which the public-houses opened in Thames Lockdon, the guests would hear the click of the front door being shut and the sound of Mr. Prest's footsteps receding down the street.

This noise, just heard, signalised to them the beginning of the evening proper, the hope of in the not-too-distant future preparing themselves for dinner, of having dinner itself, and of Miss Roach returning.

Without knowing it, the guests looked forward to Miss Roach's safe return each night—perhaps because she was their only wayfarer and adventurer; perhaps because, in this capacity, she might conceivably bring late and exciting news from the world of war and affairs; perhaps because, in their extreme of *ennui*, and regardless of her feelings, they even hoped to witness and share in the excitement of a battle between herself and Mr. Thwaites. They liked Miss Roach, and admired the way she stood up to him.

CHAPTER SIX

I

SOMETIMES, during her week-ends down at Thames Lockdon, if there was a moon to light her, Miss Roach would take a walk by herself between tea and dinner.

Walking along the tow-path the other side of the river for about half a mile, she would climb up into the fields and hills which lay to the north of the town, and stopping, perhaps at a stile or gate, would look at the moon and listen carefully—would put her ear, as it were, to the keyhole of agricultural tranquillity, and eavesdrop.

At such moments the countryside, stealthily informing her of its immense size, would seem, of course, in grandeur, wildness and stillness, completely to dominate and submerge all things appertaining to men and towns, and to reduce, in particular, to microscopic, thread-like smallness the railway-tracks by which these communicated with each other—the noise of the trains thereon distantly falling on her straining ear like something less than minute rumblings in the enormous belly of the enormous supine organism enveloping her and everything. By this adjustment of her sense of dimensions, Miss Roach's spirit, bathed in moonlight, would be composed, consoled, and refreshed.

The train, on the other hand, which Miss Roach normally took down from London to Thames Lockdon, had opposite ideas. So far from being aware of its doll-like magnitude in the night, of being diminished practically to the point of extinction by the surrounding void of fields, woods, and hills, it came crashing on, like a huge staggering bully, from station to station, lashing out right and left at the night, on which the tables were turned, which was itself relegated to nothingness, and whose very stars had less importance in the eyes of the train than one of the sparks from the funnel of its engine. In the same way Miss Roach's attitude was completely reversed, and when at last she alighted at Thames Lockdon station, instead of feeling composed, consoled, and refreshed, she was invariably filled with anxiety, apprehensiveness, and dejection.

2

The night was Wednesday, and Miss Roach walked down the platform. This was the "famous" Wednesday, as she and Vicki Kugelmann had called it when they had met in the town over the week-end—the Wednesday upon which Vicki was to enter the Rosamund Tea Rooms as her abode.

"I shall be very shy," Vicki had said, and Miss Roach had promised her that they should embark upon the adventure together. Vicki was to meet her at the station, or, if the night was too cold or the train was late, at the River Sun. Then, having had a drink, they were to get a taxi from the station, go to Vicki's place to collect her luggage, and proceed to Church Street.

As Miss Roach walked down the platform she realised that she was not looking forward to all this, and would be glad when it was over.

Though the cold was not unduly severe, and the train scarcely unpunctual, there was no sign of Vicki at the barrier. A little surprised at this, and with a faint premonition of something faintly unexpected having occurred, she followed the light of her torch round to the River Sun.

Here she was again surprised, in the first place because the saloon lounge, instead of being practically empty as it nearly always was at this time of night, was, owing to some obscure cause, filled with people; and in the second place because a single rapid glance informed her that Vicki was not present, but that the Lieutenant was, and this in a corner in the company of one of the shop-girls she had met previously.

She went to the bar with the attempted air of one who had neither seen nor been seen, but with the actual air of one who was fully aware that both these things had happened, and with two pink gins in her hand managed to procure a table at the opposite end of the room from the one at which the Lieutenant sat.

She was next surprised by the length of time she had to wait for Vicki, who did not actually appear until ten minutes later. This was, apparently, to be an evening of surprises. While waiting she indulged in speculations, speculations of considerable depth, cynicism, and audacity, in regard to the Lieutenant and the shop-girl—even going so far as to wonder whether the shop-girl, instead of herself, might not ultimately be destined to achieve the crown of Laundry queen, or, along with other candidates unknown to Miss Roach in the town, be secretly aspiring to such an office. At the moment she felt curiously indifferent as to whether this was so or not.

When Vicki at last appeared she made no apology for being late, but by this Miss Roach, aware of personally carrying notions of punctuality to excess, did not permit herself to be in any way annoyed.

They greeted each other with cordiality, but after this their conversation was a little forced and embarrassed in its gaiety. This, Miss Roach felt, was to a certain extent due to their both knowing that this was the "famous" evening, and that, although they would not admit it, something of a sharp ordeal lay ahead of them at the Rosamund Tea Rooms. It was also due, however, to the fact that Vicki (unlike Miss Roach, who had her back to them) was so seated that she could see the Lieutenant and the shop-girl the other side of the room, and was continually glancing over in that direction while answering Miss Roach in a slightly distracted way.

At last Miss Roach determined to break the ice by mentioning what she knew was on both their minds.

"Well—are you all packed and ready round at your place?" she said. "We must have another drink before we go."

"Ah no!" said Vicki, with sudden vivacity, and almost as if surprised that Miss Roach did not know. "That is all right, my dear! I changed my mind. I went round there this afternoon!"

"What? Are you in there already?"

"Yes indeed. I went round there this afternoon. I had a most interesting tea."

"Tea?" said Miss Roach.

"Yes," said Vicki. "Most interesting. I am now quite one of the circle, my dear!"

3

"Oh well—that's fine," said Miss Roach. "I'm glad you've got in." But this was not what she wanted to say, and, in the pause that followed, if Vicki had looked carefully enough, which she made no attempt to do, she would have observed a thoughtful look in Miss Roach's eye.

Miss Roach had had a premonition that this was to be an evening of surprises, but for this surprise, at this moment, she had not bargained. She was aware of being hurt. She was not sure that she was not more than hurt. She was not sure, for a moment, that she was not angry, decidedly angry. It was not so much that Vicki Kugelmann had gone into the Rosamund Tea Rooms of her own accord: that, taken by itself, she had presumably every right to do if it suited her convenience—though, in view of her pretended timidity and their friendly engagement to brave the perils of the boarding-house together, it seemed a curiously inconsequent, independent, and perhaps insensitive thing to have done. It was, rather, the fact of her having done this taken in conjunction with other facts which awakened Miss Roach's annoyance the fact that she had not turned up at the station to meet Miss Roach as she had promised, that she had arrived more than ten minutes late at the River Sun, that she had made no apology for either of these things, and had finally sprung this news in the coolest manner possible after having spoken about other things, and after having most irritatingly kept on casting surreptitious glances over at Miss Roach's personal friend, the Lieutenant. . . . It was the *coolness* of it all which surprised and irritated Miss Roach most of all. So she had had tea with them all, had she? And now she was quite one of the circle, was she? What an extraordinary woman she was, and what an extraordinary capacity for crushing Miss Roach's aspirations as a fairy-godmother!

"So you had tea—did you?" said Miss Roach, if only in order to interrupt another surreptitious glance at the Lieutenant, and as amiably as she could. "Were they all there?"

"Yes. All there. Mrs. Barratt, Miss Steele, Mr. Thwaites . . ."

"And how did you get on with them?"

"Oh, very well," said Vicki. "We got on famously. They are nice old frumps."

("Nice old frumps"! There she went again! Somehow, at some time, if hereafter Miss Roach was going to live under the same roof as her friend, she would have to get her out of the habit of gaily throwing off these fearful expressions, explain how hideous their utterance was in her faintly foreign accent, make her somehow aware of the total and appalling frumpishness attached to their use!)

"And what about Mr. Thwaites?" said Miss Roach. "How did you get on with him?"

"Ah! Mr. Thwaites! Very well indeed," said Vicki. "I think he is already a little smitten, the poor old gent!"

And, as Miss Roach's blood froze in her veins, Vicki Kugelmann again glanced over surreptitiously in the direction of the Lieutenant. . . .

CHAPTER SEVEN

I

"NICE *old frumps.*" "*Already a little smitten, the poor old gent.*" Yes, thought Miss Roach, lying in the sleepless darkness of her room, that was where the evening had, properly speaking, started, begun to warm up, acquired its peculiar tone! . . .

Miss Roach switched on her light, went over to the wash-basin for a glass of water, saw by her leather electric clock that it was twenty to two, switched off the light again, and decided, this time, to sleep.

"*Already a little smitten, the poor old gent.*" . . . And a moment after that Lieutenant Lummis had entered, and gone over (she could see by Vicki's eyes) to join the shop-girl and her own Lieutenant.

And then a few minutes later (and again informed of what was about to happen by Vicki's expression) she had felt the Lieutenant's hand on her shoulder, and heard the Lieutenant's voice. "Well—how are we tonight?" he had said. "I saw you come in."

"Hullo!" she had said, looking up and smiling. "Yes. I saw you too."

"I've been holding the fort," he said, and looked at her in a slightly embarrassed way. He bore this look of embarrassment, she believed, for two reasons. In the main it was because he was definitely trying to explain away the shop-girl, to convey to Miss Roach that in sitting with her he had only been holding the fort until his friend had come in and released him from an invidious situation, and for this reason Miss Roach was, in spite of herself, minutely relieved. For, however critical, and at times ironic, her attitude was towards the Laundry business in Wilkes Barre, U.S.A., she still liked to feel that it was a domain in which she alone had at present the right to entertain speculations and fancies. The Lieutenant, however, was also looking embarrassed because she had not yet introduced him to Vicki.

"Oh—do you know Vicki Kugelmann?" she said, and "No—I don't think I do," he said, and "No—I don't think we've met," said Vicki, and they shook hands. "Well, can I join you if I buy you a beautiful drink?" said the Lieutenant, and when they assented, he asked them what he should buy them. "You can buy me a beautiful pink gin if you will," said Vicki, looking at him humorously with her rather nice eyes. "Beautifully pink, or beautifully ginny?" asked the Lieutenant. "Beautifully pink," said Vicki, and after these undistinguished but amiable sallies he went away to get them.

Of course he had brought large ones, and of course, as soon as he could get them to finish them, he had brought them more, and in half an hour's time they were all talking away with the liveliest amity and humour. The Lieutenant, at first slightly shy of the German, and beginning by looking dependently at Miss Roach and addressing most of his remarks to her, soon lost his nervousness and began to speak, if anything, more to the German than to Miss Roach. There finally arose, indeed, amidst the general cordiality, one of those rather queer situations, common to three-cornered meetings of this sort, in which the two who have just met begin actually to take sides against the character who has introduced them and whom they both know so well, humorously aligning themselves against this character, from their common knowledge comparing notes in regard to its idiosyncrasies, saying, "Oh, of course she's awful in that way," or "I must say she's very good about that," or "Have you noticed how she always does that?"—and so on and so forth. This funny game, apparently so affectionate, but whose origins perhaps lie hidden deep in the nastier side of human nature, passes the time well enough if not taken too far, and Miss Roach was not aware of this happening and was in no way displeased. She was, however, as the third party always is on these occasions, somewhat bored and isolated, and for this reason was the first to look at the clock and suggest that it was time to go.

Of course the Lieutenant had said that he would not hear of this, and demanded that they should stay to dinner with him. But, in taking a stand against this, Vicki, after seeming to hesitate, joined Miss Roach. Only when she did so did the Lieutenant succumb. Vicki, in some peculiar way, was now the dominant power, the one looked to, the giver of deciding votes. The Lieutenant still, of course, wanted them to have another drink, and although Miss Roach did not want to do this, and said so, the Lieutenant argued forcefully, and it was Vicki who effected a compromise by saying they would have a small one, only a small one, and then go at once.

At last the Lieutenant allowed them to leave, and she and Vicki were walking along in the blackness in silence—a silence and blackness contrasting strongly with the light and noise they had left, and causing momentary speechlessness. But at last the Lieutenant was mentioned and Vicki said that she thought him "very good fun".

"He's a bit of a handful," said Miss Roach, "isn't he?" And Vicki paused a moment before replying.

"Oh yes. Perhaps," she then conceded. "But not if you know how to handle him."

And Miss Roach did not like this.

2

Nor did she exactly like the way, after they had each gone to their rooms in the five minutes or so they had to prepare for dinner, Vicki came into her room without knocking, and a moment afterwards, with a peculiarly affected sigh, flopped down on her bed and carefully watched her at the mirror making her modest toilette.

Suddenly visualising, and already contemplating subtle

methods of combating, a state of affairs in the future in which Vicki Kugelmann might, at any moment of the day or night, enter her room, flop down on her bed, and look at her, Miss Roach, an ardent lover and pursuer of privacy, became absent-minded in her answers.

Nor was Miss Roach's apprehensiveness decreased when, after they had heard the gong below being hit by Mrs. Payne, Vicki arose from the bed (without making any attempt to adjust the rumpled art-silk coverlet, or to smooth out the dent which her body had made in the bed) and, going over to Miss Roach's dressing-table, picked up Miss Roach's comb, and began hastily to comb her hair in the mirror—combing in that dashing, vigorous, head-shaking style which seems to a super-sensitive watcher to be spreading dandruff everywhere even if actually it is not....

Then Miss Kugelmann, humming to herself, looked at herself in a general way in the mirror, made a neat adjustment here and there, seemed decidedly pleased with what she saw, and with a smiling "Well—I suppose we must not keep the old fogies waiting" joined Miss Roach at the door, going out of the door before Miss Roach.

3

That had been a curious dinner. It had seemed as though they were all, with the exception of Mr. Prest in his corner, slightly dressed up as if for an occasion. Miss Steele and Mrs. Barratt were both slightly dressed up. Even Sheila was dressed up—neater, more ceremonious. The food itself was dressed up, better served. A new guest seldom fails to exercise this stimulating effect upon a boarding-house immediately upon arrival. Mr. Thwaites had certainly been dressed up (though Miss Roach could not quite analyse in what way), and on their appearance in the room, rose, in the most continental manner possible, in his seat. Miss Kugelmann begged him to be seated. Miss Roach did not have to hear Vicki and Mr. Thwaites talking to each other for more than thirty seconds to realise how well they had got on at the tea which had been briefly described to her. Was it conceivable that Mr. Thwaites was, after all, and in complete abandonment of his previously chauvinistic attitude, a little smitten?

Then the whole atmosphere and tempo of the dinner had been changed. Instead of the vast, pin-dropping silences, broken only by the long nasal booming of Mr. Thwaites and the agonised replies of a tortured and evasive Miss Roach, by the rumble of the lift and the sound of Sheila collecting plates—instead of this Miss Kugelmann's voice cheerfully prevailed above the atmosphere, rendered that of Mr. Thwaites a mere assenting and slightly bewildered bass, and went on unself-consciously and almost unintermittently as she put polite questions to both Mr. Thwaites and Mrs. Barratt and answered graciously and serenely whatever questions they put to her. Miss Roach got, indeed, an impression of the Rosamund Tea Rooms being a sort of mixed school for young people into which a new mistress had been suddenly introduced, a new German mistress with foreign methods, whose business it was cheerfully to question the boys and girls—to find out how much they knew and where they stood generally—so that she might liven things up and put their education on a new footing. And this was the poor lonely German girl whom Miss Roach had once befriended against a multitude in the mood to stone her! It was really very remarkable. She was, evidently, one of those people who at once take for granted what good comes their way, and go on without pause greedily to pursue their next advantage. You never knew what people were really like, did you?

It was clear at once that in this school for boys and girls Miss Kugelmann's favourite pupil was Mr. Thwaites—her favourite if only because the most backward or difficult—challenging her capacities to bring him out. She put on a particular expression when Mr. Thwaites spoke—and it was Mr. Thwaites this and Mr. Thwaites that.

It was easy to see that she had quickly realised that Mr. Thwaites was the key-man and dominant figure of the boarding-house, and had made up her mind to conquer him. Whether Mr. Thwaites was in fact to be conquered, whether he had, perhaps, at last met his match, remained matters of doubt to Miss Roach. Knowing his character, she believed that although at the moment somewhat dumbfounded, hesitant, and perhaps indeed a little "smitten", he was not without much in reserve, and was not the sort of man to have his ultimate dominance easily wrested from him.

Before five minutes had passed Vicki Kugelmann had already found occasion humorously, nay flirtatiously, to disagree with Mr. Thwaites on the matter of cigarette-smoking—Mr. Thwaites saying that this was in all cases poison to the system, and Miss Kugelmann making an exception of Turkish cigarettes, which she said were a different thing altogether. She had, she said, her "very own special brand", and after dinner she would make Mr. Thwaites try one.

Then again, a little later, she had occasion to disagree with Mr. Thwaites on the subject of hot-water bottles, which Mr. Thwaites declared were symptoms of decadence, but the use of which Miss Kugelmann, leading Mrs. Barratt and Miss Roach, warmly supported. Mr. Thwaites, she said, was a little conservative—was he not—no?

Then again, a little later, the topic of card games having arisen, various types of patience were discussed, and Miss Kugelmann once more held out for her "very own brand". This she said she would teach Mr. Thwaites, after dinner, if he cared.

"I see," she said, after a few more of these pleasant disagreements, "that I shall have to take you in hand, Mr. Thwaites."

"Yes—I see you will," said Mr. Thwaites, looking very odd, but by no means displeased.

In the middle of dinner Miss Roach heard the telephone distantly ringing in Mrs. Payne's room, and a moment afterwards Sheila came in and told her that it was for her. She rose and went into Mrs. Payne's room, from which Mrs. Payne happily was absent. It could be no one, she knew, but the Lieutenant, and the Lieutenant it was.

"Hullo," he said. "Have you finished dinner round there?"

"No," she said. "We're right in the middle of it."

"Well, will you hurry up and finish it and come round here?"

As the Lieutenant, when he had departed from them five and twenty minutes ago, had made no mention of ever seeing them again at any time in the future, here was more of his inconsequence, and she suspected that he was drunk.

"Oh," she said, "I don't think I can do that"; and "Aw, why not?" said the Lieutenant. "Come on. I'm lonely."

"Well, I've got to stay with Vicki, for one thing," said Miss Roach. "It's her first night here, and I can't very well leave her alone—can I?"

"Oh, I meant bringing her," said the Lieutenant, with unexpected promptness, and there was a pause. . . .

"She's kind of cute, isn't she?" said the Lieutenant. "I like her. I mean bringing her."

"Well, I don't think we can," said Miss Roach; and "Aw, come on," said the Lieutenant. "Bring her around. I guess she's kind of cute."

"No, we really can't," said Miss Roach, and after more argument on his part, "No, we *really* can't" and "No. We can't. *Really*. No!" And a few moments later she had rung off, conscious of having refused the Lieutenant something for the first time, and of having had, perhaps, her first brush with him.

Feeling oddly upset, she returned to the dining-room. Vicki, along with the others, glanced at her curiously as she sat down, but she said nothing.

Why, she wondered during the remainder of the dinner, had she so immediately and resolutely turned down the Lieutenant's offer? Were they in fact bound to stay at the Rosamund Tea Rooms that evening? Were they under any obligation to the boarding-house, and would they in fact have come to any harm outside? Was it really because she had believed that the Lieutenant had been a little drunk? And would not her friend herself have been delighted to go?

Why, in that case, had she not consulted Vicki? Why, now, was she saying nothing about it and not intending to say anything about it? Why, above all, when the Lieutenant had been talking to her, had she found herself saying to herself that she would be *damned* if she would take Vicki round with her to meet him?

Was she jealous? She dismissed the idea with an easy conscience as grotesque. But what was this strange woman doing to her? She was doing something.

4

Miss Roach had rather hoped that circumstances, to save her from being further pained and embarrassed, might somehow cause Miss Kugelmann to forget her promise to make Mr. Thwaites smoke one of her special brand of cigarettes after dinner, and to teach him her special brand of patience. But not at all. Almost as soon as the coffee had come in Miss Kugelmann had exclaimed "Ah!" reminiscently, left the room, and returned a few moments later with an extremely smart cigarette-case in a chamois-leather cover. This cigarette-case was a late nineteen-twenty model, and exhibited within, in addition to cigarettes, the half-revealed snapshot of a man, and metal clips which had pinched the cigarettes in the middle and made them look as though they had been wearing stays which were too tight for them—this after they had already been crushed flat by the pressure of the two sides of the case when closed. It was handed round to all, but all made polite excuses with the exception of Mr. Thwaites, who was committed.

Miss Kugelmann then lit Mr. Thwaites' cigarette for him in a charming and girlish way, and afterwards took out one for herself and sat down on the settee and smoked it with all the grace and elaboration she alone knew how to bring to this normally unstudied pastime—seductively crossing her legs, vigorously tapping the cigarette on the case, putting the cigarette with delicacy and precision into a holder (and the holder with equal delicacy and precision into her lips), lighting up with finesse, at once blowing out sophisticated smoke through her nose, throwing back her head, emitting thin smoke-streams into the air with the mouth of a whistler, or clever smoke-rings with the mouth of a fish, neatly tapping away ash, finding minute or imaginary specks of tobacco on her lips and daintily removing them with her third finger and thumb, etc., etc., etc. Mr. Thwaites, himself smoking awkwardly, watched her, charmed. Miss Roach watched her, fascinated.

Even more charming and fascinating was Mr. Thwaites' subsequent initiation into Miss Kugelmann's game of patience—charming the way in which she overrode Mr. Thwaites' original shyness and reluctance—his "laziness" as she called it—and overcame all material difficulties, she herself going downstairs to find some cards from Mrs. Payne, herself getting the card-table from the corner and placing it under a suitable standard-lamp, herself arranging two chairs each side of it and primly commanding Mr. Thwaites to sit on one of them while she sat on the other.

Charming the way, too, with two packs of cards, she set up two games, one for Mr. Thwaites, which she could supervise upside down, and one for herself. Charming the meticulous care with which she expounded the rules, and the patience with which she bore Mr. Thwaites' initial mistakes. Charming the difficulties caused by this upside-down way of teaching him, the laughable errors which, because of this, she herself made as well as he.

Charming the way, in her efforts to get a proper visual angle on his cards, her hair would sometimes fall right down over her face, only to be tossed back into place with an unconsciously impetuous jerk of her head—or the way, when she was doubtful exactly where to place a card, she would let it hang hesitantly in the air, or place the tip of it on the tip of her lower teeth, looking admonishingly and shrewdly at the cards in front of her.

Charming, when Mr. Thwaites began to get the hang of the game, the words of encouragement, the challenges, the reproaches, the commiserations, the sighs, the little cries of happiness—all this in an uninterrupted little stream of sound, forming a burbling background or foreground to the consciousness of the guests who sat over by the fire and read or knitted.

"I think our newcomer's charming," Mrs. Barratt murmured to Miss Roach when this had been going on for about half an hour. She said this as if to please Miss Roach, and so Miss Roach was compelled not only to smile but to look pleased. Mrs. Barratt had evidently got the point which Miss Kugelmann had been making.

Miss Steele was the first to go to bed. "Well—good night," she said, singling out and smiling at Vicki. "I see you're going to liven us up."

Just for a second Miss Roach thought that she detected a note of sarcasm or faint revulsion in this remark, and her spirits rose in the dim hope of having conceivably found one who might, since dinner, have been seeing eye to eye with herself. But the next moment the hope departed.

"It's just what we old fogies are wanting," said Miss Steele, with conviction and delight, and left the room.

5

How long she had had to stand it after that she did not know. The burbling from the card-players had continued, but had grown slowly quieter and more self-absorbed: the heat in the room grew heavier and heavier, and gas-fire drunkenness supervened for what seemed hours.

At last Mrs. Barratt rose, and began to collect her things, and Miss Roach rose too, went to the mantelpiece, and looked over at Vicki. Vicki saw her, understood her glance, yawned prettily while looking at Mr. Thwaites (she brought even to yawning the same sort of preciosity as she brought to smoking), and signified that they had both had enough. Five minutes later they had said good-night to Mr. Thwaites, and were on the stairs on the way to bed.

"Come in and see my room," said Vicki, when they were on the top landing, and Miss Roach went in.

There was, actually, little to be seen in Vicki's room, which was even drearier and darker under the dim electric light than Miss Roach's own, but the first things which Miss Roach actually saw were two portraits of men on the dressing-table—one large silver-framed one of an extremely good-looking young man of blond and German appearance, and one smaller one of what appeared to be a middle-aged English naval officer—and she at once got a distinct impression that in asking her to come in and see her room Vicki had in reality been asking her to come in and see these. She got this impression because Vicki, after lighting her gas-fire, immediately went over to the dressing-table and began to comb her hair in the close vicinity of these photographs, almost pointing at each of them with dripping hair and brisk comb, while she talked in a rather self-conscious voice of other matters. But as, at any rate, it wasn't Miss Roach's comb, or Miss Roach's dressing-table, Miss Roach didn't mind.

It was soon found that Vicki's gas-fire was not working properly, and Vicki, who had now taken off her dress and put on a large, comfortable blue dressing-gown (actually a man's dressing-gown, edged with cord, which might have been borrowed from a man), suggested that they should have a final cigarette in Miss Roach's room. This they did, speaking *sotto voce* as they crossed the landing and closed the door.

Naturally the subject of Mr. Thwaites arose, and Vicki gave her verdict.

"Oh," she said, flopping the whole weight of her dressing-gowned body down on to Miss Roach's bed once again, "he's all right, poor old bean: the old gent only wants a little handling."

If this woman (thought Miss Roach, as she sat on the wicker-chair and seemed placidly to smoke the last cigarette of the day with her friend) goes on talking about "beans" and "gents": if she makes any further mention of "handling" people or taking people "in hand": if she combs her hair over any more people's photographs, or flops her body on to any more people's beds, or, as she was now doing, flicks her cigarette-ash over any more people's bedside tables, then she, Miss Roach, was at some time in the distant future, or even in the very immediate present, going to start to scream or going to start to hit. But she showed nothing of this, save for a faintly absent-minded look in an otherwise cheerful and cordial countenance, and their cigarettes at last came to an end.

"Well—a very successful evening," whispered Vicki, as she said good-night at the door. "I am going to like it here—a lot." And Miss Roach agreed that things could not have gone better.

That was hours ago now, and still she could not sleep. She must calm down. She was exaggerating things. She always exaggerated things at this time of night—at this time of morning. There was no harm in the woman. She was just a little old-fashioned, skittish, that was all—perhaps rather absurdly old-fashioned and skittish at times. The Lieutenant had thought she was kind of cute. She was madly exaggerating things. She was a born exaggerator. This was her fault in life. . . .

"A very successful evening." Yes, indeed, a very successful evening. You might almost say a knock-out.

CHAPTER EIGHT

I

To the endless snubbing and nagging of war, its lecturing and admonitions, Miss Roach was subjected from the moment she left the Rosamund Tea Rooms in the morning to the moment she returned at night, and these things were at last telling upon her nerves and general attitude.

Immediately she stepped forth into Thames Lockdon (which itself was not even permitted to be Thames Lockdon, all mention of the town having been blacked out from shop-fronts and elsewhere for reasons of security) the snubbing began with:

NO CIGARETTES.
SORRY

in the window of the tobacconist opposite.

And such was Miss Roach's mood nowadays that she regarded this less as a sorrowful admission than as a sly piece of spite. The "sorry", she felt certain, had not been thrown in for the sake of politeness or pity. It was a sarcastic, nasty, rude "sorry". It sneered, as a common woman might, as if to say "Sorry, I'm sure", or "Sorry, but there you are", or "Sorry, but what do you expect nowadays?"

There were other instances of this sort of thing on the way to the station, where, on boardings, the lecturing and nagging began in earnest. She was not to waste bread, she was not to use unnecessary fuel, she was not to leave litter about, she was not to telephone otherwise than briefly, she was not to take the journey she was taking unless it was really necessary, she was not to keep the money she earned through taking such journeys where she could spend it, but to put it into savings, and to keep on putting it into savings. She was not even to talk carelessly, lest she endangered the lives of others.

Depressing, also, to Miss Roach, were the unadvertised enforcements of these prohibitions—the way that the war, while packing the public places tighter and tighter, was slowly, cleverly, month by month, week by week, day by day, emptying the shelves of the shops—sneaking cigarettes from the tobacconists, sweets from the confectioners, paper, pens, and envelopes from the stationers, fittings from the hardware stores, wool from the drapers, glycerine from the chemists, spirits and beer from the public-houses, and so on endlessly—while at the same time gradually removing crockery from the refreshment bars, railings from familiar places, means of transport from the streets, accommodation from the hotels, and sitting or even standing room from the trains. It was, actually, the gradualness and unobtrusiveness of this process which served to make it so hateful. The war, which had begun by making dramatic and drastic demands, which had held up the public in style like a highwayman, had now developed into a petty pilferer, incessantly pilfering. You never knew where you were with it, and you could not look round without finding something else gone or going.

2

Having thus timidly run, on her way to the office, a sort of gauntlet of "No's" and "Don'ts" thumped down on her from every side, Miss Roach looked forward to finding in her work something at least positive in which she could temporarily submerge herself. But here, in the publishing firm of Reeves and Lindsell, slowly but surely another enormous and menacing No was creeping forward—no paper. This, even if it had not as yet shown any signs of bringing about the final calamity of no publishing at all, had already caused Reeves and Lindsell (with practically no staff) to publish upside down and inside out (like card-players playing a *misère* hand), and a very funny atmosphere prevailed in the office, in half of which there was no glass, and consequently no daylight, owing to its having been affected by enemy action in the vicinity.

Mr. Lindsell, the partner with whom Miss Roach had most dealings, now only came to the office three days a week, and when he came (Miss Roach instinctively felt this, without being able to grasp anything definite) he did not stay exactly as long as he used to, or observe quite the same punctuality and rituals as he had before the war.

Also she was becoming increasingly aware, when she went into his room, of the occult yet permanent presence of a bottle of sherry, and some small glasses, lodged in his cupboard and untouched until twelve o'clock, but after that hour more often than not brought forth for the entertainment of one of his many visitors. It occurred to her that Mr. Lindsell, under the stress and strain of the war, had changed very much as she had changed, and found in sherry at midday exactly what she found in gin and french at the River Sun in the evening. It was the same everywhere: everyone, in the same way, was different: this was the war, the war, the war. . . .

3

One morning Mr. Lindsell, a thin, pale, spectacled, exhausted-looking man with sandy hair going thin, whom Miss Roach liked very much, invited her into his room and offered her sherry. As he did not usually do this except at Christmas, she was at first a little alarmed. All he had to tell her, however, was that he was making certain new arrangements and that, in view of the present situation, if she wished, she need only come to the office once, or perhaps twice, a week. The rest of her work, along with the reading of manuscripts, which she did already and more of which he wanted her to take over, she could do at home. She accepted gladly, and the prospect of freedom from the daily journey seemed, in the light of two sherries, indeed golden and glorious.

CHAPTER NINE

I

THE meal was breakfast: the subject, utility clothing. "As for the stuff they're turning out for men nowadays," said Mr. Thwaites bitterly, "I wouldn't give it to my Valet."

Mr. Thwaites' valet was quite an old friend. An unearthly, flitting presence, whose shape, character, age, and appearance could only be dimly conceived, he had been turning up every now and again ever since Miss Roach had known Mr. Thwaites. Mostly he was summoned into being as one from whom all second-rate, shoddy, or inferior articles were withheld. But sometimes things were good enough for Mr. Thwaites' valet, but would not do for Mr. Thwaites. Mr. Thwaites' spiritual valet endowed Mr. Thwaites with a certain lustre and grandeur, giving the impression that he had had a material valet in the past, or meant to have a material valet in the future. Mr. Thwaites also occasionally used, for the same purposes, a spiritual butler, a spiritual footman, and, in moments of supreme content, a spiritual stable-boy. He had at his disposal a whole spiritual estate in the country.

"Ah—you men complain," said Vicki. "But what about us? What do you think we poor things go through?"

It was odd, thought Miss Roach, the way that Vicki always managed, when talking to Mr. Thwaites, to turn whatever subject came up into a sort of contest between male and female, to somehow oppose feminine weakness and fastidiousness to masculine strength and insensibility.

"Well—*what* about you?" said Mr. Thwaites. "*You* still seem to keep up appearances, as far as I can see."

And by the look in Mr. Thwaites' eyes it was not easy to tell whether, by his stressing the "*you*", he meant Miss Kugelmann personally, or Miss Kugelmann as representative of her sex.

Vicki had now been at the Rosamund Tea Rooms nearly three weeks, and Miss Roach had noticed that these ambiguities on the part of Mr. Thwaites had been growing more and more frequent.

"Though it's not the Clothes . . ." said Mr. Thwaites, a moment later, but as no one understood exactly what he meant by this, no one made any attempt to reply.

"I said it's not the Clothes . . ." said Mr. Thwaites, and it was left to Vicki to take him on.

"What is it, then, Mr. Thwaites?" she said.

"It's what happens to be inside 'em," said Mr. Thwaites. "Or that's what *I* was taught, when *I* was at school."

"Really, Mr. Thwaites," said Vicki, "you're very gay for so early in the morning."

"I'm a very gay fellow," said Mr. Thwaites, and Miss Roach, looking at him, realised that there was a certain amount of truth in this. Since Vicki's arrival there had definitely been a certain gaiety and difference in Mr. Thwaites. At first a little embarrassed, puzzled, and sheepish under Vicki's "handling" of him, after two or three days he had noticeably begun to react. It could not be said that he had begun to dress better, for Mr. Thwaites was always, in his old-fashioned clothes, immaculate, but there was something in his whole demeanour more alert, lively, and responsive when Vicki was present.

"Certes, the damsel," Miss Roach had once heard him saying, in his awful language, when the subject of Vicki had been brought up when she was absent from the Lounge—"Certes, the damsel doth not offend the organs of optical vision. Moreover she hath a way with her, withal."

And one could see him awaiting, and even listening for, her return, slightly bracing himself in her presence, referring his conversation to her, even getting up and making room for her on chairs and sofas.

Was it possible, Miss Roach wondered, that Vicki was right—that she knew how to "handle" him? And if this was so, might she not come to be grateful to Vicki, as taking Mr.

Thwaites' mind off herself? Unfortunately, at present, Mr. Thwaites still found time to remember and duly torture her. Indeed, Miss Roach sometimes thought that there was a new savagery and sarcasm in his manner towards her, as if he were angrily comparing her and Vicki.

He now stared at Miss Roach in a prolonged manner. He stared at her in a prolonged manner at least once a day, but nowadays his stares were getting longer.

"I fear our Lady of the Roach," he said, "is somewhat shocked by my ribaldry—is't not so?"

"No, not at all, Mr. Thwaites," she said, and Mr. Thwaites went on staring at her.

"Wherefore doth she thus grace our breakfast table this Moonday morn?" he went on. "Doth she not e'en go forth, unto the populous city, to earn her daily wage?"

Miss Roach had wondered when this was coming. Mr. Thwaites was the only one who had not yet been informed of her new arrangement with her firm, and today was her first day at home.

"No," she said. "I'm only going up once or twice a week nowadays."

"What?" said Mr. Thwaites, reverting as usual, when surprised or displeased, to plain language. "What's happened, then."

"Oh—I've come to a new arrangement."

"What new arrangement? Aren't you going to work any more?" It was clear that Mr. Thwaites did not like the idea of this at all.

"Oh yes. But I'm going to do it at home."

"Oh. Are you? What are you going to work at?"

"Oh—reading manuscripts mostly," said Miss Roach. "I can do it just as well at home."

Although Miss Roach was actually going to do a lot of secretarial, accounting, and other work at home, she stressed the manuscript-reading side practically to the exclusion of the others, because this gave her a certain colour and dignity. It gave her, in fact, almost an atmosphere of being a qualified literary woman or publisher herself. She was surprised by her own pettiness, but she had felt for a long while that it was about time she stuck up for herself a bit and gave back some of the digs which were given her.

"Reading manuscripts?" said Mr. Thwaites, in his bad temper hardly thinking what he was saying. "I thought you *published* manuscripts. I didn't know you read them."

"Well, you have to read them before you publish them, don't you?"

Looking sideways at Vicki, she had a fleeting impression that Vicki also did not altogether like her as a reader and judge of manuscripts. This was not the first time that she had sensed in Vicki, the vet's secretary, a certain distaste in regard to her connection and activities with a publishing firm in London. But this might be pure imagination.

"And they leave that to you?" said Mr. Thwaites.

"Well—not only me. There are others."

There was a pause.

"*I'm* going to publish a book one of these days," said Mr. Thwaites, with vast resentment, and there the matter was left.

2

Miss Roach, who had decided to give herself a day's holiday, discovered a certain elation and sense of mystery in walking about the town as her own mistress on a Monday morning. It was as though she saw the town, as it really existed, for the first time—not as a week-end Saturday locality in which she was a week-ender. Remaining, as yet, a week-ender in all the reflexes of her spirit, she was able to feel the shock and to observe the uncanny difference between the weekday and the week-end. It was as though the town was becalmed, steeped in an air of non-

Saturday lethargy, indifference, desultoriness; the shops, the people, the streets were all subtly altered—particularly the shops. In place of the eager, exhilarating, panic-stricken bartering of Saturday, or the aloof, shuttered shutness of Sunday, there was something between the two—the shops being open without urgency, active without anxiety—a general loitering, puddling, pottering. . . .

Most peculiar of all was the atmosphere of the station, which seemed to have lost all its intense seriousness and obsessed preoccupation with London, and was playing, instead, a silly game of dreamy shunting, inadvertent whistling, absent-minded trolley-rolling, offhand loading, casual booking, and general woolgathering—all as if it had never known what war or trouble meant. Looking at the station thus, one was made aware that Thames Lockdon was, after all, a mere village right off the map.

Seeing these placid things, she foresaw a placid future down here with her work. She had had misgivings about having to spend all the day under a roof resonant with Mr. Thwaites, but she believed now that she could cope with this, particularly as she now had Vicki, if not exactly on her side, at any rate there, to absorb a certain amount of his personality. (It was queer how Vicki could not be induced quite openly to take her side against Mr. Thwaites. A sort of reticence came over her when Miss Roach spoke about him disparagingly. She would answer Miss Roach, or look at her, as if Miss Roach was somehow at fault for not knowing how to "handle" him.)

She had had her misgivings, of course, about Vicki too—but even these were diminishing. Now that Vicki was established in the Rosamund Tea Rooms, now the excitement of that first night was over, they saw less of each other, had not found any occasion to go out together to the River Sun, and practically only met at meals, in the Lounge, or in each other's rooms a few minutes before going down to meals.

Also Miss Roach had taken the precaution of putting her comb away in her drawer when not using it, and this had made a lot of difference. It was that comb-using which had put Miss Roach off—she was sure of that—it was amazing what a small thing like that could do. Vicki was all right. As long as she was kept from using Miss Roach's comb she was perfectly all right. In fact, apart from her slightly affected ways, which were not really her fault, she was really very nice. Miss Roach liked her. Now that they were going to be together more, she must make up her mind to like her more.

Thus made calm, happy, and resolute in her walk in the strange weekday town, Miss Roach returned to the Rosamund Tea Rooms at about twelve.

"There's been a phone call for you, Miss Roach," said Sheila, but on being questioned could not say from whom the call had come. Mrs. Payne had taken it, but Mrs. Payne was now out of doors.

Miss Roach at once had a feeling of terror, suspecting that an important call had come from the office while she was out playing, and she spent an uneasy three-quarters of an hour until Mrs. Payne returned.

"Oh yes—only Lieutenant Pike," said Mrs. Payne. "He says he'll call you again at one o'clock."

Enormously relieved, Miss Roach went upstairs to her room to prepare for lunch.

3

The Lieutenant! A problem she had almost forgotten!

"And where is the nice big American?" Vicki had asked her, only a few days ago, and she had answered, quite truthfully, that she did not know, she hadn't seen or heard of him for nearly a fortnight.

She had found a curious pleasure in telling Vicki this—she did not exactly know why, any more than she had exactly known why she had refused to take Vicki out to meet the Lieutenant again that night.

She had, actually, seen the Lieutenant only once since that occasion—and that had been on a Saturday morning when she had run into him quite by accident in Church Street. Believing then, because he had not rung up for a week, that she had offended him by her obduracy over the telephone, and that he had no intention of meeting her, let alone taking her out and kissing her in the dark any more, ever, she had been surprised by the profuseness of his cheerfulness and cordiality.

They had only spoken to each other for half a minute, for each was hurrying elsewhere, but in that short space of time he had made it clear that she was now forgiven—if, indeed, she had ever been out of favour. He had said that he had been "up to his eyes", that he had been having "the goddarnest awful time", and that he had been meaning to phone her, and that he would now do so "just as soon as ever he got a moment to get round to it".

That was a fortnight ago. He had not phoned until just now, and in the intervening period she had had time to wonder to what he alluded when he had said that he was "up to his eyes". As she had gathered from other sources that nothing unusual had taken place or was taking place in his unit, as she knew, in fact, almost for certain, that he was entirely free every evening of the week, the problem grew more and more perplexing. But she was by now resigned to being perplexed by the Lieutenant—whose appearances and disappearances, whose enthusiasms and fluctuations, whose bland mental reconciliation of almost explicit offers of marriage with almost complete withdrawal of his person from the recipient, whose burning faith in the Laundry business, and whose habit of drinking much too much, could be withstood and surmounted by resignation alone.

4

The Lieutenant having said that he would phone again at one o'clock, it was hardly likely that he would phone at all. Least of all was it likely that he would phone precisely at one o'clock. He phoned, in fact, at five and twenty past one, in the middle of lunch. Sheila announced the fact, saying "Lieutenant Pike, miss" at the door in front of everyone, and she left the room.

On her way to Mrs. Payne's room she found herself experiencing, in spite of herself, a certain amount of relief and pleasure. Cynical as she was in regard to all things appertaining to the Lieutenant and his behaviour, she had not, in the last three weeks, looked upon the prospect of his total disappearance from her life with complete equanimity. If only as a diversion, the Lieutenant had his uses, and his charm. She was glad, too, to find him keeping his word twice running—first in phoning her at all after his promise to do so when he had talked to her in the street, and now again after telling Mrs. Payne that he would ring at one o'clock—the inexactitude of five and twenty minutes being neither here nor there, part of the very character of the man. Perhaps, after all, he had a liking for her. Perhaps she had a liking for him.

"Hullo," she said, and, as he answered, listened eagerly to detect how much he had had to drink. "Gee—it's nice to hear your voice again," he said, and she could detect nothing of drink. "Same here," she said. "How are you?" "Oh—I've been having an awful time," he said. "How are you?" And each went on repetitively asking how the other was, as people will who are embarrassed both by a long absence from each other and by mere embarrassment.

He stressed the "awfulness" of the time he had been having, and she was bold enough to ask, "Awful in what way?" "Oh, just awful," he said evasively, and she quickly realised that he had not really been having an awful time, but was throwing out a mist of vague awfulness to conceal his real activities. This smoke-screen was also a form of apology and a form of compliment—the implication being that what he had been doing apart from her had been entirely under compulsion (since he would obviously not have endured anything so awful of his own free will), and that it was particularly awful because it had removed him from her company. He had probably been having the time of his life. However, the fact that he was taking the trouble thus to placate her proved that he was anxious to some extent to return to the fold, and her feelings towards him were cordial.

"Well, can you get away tonight?" he said. "I was thinking we could get a car and go over to the Dragon." The Dragon was a well-known country-inn-cum-restaurant about five miles outside Thames Lockdon, which still served steaks and to which the well-to-do resorted in cars.

"Well, that sounds very nice," she said, and added, in a hesitating way, "Yes. I think I could . . . I think I could. . . ." And there was a pause.

Miss Roach was actually speaking in this hesitating way simply because she was generally reviewing the situation and specifically wondering what she was going to wear at the Dragon. But the Lieutenant took it for something else.

"Is the German girl still there with you?" he said.

This was a seemingly irrelevant query, but she saw his mental processes clearly. The last time he had phoned her she had in the first place refused to come out for the reason that she had to stay in with her friend. He was now, in the back of his consciousness, remembering this, and, hearing her hesitant again, had quite automatically and unthinkingly mentioned the German girl.

Or was she completely mistaking his mental processes? Was he ringing her up purely as a means to renew his friendship with the German girl?

"Yes, she's still here," she said. "She's still here all right. . . ." And there was another pause.

For whatever reason, Miss Roach realised, the German girl had now appeared upon the scene, and something had to be done about her. She waited for him to speak.

"Would you like to bring her along?" he said, and she had

no idea what his voice conveyed—indifference, reluctance, or eagerness in disguise.

"Well—what do you think," she said. "It's your party."

"No. It's just as *you* like."

"No. It's just as *you* like."

"No. It's just as you *like*," said the Lieutenant.

"Oh—all right then," she said. "Let's all go out together."

"Fine," he said, and, after arranging to meet at the River Sun at half-past six, they rang off.

5

As she returned to the dining-room she felt glad at what she had done. Only this morning she had made up her mind to like Vicki better in the future, and now she had set the machinery going in the right way.

"That was the Lieutenant," she said to Vicki as she sat down. "Would you like to go to the Dragon tonight?"

"Me?" said Vicki. "The Dragon?"

"Yes. That's right. Are you free?"

"Yes. I'm free. I'd love to. It's very nice of him to have asked me."

Impossible to tell Vicki that he had *not* asked her, that she had not really been asked at all, or that, if anyone had asked her, she had!

"Is that the place," asked Mr. Thwaites, "out at Hearnsden?"

"Yes. That's right," said Miss Roach.

"Where you get black-market steaks and are charged five shillings for a small cocktail?" continued Mr. Thwaites, looking at her.

"Well—I don't know about five shillings."

"And where the cars are lined up ten deep outside on black-market petrol?"

"Well—I don't know . . ."

"While the country's wanting every ounce of petrol it can get to prosecute the war?" asked Mr. Thwaites.

"Well . . ."

"I only wanted to know," said Mr. Thwaites, with majestic neutrality, and continued his meal, the rest of which was eaten in cowed silence by all—by Miss Roach, Miss Kugelmann, Mrs. Barratt, Miss Steele, and Mr. Prest in his corner.

CHAPTER TEN

I

IT was not so much what Vicki did that night: it was what she said. It was not her behaviour: it was her vocabulary!

Vicki, who had been remarkably sprightly and cheerful throughout tea, took a long while over her dressing, and Miss Roach went into her room to tell her that if they did not hurry up they would be late.

"Oh—keep him waiting," said Vicki, who was combing her hair. "I always believe in keeping them waiting."

An extraordinary attitude, thought Miss Roach, for one who had been invited to this meeting in the precise way she had—that was to say, not invited at all! Extraordinary, too, the way she seemed always to regard herself, rather than Miss Roach, as the one controlling and dominating the Lieutenant. But then she wasn't really to know that she had only been invited by accident, and she wasn't to know, really, that Miss Roach had any particular claim on the Lieutenant by virtue of kisses in the dark and other matters.

They were ten minutes late at the River Sun, and the Lieutenant was waiting for them.

"Good evening, Mr. Lieutenant!" said Vicki. "And how are you?"

And the way she said this was controlling and dominating—the "Mr." seeming to challenge him, slightly ridicule him, and take him in charge.

From the first moment, too, she took on the part of the leading spirit of the party—an attitude of being the guest of the evening, of giving forth, at once as a duty and charming condescension, her vitality and wit.

The very way she crossed her legs and lit her first cigarette, or rather allowed the Lieutenant to light it for her, expressed—in its extra neat self-satisfaction, in its extra primness and authoritativeness, in the proficiency of its extra elaborations—this attitude. Miss Roach looked at the Lieutenant, to see if he was at all taken aback, but he showed no sign of this. He seemed, on the contrary, to be charmed.

As soon as they had finished their second round of drinks Miss Roach had an idea that both Vicki and the Lieutenant were getting a little silly with drink, whereas she was remaining where she was, and she felt, accordingly, a little bit out of it. She had felt something of the same thing when these two had met before.

The Lieutenant having asked them whether they would like to make a change from the gin and french they were drinking, Vicki said, "Why, yes. I'd really like a nice cocktail. Only you silly English don't know how to make a proper cocktail, do you?"

"Well, I'm not English," said the Lieutenant, and "Oh no, so you're not," said Vicki, and although it was obvious that no rudeness to herself was intended, this made Miss Roach feel more out of it than ever.

This was the first time that Vicki had alluded to the English in this way, and Miss Roach was not at all certain that she liked it. Willing enough as she was herself, at certain times, to disparage the English in a more or less conventional way—to deplore their manners, their cooking, their complacency, arrogance, and dullness—she yet found something peculiarly ugly and suspect in this disparagement of the English on Vicki's lips in the world of the present moment. If she didn't like the English, who did she like? The Germans? And if the Germans, what sort of Germans? The Nazi Germans? She was a funny one, this Vicki. She wanted watching. Or was she, Miss Roach, as usual letting her imagination run away with her? Almost certainly she was. No doubt Vicki detested the Germans and was thinking of the French, the Belgians, or the Dutch as supreme makers of cocktails.

"Why," said the Lieutenant, "can you make a cocktail?"

"Can I make a cocktail?" said Vicki. "Oh, boy, can I make a cocktail!"

"From which I take it," said the Lieutenant, apparently delighted rather than nauseated by this excursion into his own idiom, "that you can make a cocktail!"

"Can I make a cocktail?" said Vicki, conscious of having made a success, and so enlarging upon it, "or can I make a cocktail? Uh-*huh*! Oh, boy! Wizard!"

(*"Uh-huh!" "Oh, boy!" "Wizard!"*) The mere mention of "cocktails", in 1943, was frightful enough, but with the addition of "Uh-huh", "Oh, boy", and "Wizard" a depth was reached of which Miss Roach had not even thought Vicki capable.

"Well, let's have a cocktail now," she said, to hide her shame at this new depth.

2

It was Vicki Kugelmann's evening all right—there was no doubt about that. With every drink they took this became more evident.

By half-past seven Miss Roach was already feeling hungry and wondering when they were going to stop drinking and go to the Dragon. She even had the courage to mention this, but she did not get any answer, for at the moment of asking the Lieutenant and Vicki were playing upon the electric ball-machine in the corner of the lounge, and one of Vicki's cries of triumph completely drowned her timid plea.

Never was such an enchanting liveliness and responsiveness brought to any game as Vicki brought to this. To observe her childish glee and animation as she set the ball going, the way she lifted her hands in agonised suspense as it began its downward journey, the way she cried out with pleasure or disappointment at each electric jab, the way, in the intensity of her excitement, and as if to urge the ball to go in the direction she required, she leaned right over the glass (thus letting her hair fall over her forehead with exactly the same charming waywardness it had shown when she had been playing patience with Mr. Thwaites), the way she tossed it back, the way she clapped her hands at unexpected successes, the way she imitated a little girl crying at unexpected failures—to observe all these things was to observe something very remarkable indeed.

Equally remarkable was her generous and vociferous reaction to her rival's game. "Oh—sporty! *Sporty!*" she would cry, having apparently got it into her head that this was the word above all words with which the English express their admiration of skill or luck at games. Or "Oh—sporty shot, sir! Sporty play!" Or "Oh, wizard shot! Wizard!" Or, to the Lieutenant, "Oh—good for you, big boy, good for you!" Or "Oh—hard lines, old fellow! Hard lines!" Or "Oh—hard cheese—hard cheese!" Miss Roach felt she could sink beneath the earth.

"Now I buy you a drink," said Vicki at last, and, on the Lieutenant protesting, "No—I stand you a round. I stand you all a round!" And she went away to the bar to get it.

Miss Roach felt certain that the Lieutenant must be experiencing something of the same feeling as herself, and thought that now was the moment to say something about it. But she did not quite know how to put it. "I'm sorry about all this," was what she wanted to say, but something stopped her. Instead she said, "I'm afraid Vicki's getting a bit tight. You mustn't let her have too much."

The Lieutenant, who was playing the machine, paused a moment before replying.

"Tight?" he said. "She's not tight. I'm glad you brought her along. She kind of lightens things up."

Vicki's return with the drinks prevented Miss Roach from indulging in any too intense introspection concerning this attitude on the part of the Lieutenant. They all lifted their glasses.

"*Skol! Prosit! Santé!*" said Vicki, and, having thus established her familiarity with continental toasts, she took a sip, and revealed again her esoteric knowledge of informal English. "Cheers, old chap!" she said. "Here's how! Mud in your eye! Down the jolly old hatch!"

And then, having taken another gulp, she expressed her appreciation.

"Spiffing stuff!" she said. "Abso-blooming-lutely. No? What?"

3

Vicki having bought a round, Miss Roach had to buy one too.

Returning from the bar with the drinks in her hands, she found an ill-looking man in a long, shabby overcoat talking to the Lieutenant. This was the driver of the car which was to take them over to the Dragon.

"All right. We're coming," said the Lieutenant, who was now drunk. "Just be patient. We're coming." And the ill-looking man went away.

Soon after this the drink went to Miss Roach's own head, and everything became very hazy. They went on playing at the machine, but none of them were quite aware of what they were doing and no longer took any account of the scores they were making, and before long they were joined by Lieutenant Lummis. With him were two strange women, and three strange American officers, and the whole atmosphere was changed into one of a general *mêlée*.

At one moment she was sitting between two American officers, who were expatiating upon the depth and warmth of English hospitality, and then something happened and she was sitting next to one of the two women, with whom she was exchanging notes and anecdotes about the blitz in London. The Lieutenant had disappeared to the other end of the lounge, and Vicki was talking eagerly to one of the American officers. While all this was happening more than one drink, at which she barely sipped, was put in front of her, and the ill-looking man in the overcoat, who was driving the car, came in more than once, miserably, and went away again.

It was half-past eight before they made a move from the River Sun, and how it came about she never remembered—possibly the ill-looking man had at last taken to threats, though he looked too ill to threaten anybody. All she knew was that she was out in the moonlit air, and that two of the American officers were going to share the car to the Dragon. By this time Vicki Kugelmann was mistering everybody and ordering them about. It was "Mr. Major" to one officer, and "Mr. Captain" to another, and "Mr. Lieutenant" to the Lieutenant. She ended up with "Mr. Car-driver". "Come on, Car-driver," she said. "I'll sit in front with you."

They all crammed into the back of the car, and Miss Roach sat on the Captain's legs, and the Major sat on the Lieutenant's. The car moved away. They all talked incessantly, yelling each other down, and in due course began to sing in unison.

Oh, this world (thought Miss Roach as they sped along) into which I have been born! And oh this war, through which it is my destiny to pass! (Though pass was not the word, for she could not conceive any end to it.) This, she saw, was as much a part of the war as the soldiering, the sailoring, the bombing, the queueing, the black-out, the crowding, and all the grey deprivations. No imaginable combination of peace-time circumstances could have brought about such a composition of characters as now filled the car and sat on each other's knees—the ill-looking driver, the German woman, her lonely self, and the three Americans, of presumably totally different classes in civil life, and presumably going to their deaths when the second front began. And yet, she was aware, all over the countryside around, all over the country, cars were racing along with just such noisy loads to just such destinations. If it wasn't Americans, it was Poles, or Norwegians, or Dutch, and if it wasn't sitting on each other's knees it was singing, and if it wasn't singing it was sitting on each other's knees, and whatever it was it was drinking and drinking and screaming and desperate. The war, amongst the innumerable other guises it had assumed, had taken on the character of the inventor and proprietor of some awful low, cosmopolitan night-club.

She did not join in the singing, but looked out through the window at the stars. These stars gave her no sense of peace, were themselves war-stars, and told her severely, in pinpoints of pellucid light, that the war would have no ending.

4

Needless to say, although it was after half-past eight, it was not good enough to go straight to the Dragon. They had to pull up at a small inn on the way and have some more drinks. The ill-looking man drew up silently and obediently, and one of the Americans invited him inside.

"Yes, come in, Mr. Chauffeur!" said Vicki. "Come in and join in the fun of the fair!"

They entered the public bar, battering into complete dumbness, with the arrogance of their uninhibitedness, loquacity, and intoxication, the few local beer-drinkers, who sat in corners and watched them in a dog-like way.

There was no whisky here, but as much gin as they wanted. Doubles were passed round, and soon they were making more noise than ever. The ill-looking driver asked for a beer, and sat on a bench next to Miss Roach. There was already a sort of bond between the ill-looking driver and Miss Roach.

Miss Roach bore the unfortunate Christian name of Enid.

"Poor old Eeny doesn't seem to be enjoying herself," said the Lieutenant. "Why's she sitting all by herself?"

"No—she doesn't—does she?" said Vicki. "Come on, old dear—snap out of it."

"No—I'm all right," said Miss Roach, "but I wish you wouldn't call me Eeny."

"Well, what am I to call you?" said the Lieutenant. "I can't very well call you Roach."

"Well—I'd rather that than Eeny."

"All right, then. I'll call you Roach. How are you, Roach?" And he shook hands with her.

"Yes. We will call her Roach," said Vicki. "How are you, Roachy, old thing." And she shook hands with her as well.

From that moment it was Roach, Roachy, Roach. They made her drink the whole of her gin, put another in front of her, and everything, hazy enough already, got hazier and hazier.

There was a wireless blazing away in a corner of the room; a dance-band came on; and soon Vicki was demanding that they should all dance. First of all she whirled round the middle of the room with one man after another, and then she danced solo, while everyone watched her. Her manner of dancing was to lift her skirt to her knees with her left hand, and to put forth her right hand high into the air, shaking its forefinger to and fro.

5

Miss Roach never remembered how they got out into the air again, but she remembered sitting in front with the ill-looking driver, and talking quietly and soberly to him, while Vicki, sprawled out on more than one pair of knees behind, talked, rallied, challenged, sang German songs, sang French songs, demanded a cigarette, demanded a light, was queenly, was coy, rebuked, threatened to smack, and smacked. . . . Yes, it was Vicki's evening all right. . . .

Then they were in the packed saloon bar of the Dragon, and fighting their way to the counter. . . . Then the Lieutenant was making a scene because there were no more spirits left, and then they were drinking odious glasses of bitter beer, unable properly to stand on their feet because of the jostling crowd, and hardly able to hear each other talk because of the noise.

Then they were all in a corner of the dining-room of the Dragon, which was deserted except for themselves, and whose lights were mostly turned down, and whose waiter, ill-looking and deferent, like the car-driver, sorted out and made some sort of sense of their conflicting demands. "Listen to me, Mr. Waiter!" cried Vicki. (She also called him "*Garçon*" and "*Herr Ober*".)

They had some cold soup and some cold chicken, and someone bought two bottles of champagne. At the end of the meal the Lieutenant drank off the remains of one of these bottles, amounting to about half a pint, from the bottle. But he could not quite manage it all, and Vicki finished it off for him. . . .

Then they were in the crowded bar again, drinking the odious bitter. The ill-looking driver again appeared in the crowd to appeal to the Lieutenant, but was again dismissed. The order of the day now was to go down to the river before going back. Hearnsden was a river beauty-spot, and it had to be seen. "We'll go and bathe," said the Lieutenant. "Let's all go and bathe." "Don't be silly," said Miss Roach. "You can't bathe in the middle of the winter." "Can't you?" he said. "I can." And he turned to Vicki. "You'll come and bathe with me, won't you?" "Yes, of course I will," said Vicki. "We'll all go and have a jolly old bathe."

Confused as she was with drink and noise, Miss Roach could clearly enough see how Vicki was sucking up to the Lieutenant, hanging on to his words, playing up to his vanity. At moments she felt a wave of anger rising at this, but she held it back. She's drunk, of course, she said to herself, they're both drunk, and I've got to keep my head. All this will seem different in the morning, she thought, and if only I can get them home it'll be all right.

Then they were out in the moonlit air, with the Lieutenant in the middle taking their arms, and walking towards the river.

The two other American officers had completely disappeared, and never appeared again.

Miss Roach had been fairly certain that when they reached the waterside the Lieutenant would reverse his decision to bathe, but this did not happen. He sat down on the grass and began to take off his shoes. "Don't be absurd. You can't! You can't!" said Miss Roach, in desperation, and even Vicki looked a little abashed and said nothing.

"Well, let's paddle anyway," said the Lieutenant, who had got off his shoes and socks and was rolling up his trousers, and "No—don't be silly—don't be silly!" said Miss Roach. "You'll catch your death!"

"No. Let's paddle. We'll paddle," cried Vicki. "Come on, Roachy! We'll all paddle." And she also began to take off her shoes.

"Don't be silly," said Miss Roach. "Stop him. Don't be silly!" But Vicki was now taking off her stockings.

"Don't be silly, you silly old Roach," she said. "Don't be such a silly old spoil-sport!"

"Well, I'm not going to, anyway," said Miss Roach, and she began to walk away.

"Come on, Roachy—silly old spoil-sport-Roachy!" cried Vicki. "Come on in and paddle!" But Miss Roach walked further away.

When she was about two hundred yards away, she looked back. It was, of course, quite impossible to paddle in the river, as the bank fell sheer into deep water. Instead, the Lieutenant and Vicki were sitting on the bank and putting their feet into the water. In the bright moonlight the Lieutenant was to be seen sitting in a sort of stupor, and Vicki was clinging on to him and screaming girlishly with pain and pleasure.

"I'm going back to the car. I'll wait for you there!" she shouted.

"All right, Roachy, old thing—you wait in the car!" Vicki shouted back. "Toodle-oo! Chin-chin!"

6

She was sitting in front again, talking quietly to the ill-looking driver, when they returned. It took some time to convince the Lieutenant that the Dragon was closed, and that he could not drink anything more, but at last he got into the back of the car with Vicki, and they drove off.

As they drove back she did not quite know what was going on in the back in the way of hand-holding or hugging, and nothing would induce her to look. But something was going on, and hardly a word was uttered until they were approaching Thames Lockdon. . . .

"Well—that was a very pleasant evening, Mr. Lieutenant," said Vicki, at last, "and a very pleasant paddle. Thank you very much for both, my friend."

"Not at all," said the Lieutenant. "You're cute. I always said you were cute, I always said she was cute, didn't I, Roachy?"

"Yes, you did," said Miss Roach, and a few moments later the car drew up outside the Rosamund Tea Rooms, and the Lieutenant paid the ill-looking driver, who passed out of Miss Roach's life for ever.

"Come on, now we're going for a walk," said the Lieutenant, taking both their arms again.

"No, we really must go in," said Miss Roach, and "No—let's go for a walk," said Vicki, and "No, we must go in, *really*!" said Miss Roach, and "Come on," said the Lieutenant, and "Yes, come on," said Vicki. "Be sporty. For heaven's sake be sporty, you silly old Roach!" "It's not a question of being—" Miss Roach could not bring herself to bring out this terrible word and so did not finish her sentence. "Oh—quit arguing," said the Lieutenant, pulling at both of them, and in order to avoid a sort of free fight in the street, Miss Roach gave in.

It was queer how she knew from the beginning where the

Lieutenant was going to take them. He was going to take them where he always took her when he wanted to kiss her—he was going to take them to the Park. She was fairly sure, in fact, that he was going to take them to the same seat, and this, she felt, was going to be going a bit too far. She might be mistaken, however, and in the meantime she tried to make herself as agreeable as possible.

This was not difficult to do, because most of the time, as they walked along, Vicki was singing German, French, or Hungarian songs, and in these, of course, neither the Lieutenant nor Miss Roach was able to join her.

Sure enough, the Lieutenant steered them, with the certainty of a somnambulist, in the direction of the Park, and the seat in question came in sight.

For one delightful moment she thought the Lieutenant was going to pass it. It was, in fact, possible that some premonition of danger entered the Lieutenant's befuddled head. But, having got three or four yards past the seat, he defied this premonition, if he had ever had any such thing, and stopped.

"Come on," he said. "Let's sit down a bit."

"No, don't let's sit down—let's go on walking. It's nice," said Miss Roach, and "No," said the Lieutenant, "let's sit down," and "Yes," said Vicki, "let's sit down and look at the river."

"No," said Miss Roach, "*I* don't want to sit down," and "Aw, come on," said the Lieutenant, and "Yes, come on," said Vicki.

"Well, *you* sit down, I'll go on walking," said Miss Roach, and "Aw, come on," said the Lieutenant, "quit being obstreperous." And with these words he practically hauled her down on to the seat.

"Yes, she's very obstreperous tonight, isn't she?" said Vicki, who was sitting the other side of the Lieutenant.

"Obstreperous, is she?" said the Lieutenant, and he began to look at her gravely. . . .

No—he *couldn't*. Drunk as he was, he couldn't! Surely he couldn't!

"Look at that swan," she said desperately. "He seems to be making a night of it, too—doesn't he."

But all the Lieutenant did was to repeat, "Obstreperous, is she?" and to look at her more gravely still.

"I suppose . . ." she began, but by this time he had taken hold of her in his arms and was kissing her on the mouth.

"How's that for obstreperousness?" he said when he had finished, and then he turned to Vicki. "What about you?" he said. "Are you obstreperous too?" And he kissed Vicki in the same way.

Miss Roach rose. "Look here," she said, "I'm going home. I'm sorry, but I want to go home." "Don't be silly," said the Lieutenant, taking her arm. "Come and sit down." "Yes, don't be silly," said Vicki. "Come and sit down."

"No—I want to go home," said Miss Roach, and the Lieutenant, still holding her arm, rose. "Come on," he said. "Come and sit down."

"Yes," said Vicki, who had also risen. "Come and sit down. Be *sporty*—old thing! Be *sporty*!"

And now a sort of panic seized Miss Roach, and they were all talking, or rather shouting, together, and in a sort of tussle. "Listen. I want to go home. I'm serious," said Miss Roach. "Come on. Be sporty! Be sporty!" cried Vicki. "Come on. Come and sit down," said the Lieutenant.

Somehow she freed herself from the Lieutenant's grasp. She calmed down.

"It's all right," she said. "I'm sorry. You stay—but I want to go home, that's all."

"Oh, come on," said Vicki, also calmer, and approaching her. "Be sporty—can't you? You don't want to spoil the sport, do you. Can't you be a sport?"

"No, I'm very sorry. I want to go home. Goodbye."

And all at once, after looking at them both, she was running away.

And, except when she walked for a moment or two, to recover

her breath, she did not stop running all the way back to the Rosamund Tea Rooms. She did not know why: she had to run all the way back: nothing else would do.

7

She was in by half-past eleven. She undressed, took three aspirins, put out the light, and lay in bed.

At five and twenty past twelve she heard the Lieutenant and Vicki arrive outside the Rosamund Tea Rooms and say good-night in low tones. Then she heard Vicki letting herself in.

About half a minute later there was a soft knock on her door. She did not answer this, and the knock was repeated more loudly.

She said "Come in" and Vicki entered, at once switching on the light. The light blinded Miss Roach, and she glared up at Vicki at the door.

"Are you awake?" said Vicki. "Can I come in?"

"Yes, I'm awake. Come in."

"What made you run away?" said Vicki, in a more or less conciliatory tone, coming to the bed and looking down at her. "You didn't have to run away like that."

"Oh, I was just fed up, that's all," said Miss Roach, in the same tone. She noticed that Vicki was now quite sober. "I can't stand that sort of thing—that's all."

"What sort of thing?" said Vicki, and moved over to Miss Roach's dressing-table.

(Oh God—thought Miss Roach—I've left my comb out! Oh God—please don't let her use my comb!)

"What sort of thing?" repeated Vicki, in a curious voice, and she picked up Miss Roach's comb, and began to comb her hair and look at herself in the mirror.

"Oh, just *that* sort of thing," said Miss Roach. "How did you get on when I left?"

"Oh, very well indeed," said Vicki, combing away and faintly and complacently smiling to herself. "He has technique—your Lieutenant. . . ."

She was trying to control herself, but this was too much. The combing, the complacent smile, the disgusting use of the word "technique" to describe the drunken kisses she had obviously been recently receiving from the Lieutenant—the three together were too much.

"If you call it technique," she said. "I'd call it just plain drunkenness."

There was a pause. Vicki went on combing her hair.

"Ah," said Vicki. "You are angry. I thought you were angry." And it was plain that Vicki was angry, too.

"No, I'm not angry," said Miss Roach, controlling herself again. "I'm just tired, that's all. I think we'd better go to bed."

"Yes, you are angry," said Vicki, her temper rising, yet still combing, and looking at herself in the glass. As her temper rose her German accent grew stronger. "You are angry. You are not sporty. You must learn to be sporty, Miss Prude."

"You do use some funny expressions," said Miss Roach. "Don't you think we'd both better go to sleep?"

Vicki Kugelmann now flung down the comb on to the dressing-table, and turned.

"I say," said Miss Roach. "Look out for my comb."

"No," said Vicki, moving towards the door. "You are not sporty, Miss Prim." She reached the door and opened it. "You must learn to be sporty, my friend. You are the English Miss. No? . . . Good night."

The door was closed and she was gone.

With the light still on, Miss Roach gazed at the ceiling.

Now she knew she hated Vicki Kugelmann as she had never hated any woman in her life. Now she knew that she hated her, possibly, as no woman had ever hated any other woman. She hated her mercilessly. Now she knew that for week after week she had hated her in just this way. She was glad to know. She got out of bed, turned out the light, and got into bed again. She began shivering and trembling in the dark.

Then, without expecting sleep, she was granted it.

CHAPTER ELEVEN

I

SHE peered through the darkness at her leather illuminated clock. She had to put her face close to it nowadays, for it was not as illuminated as it once was. And presumably you couldn't get illuminated paint any more. Or could you? It didn't matter anyway. Even if you could, they would keep the clock three months. Or more.

It was a quarter to five in the morning. She had awakened at half-past three, and so she had been torturing herself for over an hour now. Why should she torture herself? Why should she let the filthy woman torture her? She mustn't call her a filthy woman. She wasn't filthy. But then, again, she *was*!

Her words. Her expressions. Not her behaviour, so much as her vocabulary!

"*Mr. Lieutenant*"! . . . "*Oh, boy*"! . . . "*Uh-huh*"! . . . "*Wizard*"!

"*Sporty*"! "*Sporty play*"! "*Sporty shot*"! "*Wizard shot*"! . . . "*Good for you, big boy*"! . . . "*Hard lines*"! "*Hard lines, old fellow*"! "*Hard cheese*"!

"*Skol*"! "*Prosit*"! "*Santé*"! No, that was unfair. The filthy woman had a right, as a "foreigner", to Skol, Prosit and Salut. Or *had* she?

"*Cheers, old chap*"! "*Mud in your eye*"! "*Down the jolly old hatch*"! Oh, my God!

"Mr. Lieutenant." . . . "Mr. Major." . . . "Mr. Car-driver." . . . "Mr. Chauffeur." . . . "Mr. Waiter." . . .

"Jolly old bathe." . . . "Roach." "Roachy." "Roach." "Silly old Roach" . . .

"Silly old spoil-sport." . . . "Old spoil-sport Roach."

"*Toodle-oo*"*!* . . . "*Chin-chin*"*!* . . .

"Be sporty, old thing." "Be sporty—be sporty"!

"*Technique*"*!* . . . "Technique", perhaps, was the most horrible of the lot.

"You must learn to be sporty, Miss Prude." . . .

"Miss Prim." . . .

"The English Miss." . . .

THE ENGLISH MISS! THE ENGLISH MISS!

Miss Roach sat up in bed and took a sip of water in the darkness.

2

But *was* she, after all, an "English Miss" of sorts? Was she (it was anguish merely to use the filthy woman's filthy words) a "spoil-sport?"; not "sporty"?

Was she (she must translate these odious epithets into dignified English) insular, too correct, puritanical, inhibited; one who by her lack of vitality, or lack of grace, spoiled the carefree pleasure of others?

Roach. Roachy. Silly old Roach. Here it was again, you see. "Old Roach—old Cockroach". They had called her that as the schoolmistress at Hove, and here it was again. There must be something behind it all.

Or was there just something in the surname itself—in the word Roach—the name of a fish—which somehow called forth this manner of address? Was it because of her awful Christian name—the Enid which she so detested and discouraged people from using—that people fell back upon Roach?

No—there was something more to it than that. She had been a schoolmistress, and there was still, apparently, something schoolmistressy about her.

What!—schoolmistressy, because she had retained a certain

quietude and dignity when out with a couple of drunks! Schoolmistressy, because she had objected to the notion of bathing in the river at half-past ten on a winter's night of war! Prudish, because she had refrained from sharing with a hysterical German woman the befuddled kisses of a man who had had the effrontery to choose, as a sort of kissing-station (like a petrol-station), the identical spot upon which he had previously kissed her, afterwards offering her marriage!

No—it wasn't fair—it wasn't *fair* ! She had merely been her age—she had merely been herself—a plain, nearly middle-aged woman behaving as a plain, nearly middle-aged woman should. It was those two—plain, nearly middle-aged people both of them—who had behaved like raw and raucous adolescents.

Did Vicki, by the way, think that she—Vicki—*wasn't* plain and nearly middle-aged? Well—she couldn't argue about her age, anyway—but did she have some sort of idea that she wasn't plain, irredeemably plain—*hideous*, in fact?

Now then, keep your temper—but she *was* hideous, wasn't she, and the woman *knew* she was hideous, didn't she?

What if she didn't? And what if she wasn't? What if she was, in some way which Miss Roach couldn't see, attractive? What if she was attractive to men? What if she was remarkably attractive to men? What if she, Miss Roach, the plain ex-schoolmistress, was jealous of her because she was so remarkably attractive, and was "taking" the Lieutenant away from her?

No—this was black five-o'clock-in-the-morning madness. She must get things in proportion. Vicki wasn't attractive. And she wasn't hideous. She was just a plain, nearly middle-aged woman like herself—probably just a tiny bit *more* attractive than herself—being blonde and having a nice complexion. And if, as Vicki did, you thought of nothing in the world but sex and threw yourself at men like that, of course men responded.

Perhaps *she* ought to learn to throw herself at men like that. Perhaps, then, after all, she was something of an "English Miss." . . . Here she was, back again.

3

An English Miss!

And what right, pray, had a German woman, a German Miss—at such a stage of international proceedings, in the fourth year of bitter warfare between the two nations—to allude, in such a way, to an English woman—an English woman on her own soil? Really, this was a little cool—was it not? This had not struck Miss Roach before!

What about the hospitality being extended to her? What about the little matter of the courtesy or modesty such hospitality demanded in return? What about the men dying on land and sea and air at that very moment? What about the food the filthy woman was eating, the clothes she was wearing, the air she was breathing, the liberty she was enjoying?

Oh no! Instead of being in jail, instead of being in a concentration camp, instead of being shot as a spy, she went careering about the countryside with Americans and calling people English Misses!

And after she, Miss Roach, had invited her! Or as good as invited her—had been the one, anyway, to permit her to come.

And that remark about cocktails—what was it? "But of course you English don't know how to make cocktails—do you?" *You* English! Quite apart from the drivelling absurdity of the statement! Really—if she thought about this woman much more she would get out of bed and go into her room and strike her.

Miss Roach took another sip of water, and decided to calm down.

The woman, after all, had lived in the country for something like fifteen years. She had, perhaps, a sort of right to speak of "you" English amongst people whom she considered her friends.

And then, again, she was, presumably, anti-Nazi, anti-Hitler, anti-everything of that sort.

Presumably. But was she?

Was she not, on the other hand, when you came to think of it, exquisitely Nazi, exquisitely Hitler, exquisitely everything of that sort?

4

Miss Roach took another sip at her water, and decided to think this out calmly.

Yes. In calmness she believed she had hit upon the truth: had found the solving clue to the enigma of a personality which had been irritating and puzzling her with increasing intensity for so long a time.

What about the early Vicki—the timid, the ingratiating one? Did not that original character represent one of the most famous and readily identifiable aspects of the German character—or at least the German fascist character? Was not the period when Vicki was sucking up to her, trying to get into the Rosamund Tea Rooms, posing as a delightful friend—was not this period the Ribbentrop one, nauseatingly Ribbentroppish through and through? And making, like Ribbentrop, gross Ribbentroppish mistakes?—offending the friend she sought to make by the clumsiness of her idiom and manner of thought, exposing her beastliness in a multitude of little ways, in her reluctance to pay for drinks, in turning up late without making proper apologies, in going to Mrs. Payne behind Miss Roach's back, and so on and so forth?

And then, with her object achieved, the exquisite conventional Teutonic change of demeanour! The lightning Teutonic arrogance! That first evening with the Lieutenant, when she had kept on looking over at him before he joined them. The way she had looked at the Lieutenant as they had both discussed her. Her remark outside in the street, "*Not if you know how to handle him.*" . . .

Then, the same evening, her first performance at the Rosamund Tea Rooms and with Mr. Thwaites—the patience-playing and all the rest! What arrogance, save unique Teutonic arrogance, could have conceived and achieved a performance of that kind?

And was not this Teutonic arrogance precisely the one which, flowering in the world conditions of the nineteen twenties and thirties, had developed into plain, good-old, familiar, Jew-exterminating, torturing, jack-booted, whip-carrying, concentration-camp Nazidom? Were not all the odours of Vicki's spirit—her slyness, her insensitiveness—the heaviness, ugliness, coarseness, and finally cruelty of her mind—were not all these the spiritual odours which had prevailed in Germany since 1933, and still prevailed?

Was not the woman who, six or seven hours ago, was screaming about being "sporty" and supporting a drunken American in his ambition to bathe—was not this woman one who would, geographically situated otherwise, have been yelling orgiastically in stadiums, supporting S.S. men in their ambitions, presenting bouquets to her Fuehrer? My God—couldn't you just see her!

In fact, if one interpreted Vicki Kugelmann in the light of some aspects of Nazidom, and if one interpreted some aspects of Nazidom in the light of Vicki Kugelmann, were not both illuminated with miraculous clarity?

In short, was not Vicki a Nazi through and through?

Perhaps, after all, she *was* a spy! That would be a funny one!

Or was all this Miss Roach's imagination? It was not wise to trust her imagination at a quarter past five in the morning.

As Miss Roach lay pondering upon these things she became aware of a great purring in the sky above and all around—aware of the fact that this had been going on for about ten minutes.

Our planes, going out. . . . Or coming back, she didn't know which. . . .

Coming back from burning and burying and exploding German Vickis, German small children, German charwomen and others. . . .

It was all very confusing, and she fumbled in the purring dark for another aspirin with her next sip of water.

5

So you were living in the same boarding-house with a fully-fledged unrepentant Nazi woman, who talked about "you" English, and "English Misses".

What did you do now? Leave the boarding-house? And go where? Back to London? No—she was still too scared of the bombs. They had left London alone a long while now, but you never knew when they would be back.

Go to some other country town, then? Pack up and leave Thames Lockdon behind—Church Street, Mrs. Payne, Mr. Thwaites, all of it—including the Lieutenant?

The Lieutenant! How odd that was! In all the passion and profundity of her thoughts in the dark tonight (this morning) the Lieutenant had hardly entered her head.

Why was this? And why, in view of his disgraceful, his outrageous behaviour last night, did she bear no grudge against the Lieutenant?

Was it because by now she was utterly indifferent to him? Almost certainly this was so. The poor man was a plain damned fool. Any man who could go on behaving as he did, any man who could persist in thinking Vicki Kugelmann "cute", was too immeasurably stupid to take seriously any more.

There was no evil in the man, as there was in the one he thought so cute. She did not even have any bitterness against him for the insult he had offered her on the seat by the river.

He spoke naturally and sincerely: he did not talk about being "sporty". Tomorrow morning (or rather later today) he would, if he met her, be red-eyed and ostensibly repentant, but fundamentally unrepentant and inconsequent still, and start all over again the next evening. There was just no doing anything with the man: you had to rule him out.

And had she always been indifferent to him like this? No—she saw now that she had not. She had laughed to herself about the Laundry: but she had thought about it as well. She had never quite dismissed the Laundry from the realm of practical politics. She had never shown any signs of really "loving" the Lieutenant (why did she still have to put the word in inverted commas?), but she had never altogether put from her mind the notion of "coming" to love him (inverted commas again!).

But now all that was over. He did not belong to her any more: he was no longer "her" American in Thames Lockdon. Whose was he, then? Vicki Kugelmann's? Presumably, since he thought her so wonderfully cute, and kissed Vicki Kugelmann instead of Enid Roach in the darkness by the river. Well—he was welcome to her if he wanted her; and she said that without a trace of venom.

It was queer how all her venom was directed against Vicki, and not against the Lieutenant. This was not, was it, because in the remote recesses of her unconscious mind she "loved" or wanted to marry the Lieutenant, and was wild with fury at Vicki for coming between them and spoiling the whole thing?

She thought about this, and was able in answer to furnish an easy and profoundly confident negative. But what might an outsider think? What might the Lieutenant think? What might Vicki think?

What, in fact, *did* Vicki think? Was it not clear that she was already thinking, or in a very short while would be thinking, that the English Miss was consumed with jealousy? Was not this the obvious line such a woman would take? Had she not already surreptitiously taken this line with her "Miss Prim" and "Miss Prude"—the suggestion that she (Miss Roach) was too afraid of losing a man to allow him to be friendly with or in drunken gaiety kiss another woman? And was this to be tolerated?

No, this was not to be tolerated. Somehow, she must have this out with Vicki. She must have this out at once. She must go to her and tell her that she did not care two pins about the Lieutenant—that Vicki could have the Lieutenant—that Vicki was a million times welcome to the Lieutenant.

But what would Vicki answer? Would she not reply, in her filthy slightly foreign accent, that she also was totally disinterested in the Lieutenant? And would she not, replying thus, hint that it was only Miss Roach's consuming jealousy which was making Miss Roach go to the point of avowing disinterest in the Lieutenant? And would not this be more intolerable than ever?

Miss Roach had now reached the point (she saw) at which she was inventing conversations with Vicki, inventing Vicki's answers, and then getting white with anger at these invented answers. This was the point at which she must stop, or go clean off her head.

The planes were still purring in the sky, miles and miles high, it seemed, and miles and miles around. . . .

And then there was the second front to come, which couldn't possibly succeed (well, be sensible, *could* it?), and then the Lieutenant would be killed, and then the war would go on and on, like the planes in the sky. . . .

She knew she would never get a wink now, and she might as well make up her mind to it. Knowing this she felt better.

What a thing this sleeplessness was! . . . If sleep, she thought, could be compared to a gentle lake in a dark place, then sleeplessness was a roaring ocean, a raging, wind-buffeted voyage, lit with mad rocket-lights, pursued by wild phantoms from behind, plunging upon fearful rocks ahead, a mad tempest of the past and present and future all in one. Through all this the pale, strenuous mariner must somehow steer a way, until at last the weary dawn, not of sleep, but of resignation to sleeplessness, comes to calm the waters of the mind.

CHAPTER TWELVE

I

THAT next morning there was just one split second when Miss Roach thought that there might yet be some sort of means of living in the future in the Rosamund Tea Rooms with Vicki Kugelmann on some sort of terms of mutual toleration or even ostensible amity. That was when she first met Vicki, accidentally, in the passage outside her room, and Vicki faintly returned her faint smile. But the second was only a split one, and another of its kind never put in an appearance.

As she dressed that morning Miss Roach had given a good deal of thought as to how she was to address Vicki, and indeed look at her, when they met. Meetings of this sort, between two people who had quarrelled and not made it up, were embarrassing enough in any case. They were doubly embarrassing, however, when the two parties engaged had not openly quarrelled before, and had not, as in this case, even shown any recognisable signs of ever being likely to quarrel.

Moving about in the daylight, washing and dressing in her bedroom, Miss Roach was willing to agree with the supposition that she had exaggerated everything out of all proportion in her sleepless night, and, although she now knew she hated Vicki in the recesses of her soul, she hoped that the hatred need not be active, malignant, and incessant, but could be alleviated and rendered supportable by mutual civility. And as mutual civility was the thing required, she herself had better take the initiative in being civil. She decided to smile at Vicki, and greet her in a friendly way.

She somehow saw this happening at the breakfast table in front of the others: and, without being conscious of it, to make this vision come true she actually waited in her room two or three minutes after the gong had been hit, so that Vicki might go down first and she might make her mentally prepared entrance. This was not to be, however. As she left her room she ran straight into Vicki, who was coming out of hers.

"Hullo!" said Miss Roach cheerfully. "How are you this morning?"

And, in spite of the surprise of meeting her thus in the passage, the smile came, and somehow held.

Then came the moment when she thought that she might in future live on some sort of terms of mutual toleration with Vicki, for a flicker of a returning smile appeared on her face.

"Oh, very well, thank you," said Vicki. "A slight head, but otherwise all right. And how are you?"

It was that "And how are you?" which finished it. For with it the flicker of a smile had gone, and was replaced with an expression of complacence, defiance, indifference, and subtle scorn which Miss Roach was to see a thousand times on Vicki's face afterwards, and which told her, on this, its first appearance, all the story of all that was to come.

Also Vicki, after keeping this look on her face just so long that it could not be mistaken, and instead of politely giving Miss Roach an opportunity of going first down the stairs, herself went ahead in complete silence, causing Miss Roach to follow her, like a lamb, all the way down.

Then it was that Miss Roach knew that such a moment of hopefulness would never reappear. Then it was that she knew that it was war to the death—malignant, venomous, abominable, incessant, irreversible.

It was as though she was having in silence to follow her own ugly fate, her own ugly future, meekly down the stairs.

2

Mr. Thwaites was, of course, in his place, and all the others were there as well.

Mr. Thwaites naturally had to have a good look at both of them before he started on them about yesterday evening, and this took so much time that Miss Steele came in in front of him.

"And how did you two get on last night?" she said, raising her voice because speaking from another table, and so that everyone in the room could hear. "Did you enjoy yourselves?"

It was not usual for Miss Steele to begin a conversation from her own table: in fact, it was almost against Mr. Thwaites' dining-room rules. One was allowed to join in a conversation which Mr. Thwaites had started from his own table, but one was not expected to start one from a separate table of one's own.

This itself showed the importance of the occasion, revealed the fact that by going to the Dragon Miss Roach and Vicki had created a perhaps alarming, but certainly exciting precedent, and that the Rosamund Tea Rooms, in its *ennui*, intended, whatever it thought of the moral side of the matter, to take advantage of the accomplished fact, and share vicariously in the excitement. This arose from the same causes as those which made the guests, when Miss Roach had been going daily to town, look forward each evening to her return.

"Yes, it was very nice," said Miss Roach, and Vicki said, "Yes. We enjoyed ourselves very much."

"I wish I'd been with you," said Miss Steele, as usual advertising, a trifle absurdly, her anti-fogey attitude to life. "I'd have enjoyed it myself."

"Yes, I wish you had," said Miss Roach, and wondered how much Miss Steele actually would have enjoyed it. There was a short silence, and Mr. Thwaites began.

"And didst thou dance, and dally, and trip the lightsome toe," he asked, "e'en unto the small hours of the morn?"

"Oh no," said Vicki, "we were in before twelve."

"Like Cinderella?" said Miss Steele, from her table, and, Vicki not answering, Miss Roach said, "Yes. That's right. Like Cinderella."

It was characteristic of Vicki to have left Miss Roach to answer Miss Steele. Now that Vicki was established in the boarding-house, it was becoming more and more clear that she took hardly any notice of, had hardly a word for, anyone but Mr. Thwaites.

"And didst thou imbibe mighty potions from the fruit of the grape," Mr. Thwaites went on, "pursuing God Bacchus in his unholy revels?"

"Oh yes," said Miss Roach, "we had a certain amount to drink." As Mr. Thwaites was Trothing, it looked as though, on the whole, he was going to be fairly lenient.

"And hast thou one Ache, this morning," asked Mr. Thwaites, "appertaining unto Head, and much repentance in thy soul, forsooth?"

"Oh—not so bad," said Vicki. "It might be worse."

"And what did you dance?" asked Mr. Thwaites, de-Trothing in a sudden access of bitterness. "*Jazz*—I suppose!"

There was a pause.

"Oh, it's not jazz now," said Miss Steele. "You're old-fashioned, Mr. Thwaites. It's Boogy-woogy now, isn't it?"

Vicki, of course, did not answer this, and this time Miss Roach did not answer either—being too ashamed both of Mr. Thwaites and Miss Steele to do so.

"I didn't know that you could dance at the Dragon," said Miss Steele, again advertising her knowledge and tolerance of these matters. "Have they got a band there now?"

"No," said Miss Roach. "But we did dance a little—in a place on the way." And she remembered the horrible exhibition Vicki had made of herself in the small public-house.

"I suppose *she*," said Mr. Thwaites, looking at Miss Roach but obviously addressing Vicki, "did a Russian dance, didn't she?"

As Vicki was not being looked at she did not answer, and Miss Roach did not answer either.

"I said I suppose *you*," said Mr. Thwaites, "did a Russian dance—didn't you?"

"No, Mr. Thwaites," said Miss Roach. "I didn't do a Russian dance."

"Oh. Didn't you? Why not?"

He was at it again.

"Why should I?" said Miss Roach.

"Why shouldn't you? You like the Russians — don't you?"

What was so awful was that you had to find answers to these questions, and the answers were of necessity as puerile as the questions.

"Yes," she said. "But that doesn't mean I did a Russian dance."

What *else* could she have said!

"Oh—doesn't it?"

"No. It doesn't."

"Oh well—I'm glad to know that," said Mr. Thwaites. "We're not on the steppes now, you know."

"No. I know we're not," said Miss Roach.

"At least not at *present*, anyway," said Mr. Thwaites, as if it was quite clear that we very soon would be, if things went on as they were.

"I expect *you* can do a Russian dance, can't you?" said Mr. Thwaites, now talking to Vicki, "if I know anything about it?"

And now, miraculously, because he was talking to Vicki instead of Miss Roach, a Russian dance, instead of being a bad thing to do, had become a highly estimable and delightful sort of thing.

"Oh yes, I can do a Russian dance," said Vicki. "I can do all sorts of dances."

"Ah—then you must give Our Lady of the Roach some

lessons," said Mr. Thwaites. "It'll come in useful for her. You must give her some wrinkles."

There was a pause.

"Or perhaps," said Mr. Thwaites, "Dame Roach could give *you* some wrinkles. What?"

Miss Roach got his meaning at once. He meant that Miss Roach, as a less youthful or less well-preserved woman than Vicki, and having, as such, more wrinkles on her face, could well afford to dispense with them, pass them on to Vicki. She was amazed by the lengths to which Mr. Thwaites went nowadays. He had got steadily worse since Vicki had arrived: he got worse, it seemed, every day, every hour.

She hoped that the others had not fully taken in his meaning, as, if they had, it was difficult to know what she ought to do. Walk out of the room? In the silence that followed she wondered what Mr. Thwaites was going to say next.

He actually said nothing intelligible. Instead of this he imitated a cat.

"Miaow! . . ." whined Mr. Thwaites. "Miaow! . . . Miaow! . . Miaow! . . ."

3

Obscure as this might have been with one unacquainted with Mr. Thwaites' mental processes, his meaning, as usual, was clear enough to those who were familiar with these. Although he had brought up the subject of wrinkles himself, he was now, in that extraordinarily free-and-easy association of ideas which characterised him, making it appear that the two women had begun the thing, and was saying "Miaow! . . . Miaow!" in order to suggest that these two women were being "catty" to each other in discussing each other's wrinkles.

Here Mrs. Barratt took a hand. She had been reading her newspaper, and whether she had properly understood the crude affront a moment ago offered to Miss Roach, Miss Roach did not know. She did, however, come in on Miss Roach's side.

"What's the matter with *you*, Mr. Thwaites?" she said, smiling. "Are you taken ill or something?"

"No, I'm not taken ill," said Mr. Thwaites, looking at Vicki and Miss Roach. "Miaow! . . . Miaow!"

And he then pretended to look for a cat under the table.

"Pussy!" he said, snapping his fingers. "Pussy! . . . Pussy! . . . Pussy!"

Both Miss Roach and Vicki looked down their noses.

"I don't seem to be able to find him," said Mr. Thwaites. "Well, never mind that. What were we talking about?"

"We were talking about Russian dances, Mr. Thwaites," said Vicki, with a sort of primness.

"Oh. Were we? I thought we were talking about wrinkles."

"Oh well," said Mrs. Barratt, "I don't think we'd better talk about wrinkles. We know enough about them without having to talk about them."

"Yes, we certainly do," said Miss Roach.

"And do *you* assent to that statement?" said Mr. Thwaites, looking at Vicki.

"Naturally," said Vicki.

"Why?" said Mr. Thwaites. "You haven't got any wrinkles, have you? At least not as far as I can see."

"Ah—perhaps you don't see everything, Mr. Thwaites," said Vicki.

"See everything?" said Mr Thwaites. "No, perhaps I don't . . ."

At this moment something in Mr. Thwaites' measured tone made Miss Roach look up at him. Something in his words as well. Was Mr. Thwaites about to become "suggestive"? Increasingly complimentary to Vicki he had already shown sufficient signs of being in the last week or so (while increasingly harsh and bullying to herself), but so far he had not stepped further into actual sexual innuendo.

Looking at him now, it suddenly occurred to Miss Roach

that perhaps a new Mr. Thwaites was about to appear on the scene. Had he not an excitable, an almost feverish look? And did not his talk, which was certainly growing wilder and wilder, coincide with this look?

"But perhaps I'd *like* to see everything," said Mr. Thwaites, in the same measured tone, and looking at Vicki in the same measured way. "Or at any rate a bit more."

There was no doubting what he was up to now. Oh dear—thought Miss Roach—not this! Not, on top of yesterday evening, on top of her sleepless night, on top of her quarrel with Vicki and deadly feud against her—not a new Mr. Thwaites with an elderly physical passion out of control! And not for Vicki! Not, at this juncture, another feather in her cap! (For she would take it as such: she was that sort of woman.)

"I don't quite follow, I'm afraid, Mr. Thwaites," said Vicki, primly again, but by no means with a look of displeasure.

"Don't you?" said Mr. Thwaites. "I wonder if you could if I said it in French?"

This was referring back to a conversation a few days ago, in which it had been agreed that things could be expressed in French which could not be expressed in English.

"*Vraiment, monsieur,*" said Vicki. "*Pourquoi en français? Vous êtes tres gai ce matin, n'est pas? Je crois que ce serait mieux si vous continuez votre petit déjeuner.*"

She couldn't, thought Miss Roach—she *couldn't.* No woman on earth could descend to such depths as these. But she had. What, exactly, Vicki had said she did not know, for she herself could not speak French.

"Go on," said Mr. Thwaites. "I like to hear you speaking French."

"*Non—c'est assez,*" said Vicki. "*Vous allez continuer votre répas ou je ne dirais plus.*"

"And what about Dame Roach?" said Mr. Thwaites. "Can she speak French?"

"No," said Miss Roach. "I'm afraid I can't."

And, catching Vicki's eyes for a second, she realised that one of the objects of this exhibition was to reveal as even more insular and English the English Miss.

CHAPTER THIRTEEN

I

MISS ROACH had not been mistaken: this was the beginning of something new.

It seemed, almost, that Mr. Thwaites, that morning at breakfast, had sensed a fatal split between the two women, and (this coinciding with the release of some previously more or less submerged ambition or desire in regard to Vicki of his own) had rushed in to take advantage of it.

Yes—Mr. Thwaites had conceived an elderly amorous desire for Vicki. From now on there was no evading a fact which grew daily more evident. You could hardly be surprised. If you made up to an old man like that, rallied him, flattered him, challenged him, played patience with, made *moues* at him, dripped your beastly hair over him—you could hardly be surprised. Old men were notoriously unfastidious, and it was not, after all, any feather in Vicki's cap.

It was difficult to ascertain whether the force motivating the old man was actually desire or vanity. There was probably something of both. Also, curiously mixed up in it all, there was a hatred of Miss Roach. It was as if he had found another delightful rod with which to beat Miss Roach. Or it was as if, suspecting Miss Roach's disapproval, he was defying her. Or it was as if, knowing somehow of the rupture between herself and Vicki (perhaps having been privately told as much by Vicki!) he was seeking to please Vicki by striking at Miss Roach. Whatever it was, it was plain to all. He was unable to make a remark in subtle or open praise of Vicki without somehow dragging in Miss Roach. He was unable to be "suggestive" about Vicki's physical attractiveness without making some complementary suggestion about Miss Roach's lack of it.

And those "suggestions"! Whatever Vicki did, whatever Vicki said, he was on to her like a terrier. His state of self-consciousness was painful: he watched her all day, and pounced at every opportunity. He pounced without opportunity: he twisted her words, he turned her thoughts. He twisted and turned his own thoughts and words in order to create opportunities. Among other things he had developed a madness to hear her speaking in French. "Say *that* in French," he would say, or "What's *that* in French?" Vicki obliged, charmingly, rapidly, liltingly, fluently: she was an indescribably low woman. Later he asked for things in German. He could understand none of this, but he liked to watch her as she spoke her own guttural tongue. Also this was another way of striking at Miss Roach.

Oddly enough, he did not allow all this to become too obvious in front of the other guests. Like all complete fools, he was anything but a fool. Behind his puerility there was a sort of base natural cunning. He was clever enough somehow to avoid creating an open scandal in the boarding-house. It was only when Miss Roach alone was present, when just the three of them were together, that he really let himself go.

Vicki's reaction to all this was also interesting. She was too clever to show any of the definite pleasure and triumph which Miss Roach was quite certain she was in fact feeling. While leading Mr. Thwaites on with her French and her German and in other ways, she still kept up a pretence of being mildly scandalised, and of rebuking him, even if kittenishly. Her attitude was signalised mainly by a sort of growing and insufferable smugness. As Mr. Thwaites progressed in his ardour a kind of indolent look had appeared in her eyes. Her manner had become more indolent, too. Her walk, her sideways glances, the very movement of her shoulders, had become indolent. She seldom made *moues*, and she no longer let her hair drip about. She didn't have to.

Another thing which Miss Roach noticed was that, since arriving at the Rosamund Tea Rooms, and particularly since Mr. Thwaites had begun this sort of thing, Vicki's foreign accent had become much more pronounced. Nor did Miss Roach believe that it was quite the genuine accent of a German speaking English. She believed, rather, that it was something eclectic which Vicki believed to be pretty, and had adopted purely for the sake of charming.

Miss Roach, of course, personally found it hideous. Particularly did she abominate Vicki's use of the indefinite article, which was stressed, made to stand out, in the most repulsive way. Instead of "You're in a very bright mood this evening, Mr. Thwaites," she would say "You are in A very bright mood this evening, Mr. Thwaites." And instead of saying "Now, Mr. Thwaites, would you like a cigarette," she would say "Now, Mr. Thwaites, would you like A cigarette?" And she would say "Now, I think I will take A walk" and "Ah, never mind—I have what you call A hunch!" And the minute pause she made just before uttering this A was filled with indescribable self-conscious archness, and, for no particular reason, got on Miss Roach's nerves more than any other single thing.

2

It was at tea-time in the Lounge, four days after that revealing breakfast, that matters took a turn for the worse.

Miss Steele was out to tea: Mrs. Barratt hurried out after a single cup: and the three were left alone together.

Somehow the subject had got back to dancing. Somehow, ever since hearing of Vicki's dancing on that evening out with the Lieutenant, Mr. Thwaites had got dancing a little on the brain. Was this because he had some visions of holding Vicki in his arms in a dance? He had even gone so far as to say that he himself would take Vicki out for a dance one of these days. He would show her some dancing, he said.

"But I thought you said," he now said to Vicki, "that you could do all sorts of dances?"

This was typical of the present situation: he now remembered everything the woman said. Miss Roach herself remembered Vicki saying exactly this, four days ago at breakfast-time: he had got the precise words. He remembered everything, to use against Vicki, to use against Vicki in dalliance, to twist and to turn.

"Really?" said Vicki. "I don't know that I did."

"Oh yes, you did. Didn't she, Miss Roach?"

"Yes, I believe she did," said Miss Roach.

"Ah well," said Vicki, "perhaps I say A heap of things I do not mean."

("Heap", Miss Roach noticed, was an Americanism which she had obviously picked up from the Lieutenant, who used it constantly.)

"Perhaps," said Mr. Thwaites, after a pause, "you *Lead* a lot of Dances, as well."

Another twist. It was easy to see what he was getting at: at the same time it was almost impossible to do otherwise than pretend that one saw no such thing—a classical Thwaitesian dilemma.

As Vicki did not choose to answer, Mr. Thwaites repeated himself.

"How do you mean, Mr. Thwaites?" said Vicki.

"I mean perhaps you *like* leading people dances," said Mr. Thwaites. "Perhaps you make a hobby of it?"

"Lead people dances? Who, for instance?"

"Oh—the Male of the Species. What? Don't you?"

"No, Mr. Thwaites. Certainly not that I'm aware of."

"What! Don't you? And like it, too! I'd wager she does—wouldn't you, Miss Roach."

"Oh—I don't expect she does," said Miss Roach. She wondered if she could gracefully leave the room. If Mr. Thwaites was going to make love to Vicki in front of her, surely this would be the best thing to do. But at the moment she had a full cup of tea on her knee.

"But perhaps you wouldn't know anything about it," said Mr. Thwaites, looking at Miss Roach.

There were three ways of answering this. One was with the drearily familiar "What do you mean?" Another was with the embarrassing and equally familiar silence. The other (in view of the fact that his intention pretty obviously was to present her with one of the gravest affronts a man could present to a woman) was to throw her cup of tea in his face. But she had better not do this, and she had better not say "What do you mean?", in case he did explain more fully what he meant. So she remained silent. But Mr. Thwaites had better not go too far.

Luckily he altered his line.

"Some funny things go on in dances in this town," he said, "as far as I can see." He was alluding to recent scandals, concerning girls and Americans in a hotel in the town, which had got into the local newspapers.

"Yes. Some very funny things," said Vicki. "I read about them."

"Yes," said Miss Roach. "So did I."

"In fact, it hardly seems safe to go to them," said Vicki.

"No," said Miss Roach. "It hardly does."

It was then that Mr. Thwaites went too far.

"Oh, that's all right," said Mr. Thwaites. "You wouldn't have to worry."

There was a pause. Then Miss Roach, having thought it out, took up her cup of tea, put it down on the table, and walked towards the door.

"What's the matter with you?" said Mr. Thwaites. "Where are you going?"

"Nothing," said Miss Roach. "I'm going out, that's all."

"Oh—you *two*!" said Vicki. "Can't you two stop *squabbling*?"

"Come on—come back," said Mr. Thwaites, and "Stop squabbling!" said Vicki.

"No. I'm going out," said Miss Roach, and she did.

"Our Worthy Dame," she heard Mr. Thwaites saying, after she had closed the door, "seems to be in Somewhat of a Huff."

CHAPTER FOURTEEN

I

THE mystery, at this time, was the Lieutenant.

Having some experience of the Lieutenant as a mystery, his complete absence and silence hardly bothered Miss Roach: she wondered what Vicki thought about it, and if she was as little bothered.

Naturally, not a word about him passed between them, and this added to the general strain.

"Where's your American friend?" Mr. Thwaites asked them both one day, and Miss Roach said that she did not know. Vicki did not answer.

It occurred to her that Vicki might be meeting him in secret. But she did not really believe this, any more than she really believed that Vicki was in fact a German spy. But she wouldn't put either of these things beyond her.

The mystery was in some measure solved, and in some measure deepened, when, after eight days of silence, the Lieutenant rang up.

It was at lunch-time, and Sheila came up to Miss Roach, saying, "Lieutenant Pike on the phone, miss."

Miss Roach had foreseen such a situation, but she had not foreseen doing what she now did.

"Oh . . ." she said, and hesitated. "Oh . . . Will you tell

him that I'm not in? Will you tell him I'm out to lunch—or something?"

"Yes, miss," said Sheila, and went away.

In the silence that followed she dared not look at Vicki, though she knew that Vicki was looking at her. She was aware that Mr. Thwaites was looking at her. She was aware that everyone in the room, in some sort of way, was looking at her. She looked at her food, and wondered why she had done this.

Soon enough her motive became clear to her. It was nothing more complicated than revenge—a sudden impulse of revenge against Vicki—Vicki who supposed that the English Miss was jealous of the interest the Lieutenant was showing towards Vicki. This would "show" her—this would "English Miss" her! She had for days been longing to have this out with Vicki, to make her own complete indifference towards the Lieutenant quite clear. Now the result had been achieved by a single gesture. She was glad at what she had done, though rather sorry for the Lieutenant. It was unfortunate for him to have got caught up in feminine politics of this kind. She would have liked to have seen him, too.

Sheila returned.

"Please, miss," she said, speaking to Miss Roach, but glancing at Vicki, "he said if you wasn't here, could he speak to Miss Koogle?"

(It was a boarding-house joke that Sheila could get no further than this with the German woman's name.)

Vicki rose.

"Yes. I'll go," she said, and went out. Miss Roach, looking at her food, could not, of course, see her expression.

She had not foreseen this, and yet she ought to have. What now?

Complete silence reigned in the room. They, like her, were waiting to see what would happen next. She glanced up at Mr. Thwaites and Mrs. Barratt, and saw that they were not looking at her. But their way of not looking at her, she observed, was a way of looking.

Vicki returned. There was a long silence, and then Miss Steele got up and left the room. It was the end of the meal. Mr. Thwaites, oddly enough, got up and went out next. After him Mrs. Barratt went, and after her Mr. Prest. She and Vicki were alone. It was as though the guests had decided to leave them alone.

She had a little left on her plate, and in awful silence she made herself finish it. No, the silence was not awful—it was just plain silly. She decided to put an end to it.

"Well," she said, rising, and putting her napkin into its ring, "what did the Lieutenant have to say?"

"Oh, nothing much," said Vicki, also rising and doing the same thing. "He seemed to want me to come out this evening, that's all."

"And are you going?" said Miss Roach, still busy with her napkin and ring.

There was a pause. Then, with a look in her eye which Miss Roach was never to forget, and with a stronger foreign accent than Miss Roach had ever heard in her, and patting Miss Roach soothingly on the shoulder, Vicki answered.

"No," said Vicki. "That is not me, my dear. I do not Snatch. I do not Snatch the Men. . . ."

Miss Roach was about to say something, but Vicki, still patting her, went on.

"No, my dear. I put him off. Have no fear. I do not Snatch. I am not the Snatcher."

Then, with a final "No, I am not the Snatcher. Do not be alarmed. I do not Snatch," the German woman, in a dignified way, left the English one alone in the dining-room of the Rosamund Tea Rooms.

2

Oh! . . . Oh! . . . *Oh!* . . .

She was walking in the Park, by the river. She walked in a high wind and a lurid red-and-yellow sunset—one of those sunsets which seem to be imitating the postcard work of the firm of De La Rue, and she groaned at the cold and the wind and the memory of that woman's words.

"Do not be alarmed. I am not the Snatcher"! *The* snatcher! *The!* Oh . . . oh . . . *oh*! . . .

She had missed tea. She had made up her mind she couldn't face it. She had thought she would have it somewhere outside. But when she was out in the air she knew she couldn't sit still anywhere, and made up her mind to walk in the wind.

"No. I do not Snatch the men." And that indescribable glance of spite and condescension!

That condescension—above all, that condescension—the hideous twisting of the true situation into one in which she seemed to be able to condescend!

"That is not me. I do not Snatch." All the implications of that! Firstly, the calm assumption that she was in a position to snatch—that in this case the Lieutenant's inclinations had obviously been already transferred from Miss Roach to herself! Then, that such cases were continually arising in the life of this *femme fatale*, so much so that she had had to make a special rule to deal with them—that she was now (in spite of Miss Roach's warped and intemperate jealousy) maintaining her standards and heroically refraining from snatching. Then (and here was the most hideous twist), that Miss Roach had refused to go to the phone because she was angry with the Lieutenant for showing a preference for another woman—because she was too piqued even to speak to him. That was how it had been made to look—that was what the soothing pat on the shoulder had meant. Really, before long she would do this woman some harm. Miss Roach's brown eyes glowed black in the angry sunset, as she forced her way through the wind.

And then the implication that she *wanted* the Lieutenant, that the man, by now, didn't bore her *stiff*! Well, that might be exaggerating, but it was practically the truth.

As if, if she had wanted him, she could not have answered the phone and made an appointment to meet him separately! He had enquired for her, had he not—not Vicki?

This could not go on. She must have it out. Since the hint had failed, she must tell Vicki in so many words that she took not the slightest interest in the man—that she was welcome to him. She must make this clear, or she could no longer stay in the same house with the woman.

Have it out, then. When? Now? Yes—why not now—why not go back and have it out now? She turned her back on the sunset and the wind.

The silence of the wind, now it was behind her, smote her with sudden fear, but her determination remained.

Where would Vicki be now? At tea? Then she must call her out of tea, ask her if she could have a word with her alone.

What if she refused? No—she could hardly do that.

Or perhaps she would be up in her room. She usually went to her room after tea, and stayed there a long while. What she did there, nobody knew—probably sent messages to Nazi Germany on a secret wireless transmitter.

It didn't matter where she was—she must find her and have it out.

It was almost dark when she reached the Rosamund Tea Rooms. Her heart beat faster as she put the key in the door. The dim oil-lamp was burning in the hall, illuminating the hall-table, the tinny brass gong, and the green letter-rack criss-crossed with black tape.

As she climbed the stairs she heard Mr. Thwaites' voice booming in the Lounge, but as she passed the door, stopping to listen for a moment, she could not hear Vicki's voice.

On the top landing she saw a light under Vicki's door. She went into her room, switched on the light, and hastily did the black-out. Now for it! Now for it!

She walked about her room, looked at herself in the glass, and walked about again. She opened her door, listened, almost closed it, walked about the room again, and looked at herself in the glass.

All at once she heard Vicki open her door and come out. Now for it! Now for it! She went to the door.

"Oh—Vicki," she said. "Can I have a word with you for a moment?"

She was surprised, but rather pleased, to hear herself calling her "Vicki", in a calm and more or less friendly way like that. Perhaps this thing could be done in a more or less friendly way: perhaps this thing could be more or less smoothed out.

"Yes," said Vicki. "What is it?" She came into the room. She was dressed for going out.

"Oh, it's only about something you said at lunch-time this morning," said Miss Roach, swallowing slightly, but maintaining her calm.

"Yes," said Vicki, with an innocent and slightly puzzled expression. "What?"

"Oh—only something you said about—taking—men". (She could not bring herself to repeat that awful word "snatch"!).

"Yes," said Vicki, "I remember. What of it?"

"Well, it's only," said Miss Roach, again swallowing, "that with this particular man . . ." For a moment she could not go on.

"Yes," prompted Vicki. "This particular man? . . ."

"Well, it's only that I haven't got the faintest interest in him. . . . And I'm sure he hasn't got the faintest interest in me. . . . And so I didn't want you to think there was anything of that sort, that's all."

For a moment Vicki paused, looking at her. Then, with the look of charmed incredulity with which one hears a child's story, with a look of infinite benevolence, combined somehow with a look of infinite spite, she put out her hand and patted Miss Roach's cheek.

"Really!" said Vicki, again in her most guttural accent. "You are rather A dear, aren't you?"

Then she again patted Miss Roach's cheek, and went to the door.

"Yes. You are rather A dear!" she said, and was out in the passage . . .

What now? . . . Call her back? Go out and *haul* her back?—hit her in the face?—kick her down the stairs?

Instead, Miss Roach went out on to the landing and listened to Vicki going all the way down the stairs. There was something maliciously and exquisitely genial and forbearing even in the sound of her footsteps. Then Miss Roach heard the front door being closed.

Mr. Thwaites' nasal voice came booming up from behind the closed door of the Lounge. . . .

CHAPTER FIFTEEN

THOUGH the Rosamund Tea Rooms was, as regards bedroom accommodation, full up, there was still plenty of space in the dining-room, and Mrs. Payne, whose love of gain over-rode all other considerations, did not hesitate, when the occasion arose, to inflict her regular guests with the company of strangers at meals. Sometimes these strangers, temporary visitors to Thames Lockdon, would come in just for one meal, sometimes for two or three days, sometimes for as long as a week.

This was something of an ordeal for the regular guests, but more so for the strangers, who were stuck out in the middle of the room, and, surrounded by an atmosphere of silent curiosity and seeming dislike, did not dare to speak, adopted a timid and tentative attitude towards the food and the service, and were very glad indeed to get out of the room again.

The lift-rumbling, knife-fork-and-plate silence was, it seemed, particularly awful on these occasions, as even Mr. Thwaites, though speaking, spoke less—not caring to impress his personality on mere passing strangers who could not absorb it fully or adequately in the time.

Amongst these intruders was a piano-tuner, of the name of Albert Brent, heavily moustached and in late middle-age. He did not come to tune any piano, for there was no such thing at the Rosamund Tea Rooms, but he was an old personal friend of Mrs. Payne. (For, incredibly enough, Mrs. Payne had a private life, ate and drank, went out to tea, went to the pictures, loved and hated, like any other woman.) And when he was in this part of the world, doing this "territory", Mrs. Payne provided him with lunch in the dining-room, where he was given a table in the corner.

This respectable man took an interest in human nature, and, without their knowing it, studied and came to conclusions about the guests.

Thus looked at from outside, these guests—in this dead-and-alive dining-room, of this dead-and-alive house, of this dead-and-alive street, of this dead-and-alive little town—in the grey, dead winter of the deadliest part of the most deadly war in history—thus seen from a detached point of view, they presented an extraordinary spectacle.

Albert Brent, who liked talking and a glass of beer, could not understand how people could live in this way—how they could have ever reached, and could continue to suffer, such a condition of dullness, torpidity, inactivity, stupidity, and silence. It was enough, he thought, to drive anybody raving mad.

They didn't talk, they didn't laugh, they didn't seem to enjoy their food, they didn't seem to go out, they didn't seem to have any interests, they didn't seem to like each other much, they didn't even seem to hate each other, they didn't seem to do anything. All they seemed to do was to crawl in one by one, murmur a little to the waitress, mutter little requests to pass the salt, shift in their chairs, occasionally modestly cough or blow their noses, sit, eat, wait, eat, sit, and at last crawl out again, one by one, without a word, to heaven knew where to do heaven knew what. . . . It was all beyond Albert Brent, who lived for the most part in London and had been in close touch with the world of affairs and the war.

Most of them, he thought, were pretty ordinary boarding-house specimens. Mr. Prest he could not quite make out, but Miss Steele and Mrs. Barratt were easily recognisable types. The loud, nasal-voiced, foolish man was of a type too, though much more foolish than was usual. The two younger women also, he supposed, were of a type.

He studied these two—one of whom, he observed, was a foreigner. Plain women, both of them, though the darker one had a "nice" face. Not likely to marry, either of them—the spinster type—not likely to marry unless a bit of luck came their way—which might not be impossible with all these Americans about. What puzzled him was the way the awful atmosphere of the place seemed to have got these two women down as well. They were comparatively young—young enough to talk and laugh, to exhibit some sign of vivacity, of response to life. But no—instead of this they seemed to be, in some way, duller, dumber, more deadly quiet and lifeless than all the others.

It was not for Albert Brent to know the actual state of affairs. It was not for the piano-tuner to know that in this still, grey, winter-gripped dining-room, this apparent mortuary of desire and passion (in which the lift rumbled and knives and forks scraped upon plates), waves were flowing forward and backward, and through and through, of hellish revulsion and unquenchable hatred!

It was not for him to know that between these two women there existed a feud almost unparalleled in boarding-house, or indeed feminine, history—that one of them walked against the wind in De La Rue sunsets with evil, all but murderous thoughts, yet remained blameless in character.

CHAPTER SIXTEEN

I

JUST as the guests of the Rosamund Tea Rooms were occasionally observed and appraised from outside, so the relationship existing between Mr. Thwaites, Miss Kugelmann, and Miss Roach was watched from within.

Oddly enough, Mrs. Barratt, who sat at the same table with these three, observed least of all. Perhaps she was too near. In any case, Mrs. Barratt existed in a sort of dream at meal-times, and indeed at most other times. She certainly had no notion of any sort of friction, or cause for friction, between Miss Roach and her German friend. She thought it must be "pleasant" for them to be together.

She was aware, on the other hand, that Mr. Thwaites, whom she indistinctly recognised as a type of bully, but one who seldom bothered her personally, had his knife into Miss Roach. For this reason, when she saw Mr. Thwaites going too far, she made a point of coming to Miss Roach's assistance.

But frequently, when in fact Mr. Thwaites was going much too far, she did not take in what was happening, and so, out of ignorance, withheld her support.

Miss Steele saw more. She saw clearly what sort of man Mr. Thwaites was. She saw, also, that he had chosen Miss Roach as the victim of his singular persecution, and she as well tried, when possible, to come to Miss Roach's aid. But as she sat at a separate table this was not so easy to do, and although, for this reason, what she did succeed in doing was doubly commendable, she in effect did very little.

In addition to this, not being personally molested by Mr. Thwaites, she did not believe that anyone, least of all the intelligent and comparatively youthful Miss Roach, could take so ridiculous an old man seriously, could be seriously hurt or tormented by what he said and did.

In other ways, too, she noticed a good deal more than Mrs. Barratt. She noticed, as soon as it began, the unwholesome, elderly interest Mr. Thwaites was showing towards Vicki. She noticed that along with this interest there had arisen an increased and parallel persecution of Miss Roach. She could not account for this, but she noticed it.

She was not sure of her opinion of the German girl. She had at first liked her, while realising that she was a little over-bright, facetious, and talkative in a typically un-English way, and she had genuinely thought that she would be a good influence as "livening things up". But, in a funny way, instead of livening things up, she had, very shortly after her arrival, somehow contrived to deaden things down. She was no longer over-bright and facetious in the dining-room, and, in evoking what she had evoked from Mr. Thwaites, she had introduced into the boarding-house, in addition to its dullness, something rather ugly which had not been there before.

She was not certain, either, whether the German girl and Miss Roach were quite as good friends as they were supposed to be. She watched them at meal-times, noticed that they did not talk to each other unless it was absolutely necessary, and seemed to avoid looking at each other altogether. And Vicki, while not exactly encouraging, and not exactly discouraging, Mr. Thwaites' clumsy verbal innuendoes and advances towards herself, made no attempt to help her friend out when he turned his attention to Miss Roach and began to attack her. It was all rather queer—nothing definite, but rather queer.

Miss Steele, of course, knew nothing of what took place when the three were alone together, and if she had been told that in front of her eyes and under her nose there was taking place a feud between two women almost unparalleled in boarding-house history, she would have been surprised exceedingly, and incredulous.

Mr. Prest, alone in his corner, sent to Coventry, and apparently mentally deaf to all that took place in the boarding-house, in fact observed and understood more than any other spectator.

Mr. Prest thought that the old man was a noisy, nattering, messy piece of work who ought to be in a mental home. He liked and pitied Miss Roach. He thought that the German woman was about as frightful a bitch as you were likely to find anywhere, and that something pretty nasty was going on, at that table, and between those three, one way and another.

2

Miss Roach had her work to do, and this she did in her bedroom, in front of the gas-fire, mostly in the mornings, but sometimes in the afternoons or evenings. But there was not enough to occupy her in any sense fully or satisfactorily, and she often wished that she was going up to London and back again each day by train.

Miss Roach disliked, too, having to wait for her room to be done before she could go into it and work, and more still, when it was done, having to light the fire and settle down to tasks by herself, without the stimulus of external demands from fellow-workers. In fact, before long Miss Roach found herself taking a sort of aversion to her work, even dodging it as much as possible, and, on the pretext of shopping, wandering more or less aimlessly about the streets of Thames Lockdon instead.

The war, in its character of petty pilferer, had been as busy in this little town as in London, and, for a woman's personal needs, the shops had little save frustration, irritation, or delay to offer in almost every department. There were no stockings, there was no shampoo, there was no scent, there were no hair-pins, no nail-varnish, no nail-varnish-remover, no ribbon, no watch-glasses, no watches to lend you while you waited for watch-glasses which might or might not come, no glycerine, no batteries for your torch, no scissors, no darning wool, no olive oil. . . . The pilferer, who for some reason had no taste for cocoa (which you could buy and bathe in if you had the money), had been here, there, and everywhere. . . .

The pilferer was an insatiable reader, too, and Miss Roach spent a good deal of time at the library failing to find anything she wanted to take out. Here she more than once ran into Mr. Thwaites, who went almost daily to change his book in an angry and disdainful way.

Miss Roach, listening to the remarks of Mr. Thwaites, as well as those of other subscribers, found the library one of the most peculiarly depressing features of the town. "Is this book Good?" she would hear the assistant being asked. Or "Can you recommend a good Book?" Or "I want a good Historical Book." Or "I want a book for my Nephew, who's just taken his degree in Mathematics." Or "Is this book Interesting?" And, sometimes, bitterly, "That book wasn't at *all* good," as much as to say that a practically fraudulent assistant had better do better next time or get into trouble. . . .

This depressed Miss Roach because it made her wonder whether the cultural level of the subscribers was, on the whole, very many degrees higher than that of Mr. Thwaites. She was aware, also, that a large amount of these subscribers came from boarding-houses round about in Thames Lockdon, and that Thames Lockdon was only one small town amongst the thousands of its sort spread out and hidden away from the world war all over the land.

She was not, she saw, really cut out for small-town, boarding-house life during a world war.

3

A duty had been bequeathed to Miss Roach by a widowed dressmaker—a Mrs. Poulton—with whom Miss Roach had been very friendly when she had first come to the town, but who had since left. This duty was to maintain an interest in, and occasionally take out to tea, the dressmaker's seventeen-year-old son, who was in due course going into the R.A.F.

The boy—John Poulton—interested Miss Roach because he had a decided gift, for his age, for painting water-colours, and because he did not desire to go into the estate agent business to which his family connections were pointing the way. (He did not, of course, desire to go into the R.A.F., but that was beside the point.) He wanted, after the war, to make his living as a painter of water-colours, and had confided as much to Miss Roach.

Miss Roach, as well as she could, supported him in this ambition—not because she really believed that his gift for painting water-colours was decided enough for him to make a living at it, but because she thought that the ambition was, in a general way, laudable, and better than an ambition to go into the estate agent business.

He was a good-looking boy, pale, and with a slight tendency to spots appropriate to his age.

One afternoon during this period they went for a walk, and, sitting on a felled tree in a field high above the town, he became more and more naïvely confiding to Miss Roach, and enlarged, earnestly and modestly, upon what he wanted to do and the opposition which he was encountering on all sides.

"Well, you do what you *want* to do—that's the only thing in life," said Miss Roach. And looking at the unhappy, bewildered boy, and remembering her own disappointed youth, with her grave, exhilarating theories about "education", and realising that he would soon be in the R.A.F. and not likely to get out of it again for years, she felt a warm, happy, simple, sad, maternal feeling towards him.

After this she had tea with him in the town. Coming out of the shop they bumped into Vicki, who had come in to buy some cakes.

"Oh—hullo!" said Miss Roach, and managed to force a smile. Vicki returned her "Hullo" and also managed a sort of smile in return.

Then she looked at Miss Roach and the boy in a fleeting but searching way.

CHAPTER SEVENTEEN

About certain things, and about the war in particular, Miss Roach was an ostrich, and purposely and determinedly so. In many respects she believed the ostrich to be a bird wiser than the owl. If you could do nothing to alleviate a situation, what sense was there in thinking about it, talking about it, taking any interest in it?

There were, she knew, many total non-combatants who thought about, talked about, and took an intense interest in the war. There was, furthermore, still quite a large percentage of non-combatants who were enormously enjoying the war. Mr. Thwaites, for instance, if it had not been for the shortage of food and the personal bother he was having with the Russians, would have been adoring the war. Even in spite of the food and the Russians he was still liking it quite a lot. It is difficult to keep a good war-liker down.

In her revulsion against this attitude Miss Roach went to the opposite extreme. So little could she bear to think about the war that she refused to apply her mind either to its details or general shape, and if she had been forced to enter for a general knowledge test on the subject would have probably scored less marks than anyone else in the country. So miserable was she made by the mere aspect of the national uniforms generally that she could not bring herself to look closely enough to differentiate between the ranks and regiments and kinds of any of these save those of the most obvious sort. She could not, off-hand, observe the difference between a lieutenant and a captain, let alone that between a squadron-leader and a wing-commander—

and she particularly disliked non-combatant people who gloated over these differentiations. All badges, medals, and bars were a mystery to her, and if asked such questions as what the word "Wren" actually meant, or "Waaf" or "Naafi" or "Ensa", she would have been in most cases unable to supply an answer. She had never even properly questioned the Lieutenant about what he was doing now, or what part he was likely to play when the second front began. In pity and horror she didn't want to hear. She hid her head in the sand, and didn't want to have anything to do with it.

Similarly she would hardly read the war-news in the newspapers apart from the headlines. She would just ascertain whether the right side was going forward or going back or staying where it was, and leave it at that. As for listening in morning, noon, and night to the wireless (particularly in the test match spirit which Mr. Thwaites brought to this pastime), she hated it, and she would always, if possible, leave the room.

Thus hiding her head (or trying quite unsuccessfully to hide her head) from the war, she had also lately been hiding her head from another reality—the approach of Christmas. There was a period, six or seven weeks before Christmas, in which people began to talk about doing things before Christmas, or doing things after Christmas, and against this attitude Miss Roach took a resolute and ostrich-like stand. She refused to think of, mention, or even fully believe in, the approach of Christmas. It couldn't happen again, she felt. They couldn't, in the present circumstances, be so silly as to do it again.

But doing it they were. Mr. Thwaites was, of course, a pronounced and leading Christmasist, being the instinctive leader of everything irritating and depressing, and the others followed him.

"Well," said Miss Steele, alluding to the general improvement of the war news, "we ought to be happier this Christmas anyway. And perhaps by next Christmas we'll be really happy."

"Yes," said Mr. Thwaites. "We happen to have a rather funny little way of pulling through."

And a certain blend of austerity and modesty in his look and nasal voice gave the impression that he himself had been having a funny little way, and pulling through the Rosamund Tea Rooms and everybody outside it.

"Yes," said Mr. Thwaites. "I think we may be said to have cooked Friend Hitler's goose."

At this Miss Roach glanced at Vicki, and noticed a slightly discontented, evasive expression on her face, which she had seen there before when Hitler was unfavourably mentioned.

As Christmas approached there was much talk of an excursion to the pictures, which, at this season, Mr. Thwaites was going to make with Vicki. Vicki was going to "take" him, she said. Long before the time came Mr. Thwaites displayed undue excitement about this excursion, and talked about it almost every day, contriving to make suggestive remarks about even so innocent a matter as this. It was as though the thought of going to the pictures alone with Vicki, of sitting in the dark alone with her, perhaps, had gone to his head. It was as though he thought that this outing marked, or would mark, some further advance in his advancing relationship with her.

Still Miss Roach resolutely denied the approach of Christmas, but at last Christmas cards arrived in spite of everything (which Miss Roach thought ought to be stopped, what with postmen trailing round and manpower and one thing and another), decorations (could you believe it?) were put up, and dreary cotton-wool snowstorms appeared in certain shop-windows.

Miss Roach's faith wavered. She did not, however, fully take in the fact that the season of peace and goodwill to men was upon her until, on Christmas Eve, coming back from a trip to London at about six o'clock in the evening, she found the Lieutenant in the Lounge, in the company of Mr. Thwaites, Vicki Kugelmann, an open bottle of whisky, a jug of water, and tumblers.

CHAPTER EIGHTEEN

I

AH—that Christmas!—that Christmas of hatred, fear, pain, terror, and disgrace! It all began at that moment.

And coming down in the train she had made up her mind that, because it was Christmas, she would make some effort to make things go smoothly, some effort at reconciliation even!

"Hooray!—you're just in time," said the Lieutenant, who was pouring the whisky into the tumblers. "Where've you been all this time?" A question which, actually, she thought she might more fittingly ask him.

"Salaams, good lady," said Mr. Thwaites, with his usual sarcasm. He was sitting on the sofa, and she noticed, from the beginning, that he was in a state of extra excitement. This was probably to be accounted for by the fact that he had been that afternoon to the pictures with Vicki.

Vicki said nothing, and would not catch her eye.

"Well, these are extraordinary goings-on," said Miss Roach brightly, because it was Christmas and she had made up her mind to make things go smoothly. "What do you think *you're* all up to?"

And she again tried to catch Vicki's eye, but Vicki would not look at her.

"And when did you drop in?" she said to the Lieutenant, and it turned out that he had appeared only a quarter of an hour ago. Within five minutes of arriving he had gone downstairs to Mrs. Payne and procured the tumblers and water. Because it was Christmas Eve, and because it was the Lieutenant who had done it, Miss Roach presumed that they would not all be expelled for drinking whisky in the Lounge: but she had never expected to see such a thing happening.

When the Lieutenant had poured out the whisky into the glasses, and added water, a silent, slightly interesting moment occurred in which Miss Roach wondered to whom he would offer a glass first—herself or Vicki. He offered a glass first to Miss Roach, though actually Vicki was nearer to him at the time.

Then he gave a glass to Vicki, and then he went over with one to Mr. Thwaites, who at first refused it.

"Aw, come on!" said the Lieutenant, in the old way, and when Mr. Thwaites again refused, "Aw—come on! Snap out of it! It's only Christmas once a year, isn't it?"

Mr. Thwaites gave in.

With the aid of Christmas, clearly, the Lieutenant was going to get away with murder. Indeed, to judge by his appearance, which was, to one who knew him, that of a man who had been intimately associated with the bottle for several days, he had in this way been getting away with murder from the earliest possible date at which such an excuse might be considered valid.

"Well," said Miss Roach, "how did you two get on at the pictures?"

She would *make* this woman catch her eye, if she died in the attempt.

But Vicki did not answer her or look at her. Neither did Mr. Thwaites.

Were they not going to answer at all? An awkward situation was saved by the Lieutenant, who asked:

"Why—have you two been to the movies?"

"Yea. Verily," said Mr. Thwaites. "We have paid a visit unto the House of Many Shadows—the Mansion of Flickering Visions—much to the entertainment of our jaded souls."

"Good for you," said the Lieutenant.

"Afterwards consorting," said Mr. Thwaites, "unto An Tea-shop—or Confectioner's—wherein we were regaled with rock-cakes and tea, and enjoyed a tête-à-tête."

"Fine," said the Lieutenant, slightly embarrassed, and sitting down. They were all seated now, and all, with the exception of

Mr. Thwaites, slightly embarrassed. Or so it seemed to Miss Roach.

"Whereupon," said Mr. Thwaites, looking at Vicki, "inspired by the cheering fluid, and smitten by Dan Cupid's dart, I proposed to the beauteous dame!"

And with a sort of triumphant air he took a large sip at his whisky.

(Hullo, thought Miss Roach—what was this? Was this the joke it seemed to be? Or was there something serious behind this? Mr. Thwaites, she saw, behind his jocular manner, was in a greater state of excitement than she had at first thought. In fact, she did not know that she had ever seen him in quite such a state of excitement. Was it wise to give him whisky in this state?)

"Really?" said the Lieutenant. "And what did the beauteous dame reply?"

"Ah," he said. "The beauteous dame gave me neither Yea nor Nay. She keepeth her Knight-gall*ant* on Tenterhooks."

And he took another enormous sip, one might say gulp, at his whisky.

The Lieutenant noticed this.

"How's the whisky going down?" he asked.

"Passing well, I thank you," said Mr. Thwaites. "Much good fire-water. Heap good medicine. Plenty warm. Plenty fine."

"So that's what you two have been up to, is it?" said the Lieutenant, addressing Vicki.

"Oh yes," said Vicki. "I have been vamping him mercilessly, I'm afraid."

("*Vamping*"*!*)

"Yes," said Mr. Thwaites, "I should say she has! She's a tease all right, isn't she? Yes—she's a tease—isn't she?"

This was bad. Was it possible that two sips of whisky (two inexperienced and enormous sips) had gone to his head?

"Yes," said Mr. Thwaites, "she's a vamp all right! She's a tease. And she knows it, too. Doesn't she? What?"

"Really," said Vicki, appealing to the Lieutenant, "he is quite A lad, isn't he? He is quite A Knut—no?"

("*Knut*"*!*)

Even the Lieutenant, normally deaf to these atrocities, looked a little silly, and changed the subject.

"And what did you see at the pictures?" he asked.

"We saw," said Mr. Thwaites, "one Oakie—Jack of that ilk, surrounded by diverse belles. Together with one thriller—gangster—which muchly froze our blood." And he took another sip at his whisky.

"Oh, then it's the same programme I saw," said Miss Roach, trying to calm things down. "I thought the gangster one rather good."

But this did not calm Mr. Thwaites down.

"Stick 'em up, big boy!" cried Mr. Thwaites. "Step on it, kiddo! Take 'em for a ride! Give 'em the Woiks!"

"Well," said the Lieutenant, putting his finger on the mark, "the films certainly seem to have excited you, Mr. Thwaites."

"Yes," said Vicki. "I think you'd better calm down, Mr. Thwaites, or we won't be able to take you out."

"Yes," said the Lieutenant. "You mustn't disgrace us at dinner."

"Why," said Miss Roach. "Are you going out?"

"What do you mean?" said the Lieutenant. "Of course we're going out. We're all going out."

And finishing up his drink, he went to the bottle and said, "Come on. Fill up."

2

He filled up Mr. Thwaites' glass again, and Mr. Thwaites made no objection of any sort. She didn't think it right, to excite an old man like this, but it wasn't for her to say anything—in fact, as the alleged "spoil-sport" it was beyond any strength of character she might have to say anything—and she wondered what on earth was going to happen.

This was bad, but twenty minutes later things were a good deal worse.

By then the Lieutenant was drunk, calling Miss Roach Roachy, Vicki Vick, and Mr. Thwaites Thwaitey, or "Old-timer", and eagerly encouraging him to make a fool of himself.

Miss Steele coming in, the Lieutenant insisted on her having a drink, and because there was no glass for her, went downstairs himself to fetch it. What Mrs. Payne was thinking about all this, heaven alone knew.

The Lieutenant had announced that they were going to dine at the River Sun. A sudden hope came into Miss Roach's mind that, because it was Christmas Eve, there would be no table for them at the River Sun, and that for this reason the outing might have to be abandoned. She mentioned this matter to the Lieutenant, but he said that that was all right, he had booked a table for eight o'clock.

Miss Steele accepted and drank her drink manfully, but was rather frightened. When the Lieutenant began to press her to join the party she grew more frightened still, and at last, in a panic, made an excuse laughingly to leave the room.

"What's the matter with the old girl?" said the Lieutenant. "Why won't she come?" And he went over to Mr. Thwaites to refill his glass.

Here Miss Roach had enough strength of character to intervene.

"No," she said. "You mustn't. He's had enough. You really mustn't!"

"Oh gosh," said the Lieutenant. "Let the old guy have a good time for once, won't you? It's only Christmas once, isn't it? Let the old guy have a good time."

"Yes," said Vicki, "let the silly old bean enjoy himself!" And Mr. Thwaites' glass was refilled.

Only Miss Roach noticed that Mrs. Barratt put her head into the room, retiring at once in terror. Mrs. Payne would be up next, and then there was going to be trouble.

Half-past seven came, and by this time Mr. Thwaites, after another noisy period in response to his replenished whisky, had sunk into a quiet stupor. By this time, also, the bottle was not full enough for the Lieutenant's liking, and he suggested they should go round to the River Sun and have some there before dinner.

Mr. Thwaites rose, and swayed as he went to the mantelpiece to put down his glass. It seemed to Miss Roach that he almost fell.

At this a sort of panic arose. "I'm sure he oughtn't to go," said Miss Roach aside to the Lieutenant. "Let him have a meal here and go quietly to bed," and "Oh—let the old guy come and enjoy himself!" said the Lieutenant, now almost irritable, and Vicki again supported him. "Coming? Of course I'm coming," said Mr. Thwaites.

There was then another panic because Mr. Thwaites, having gone to his room, in a mysterious way failed to come out again, and, on being applied for, was found to have his overcoat on, but unable to find his cap. He was bent upon wearing a cap. A hat (of which he had two) would by no means do.

A search took place all over the room, and when at last it was found, the Lieutenant, coming out on the landing, wanted to know which was the Old Girl's room, as he desired to renew his invitation to her to join them. "Oh, come *on*! Let's get *round* there," said Miss Roach, now very much more anxious to go than to stay, and for once Vicki supported her.

Mr. Thwaites seemed to recover somewhat in the fresh air, and supporting himself between Vicki and the Lieutenant in the blackness, went on about Vicki being a Tease.

"She's a Tease all right" he said. "Yes. She's a tease all right! And doesn't she just know it—doesn't she just love it!"

And then, having repeated this several times, in several different ways, "I don't know whether to give her a jolly good kiss," he said, "or to put her across my knee and spank her."

And, thinking aloud, he contemplated these two alternatives in a lascivious way all the way round to the public-house.

This was the war, Miss Roach again reminded herself in the blackness, this was the war! Allowances had to be made—it was all the *war*. Only the war could have brought a drunken American into a quiet riverside boarding-house in such a way as to cause so wild and uncomely a scene. The war was on their nerves, on the Lieutenant's nerves, probably even on Mr. Thwaites' nerves—causing this state of excitement and (abominable as his behaviour was normally) a mode of behaviour totally alien to him. The war was on her own nerves, on Vicki's nerves, she dared say, if such a woman had any nerves.

3

On their reaching the saloon bar of the River Sun, and luckily finding a table in a corner, an angry, contemplative, and contemptuous expression came over Mr. Thwaites' face, and he became silent. For although, in the excitement caused by his outing with Vicki and the whisky, he had been lured to come here, public-houses were not really things which were supposed to take place at all, and he wasn't going to give in now, and let people think, by his expression, that they were. Mr. Thwaites was a man who maintained his standards.

Also he was hungry by now, and showed very little interest in the drink that was brought him.

It was not, in fact, until they were up in the dining-room (into which the reluctant Lieutenant was compelled, by a nagging waiter, at last to escort them) that Mr. Thwaites returned to life. The food, indeed, seemed to go to his head more than the drink, and as soon as the soup appeared he began Trothing right and left for all the room to hear.

"A goodly soup, i'troth," he said, and he Trothed at the chicken, and Trothed at the waiter, and Trothed at both the waitresses (even the one who was not serving at the table at which they were sitting), and Trothed at the cheese, and Trothed at the furnishing of the dining-room (which met with his approval), and Trothed and Trothed and Trothed. He very nearly Trothed, in the most agreeable way, at the other diners in the room, but the Lieutenant managed to talk him down.

A sudden silence descending, Mr. Thwaites then slowly began hiccoughing (this with the intensest seriousness and mental concentration), and the Lieutenant saw that it was time to take him home. "Come on, we're going home now," he said, and helped Mr. Thwaites to rise. "You were quite right," he said aside to Miss Roach. "We oughtn't to have brought the old guy out."

(That was the *trouble* with the Lieutenant. He had a sort of *niceness*. It cropped up every now and again and made you almost wholly forgive him.)

CHAPTER NINETEEN

I

A FEW minutes later they were out in the black street, and Mr. Thwaites, having swayed up against a wall, did not seem easy to move.

"Methinks it behoveth me," said Mr. Thwaites, "to taketh me unto my mansion. Doth it not? Peradventure? Perchance?"

"Yes," said the Lieutenant. "Come along then. Get a move on."

"What?" said Mr. Thwaites. "Peradventure? Perhaps? No? Whereanent? Howbeit?"

"Yes," said the Lieutenant. "Come along now. Here's my arm. Got my arm? Got it?"

"Come along, Mr. Thwaites," said Vicki.

"Ah—the Beauteous Dame," said Mr. Thwaites. "The beauteous damsel that keepeth me on Tenterhooks."

"Come on then," said the Lieutenant. "Take my arm."

"Hooks. Tenter. One," said Mr. Thwaites. "See Inventory."

"Aw, come *on*, will you?" said the Lieutenant.

"Damsel. Beauteous. One," said Mr. Thwaites. "Hooks. Tenter. Two. Yea. Verily."

"Now then," said the Lieutenant. "Take my *arm*."

"The Arm of the Law," said Mr. Thwaites. "Law. Arm. One. One. Two. Three. One, two, three, March!"

But Mr. Thwaites, in spite of saying this, did not himself march.

"Can I help?" said a stranger in the darkness, and "No—it's all right, thank you very much," said the Lieutenant. "I think I can manage him."

"April, too," said Mr. Thwaites. "Thirty days hath November."

At this he lurched forward, the Lieutenant caught him, and with Miss Roach taking his arm the other side, they all began the journey homewards.

"Hooks. Tenter," said Mr. Thwaites. "See Inventory. Pitch your tents."

"That's all right," said the Lieutenant. "We will."

"Arabs," said Mr. Thwaites. "Fold 'em up."

"Yes, that's right," said the Lieutenant, soothingly. "Arabs."

Mr. Thwaites now took a new line, saw things in a fresh light.

"Some people do," he said, "and some people don't."

"Sure thing," said the Lieutenant.

"Not that they *do*," said Mr. Thwaites misanthropically, and, as if in despair of mankind, was silent for nearly a minute.

"Do you think we'll get him upstairs?" said Miss Roach.

"Yes," said the Lieutenant. "He's not so bad on his legs. We'll manage."

"*Touché!*" cried Mr. Thwaites, out of the blue. "I'troth! A Parry!"

"Make it a bit quieter, Mr. Thwaites," said the Lieutenant, for they were approaching the Rosamund Tea Rooms.

"By the Lord Hal," said Mr. Thwaites, more quietly and earnestly. "A Veritable Thrust!"

"Now then, quiet," said the Lieutenant as they reached the door of the Rosamund Tea Rooms, and Mr. Thwaites, in some miraculous way, seemed to be able to discern the seriousness of the situation, and remained quiet as Vicki opened the door with her key and he was led indoors. Indeed, apart from murmuring "Distinguished Solicitors" four or five times on the stairs, and "Distinguished Solicitors and Collaborators" on reaching his room, he accomplished the journey with dignity and in silence.

2

Vicki had somehow vanished. Miss Roach switched on the light, and the Lieutenant got him on to his bed. "All right," he said. "Leave him to me," and Miss Roach went up to her room.

On arriving here she found that she was clutching Mr. Thwaites' cap under her arm, and wondered whether she ought to restore this.

She went on to the landing, listened, went into her room again, came out and listened, and at last, after four or five minutes had passed, went downstairs and listened outside Mr. Thwaites' door.

Hearing no sound, she knocked gently, and the Lieutenant came to the door. "Come in," he said. "He's better now."

The Lieutenant had made quick work of Mr. Thwaites, who was already in his pyjamas and sitting on his bed. The Lieutenant had his dressing-gown in his hand, and was persuading him to put it on. "Come on," he said. "Dressing-gown."

"Ah—ha," said Mr. Thwaites, who, without being by any means sober, was clearly a good deal more sober than he had been. "Dame Roach! Come in, Dame Roach!"

"Come on," said the Lieutenant, forcing one of Mr. Thwaites' arms into the dressing-gown. "Get it on."

"Enter Dame Roach!" said Mr. Thwaites, allowing the

Lieutenant to proceed peacefully with his manœuvres. "Dame Roach—the English Miss! Miss Prim. Dame Roach—the Prude. . . . The jealous Miss Roach."

At this moment Vicki entered. Whether or not she had heard what Mr. Thwaites had just said Miss Roach did not know —did not ever know.

"How is he?" said Vicki.

"He's all right," said the Lieutenant. "Come on. In you get." And he threw back the bedclothes, thrust Mr. Thwaites into bed, and covered him again with the bedclothes.

"Well, I'm going," said Miss Roach.

"Don't be silly," said the Lieutenant, tucking Mr. Thwaites in. "This is just where we go and have a drink. It's only a quarter past nine."

"No. I'm sorry. I really must go." Miss Roach was at the door.

"Aw—quit being plain silly," said the Lieutenant. "It's only a quarter past nine, isn't it?"

Then Vicki did an unexpected thing.

"Yes. Let her go. If she wants to," she said in a flat tone, and, without looking at Miss Roach, she went over to the bed. "How are you, dear old Thwaitey?" she said. "Feeling better?"

"Aw—" the Lieutenant began, looking at Miss Roach, but Miss Roach cut in on him.

"No. Please don't try and persuade me," she said, and there was anger in her voice. "I want to go to bed. I'm tired. Thanks for the dinner. Good night."

And she fled upstairs to her room.

A few minutes later, and after she had heard the Lieutenant and Vicki leaving the house together, she came out of her bedroom and went into the bathroom, where she was violently sick.

This woman, she observed, affected her physically as well as mentally.

3

Her leather illuminated clock told her it was a quarter to one.

After her sickness she had slept lightly, but now she was wide awake. Vicki and the Lieutenant had not yet returned. She would have heard that.

It was queer—how her instincts were always right. From the moment she had arrived home that evening, and found the Lieutenant there with his bottle and glasses, she had known that disaster was to follow. And here it was!

It wasn't the mere disgusting disgrace of the whole evening—the sordidness of Mr. Thwaites' excitement and his behaviour towards Vicki—the subsequent exhibition he had made of himself in the hotel dining-room, and, after that, in the walk home. All that, conceivably, might be conceded to "Christmas". It was the revelation, made at the last moment, which had made her physically sick.

"*Dame Roach—the English Miss. Miss Prim. The Prude. The jealous Miss Roach.*"

The planes were roaring over again. . . . How they roared and filled the sky for miles around. . . .

The identical words. . . . There was no question of Mr. Thwaites having thought them up himself. Those words were given to him by Vicki—those ideas were put into his head by her. The old man would almost certainly never have disclosed this unless he had had too much to drink—a thing he would not have ordinarily been likely to do—but now the cat was nicely out of the bag.

And so that was the way they talked about her when they were alone. So that was the poison that woman had seen fit to spread forth, or rather venomously inject.

To gain the knowledge that she had been talked about at all by two people was shock enough for Miss Roach (such knowledge is always a shock of a kind to any human being, unless it is at once followed and compensated for by the news that the talk is of a highly favourable nature): but to learn that two people of this sort had been talking about her, and in this way—she believed it was more than she could stand.

And she betted your life they had talked! If she knew anything about them, they had talked and talked and talked.

Really, she had thought she had gained experience of the lowest depths of this woman: she had thought she knew where she was and could just stand it. But now these depths had collapsed, opening up shifting, endless depths. She would have to get out of this place: she would have to leave, go somewhere.

But why should *she* be made to go? And where? And at Christmas?

"The jealous Miss Roach." Again, how right her instincts had been. She had foreseen, at the earliest possible date, that this was the evil course the woman was going to take. Lying awake in the dark, as she was now, she had guessed that Vicki was somehow going to contort the situation into one in which it appeared that she was jealous. She had tried to combat this. She had first of all refused to go to the telephone when the Lieutenant had called: then she had had the courage to go and have it out with the woman. And all she had got for her pains was "Really, you are rather A dear!"—and now this poison behind her back with a semi-idiotic old man.

Now it was easy enough to account for all that extra bullying, by Mr. Thwaites of herself, which had seemed strangely to run parallel with his mounting infatuation for Vicki. The old man obviously could not resist such a temptation. Led on, inspired by the woman, inspired by their private talks, he had really been able to let himself go: it had been a sort of game between the two of them.

Why should she be *set* on like this? It reminded her of her schooldays—her schooldays both as a pupil and as a schoolmistress—in which there would occur, for no apparent reason, sinister developments of this sort—gradually and mysteriously emerging plots, spites, malicious alignments against an individual, sendings to Coventry, at last open hatred and torture. Had she got to go back to school at the age of thirty-nine?

"No. Let her go if she wants to," Vicki had said. And that flat tone in which she had said it—what did this mean? Obviously that she could no longer be bothered. She had suffered, humoured the jealous English Miss long enough: now she must stew in the juice of her own jealousy.

And if she had talked in that way to Mr. Thwaites, had she not done the same thing to the Lieutenant? No—for she had not as yet had an opportunity. She had that tonight. She would be telling the Lieutenant some fine stories tonight. And would the Lieutenant believe them? Yes—almost certainly. But somehow she did not mind so much what the foolish Lieutenant was told or believed about her. He had a niceness. He wasn't in *league* against her, like Mr. Thwaites. He wasn't in the private plot—the school plot.

It was time they were back, was it not? Where were they now? Probably on the seat by the river. Vicki triumphant. Vicki with the Laundry in the bag!

The planes were still going over. . . .

She heard quiet voices below, and then, she fancied, the key in the lock, and the front door being closed.

Then, amidst the sound of the planes, she heard Vicki come up the stairs to the landing, and closing the door of her room.

This was the conclusion of the proceedings. Within ten yards of her, amidst the purring of the planes, Vicki was undressing. . . . Such had been, such was, her jolly, jolly Christmas Eve.

No—by now Christmas Day!

CHAPTER TWENTY

I

MISS ROACH assumed that, elsewhere, somewhere, there was a good deal of cheerfulness and goodness about the Christmas season, even in war-time: but this did not fall within the range of her experience. To her it had for many years only been associated with a species of dullness and even evil, of stupidity or even madness, connected with eating and drinking, which weighed insufferably upon her spirits, and from which it was hopeless to try to escape until Boxing Day and the whole holiday was over. Its colour was dirty grey: its noise was the noise made by shut shops: its odour was the odour of turkey and stuffing experienced after one had eaten turkey and stuffing.

The madness was resumed at half-past eleven in the morning. As she was sitting in front of her gas-fire in her bedroom, trying conscientiously to read an absurd manuscript, the Lieutenant knocked at her door (knocking at *her* door first, she noticed, although Vicki was in her room) and invited her to come downstairs to the Lounge, where he was opening a bottle of gin and a bottle of orange (both of which were bulging from his pockets) for the benefit of all. She said she would do this, and the Lieutenant went away and was heard knocking on Vicki's door.

Although going downstairs involved meeting Vicki and Mr. Thwaites again, which she had hoped to avoid until lunch-time, she did not really see what else she could do.

There had been a most odd atmosphere at breakfast. She had rather expected to find Mr. Thwaites repentant, embarrassed, not knowing quite where to look. But not a bit of it. He looked her straight in the eye, in just the same critical and contemptuous way, rather as if it was she who had got drunk and made a fool of herself instead of him. It occurred to her that the weak-brained man might have forgotten all about the night before.

In any case, nothing was said about this. It was particularly noticeable that Miss Steele said nothing—ordinarily she would have wanted to hear about their outing. Miss Roach remembered Miss Steele's frightened laughing exit at an early stage of yesterday's celebrations.

Miss Steele, however, gave forth bright "Merry Christmases" all round, and it was very difficult to ascertain how much precisely was known about last night, how much they were in disgrace generally, and whether the blame was allotted in equal or unequal proportions.

2

She heard the Lieutenant staying rather a long time in Vicki's room, and then they came out and went downstairs.

Miss Roach now decided to change her dress, and so it was not until some ten minutes later that she herself went down to the Lounge.

She had only to open the door to realise that already, at a quarter to twelve, the Christmas madness and evil was in full swing. Glasses of gin-and-orange had been given to everybody, and everybody was there. Miss Steele was there, Mrs. Barratt was there, even Mrs. Payne (extraordinary yet characteristically Christmas phenomenon!) was there. Above all this, Mrs. Barratt's forty-year-old son in the Air Force was there, having arrived late last night to spend Christmas Day with his mother.

He had to be introduced to everyone. The presence of Mrs. Payne, and Mrs. Barratt's son, in a characteristically Christmas way threw everything completely out of gear, and one had the sensation of being at a crowded cocktail party of strangers in London, rather than in the familiar Lounge of the Rosamund Tea Rooms.

This, seemingly, was all the Lieutenant's doing, but Miss Roach had a feeling that, even if there had been no Lieutenant, the same thing, merely because it was Christmas, would have somehow happened. The madness of Christmas is not to be resisted by any human means. It either stealthily creeps or crudely batters its way into every fastness or fortress of prudence all over the land.

The Lieutenant, of course, had shown instinctive shrewdness in bringing round gin-and-orange instead of whisky. The spirit of gin, served in a small glass with orange juice, passes as a "cocktail", which old ladies are allowed to take at Christmas. Whisky, and particularly whisky in large glasses, would have been raw drinking and impermissible.

The spirit of gin, however, is as powerful as the spirit of whisky, and soon enough old and young were getting decidedly talkative and silly. Miss Roach, mercifully in a corner with Mrs. Barratt and her son, was aware even of herself being talkative, and of feeling silly. Drink always went to her head and made her feel silly at this time of day.

There you had Christmas again, all over. She had actually foreseen that she would have to get silly, and had made plans to do so in a modest and moderate way of her own. She had arranged to meet the Poulton boy at a quarter to one at the River Sun to give him a "Christmas" drink. This, she had thought, would keep her out of trouble. And yet here she was, at twelve o'clock, and with the Poulton boy ahead of her, already silly! Christmas denied one the right to any sort of sane or premeditated adjustment either to itself or to other people.

Because of the noise and confusion she was able to slip out unobserved from the Lounge at half-past twelve, and soon she was walking through the streets—streets steeped in the grey gaiety of Christmas—the cotton-wool snowstorms in the shut-shop windows, the children wearing their Christmas-present clothes and carrying their Christmas-present toys—towards the River Sun.

Here she found, waiting for her, the Poulton boy, who had had two glasses of beer, and was, in consequence, she thought, rather silly. Also he now wanted, for his "Christmas" drink, a short gin drink, which Miss Roach thought silly, wondering whether his mother would approve.

But he was a nice, simple boy, and for a quarter of an hour she enjoyed talking to him. Then, as she had known for certain would happen, the Lieutenant came in with Vicki, and although they were the other side of the room, she was too conscious of their presence, and their glances, to enjoy herself any more. . . .

Lunch was at a quarter to two, and total Christmas confusion reigned in the dining-room. There were half-bottles of white wine on the tables—one for each person and presented by Mrs. Payne stupendously—and so that Mrs. Barratt could sit with her son, Miss Roach had been put (presumably on Sheila's initiative) with Mr. Prest. Why with Mr. Prest rather than with Miss Steele, Miss Roach did not know, and why Mr. Prest shouldn't have been brought to the Thwaites table, and Mrs. Barratt and her son put at a table by themselves, she did not know either. These were Christmas mysteries.

Mr. Prest was not a lively table-companion. She did not want liveliness, but Mr. Prest was rather less lively than she desired, causing them, in the many long silences which fell upon them, to look about the room with a disinterested, interested air, or to finger their knives and stare at the tablecloth, and even find themselves blushing.

She had often wondered what exact motive Mr. Prest had in being alive—if, and by what means, this seemingly empty, utterly idle and silent man justified his existence—and now she wondered more than ever.

The mystery was deepened by a remark he made at this meal. He had recently, for a week or more, been absent from the Rosamund Tea Rooms during the day.

"By the way," she said, trying to keep one of their small outbursts of conversation going, "we haven't seen much of you lately, have we? Have you been up to London?"

"Yes," said Mr. Prest. "That's right. I'm back at work now. Going back to London after lunch."

What did this mean? He had at one time, she gathered, been something to do with the theatre—but what work was this? And why this travelling on Christmas Day?

She did not like to ask him, and he was not the sort of man to tell her unless she asked. But she thought she had noticed a dim gleam of pride and pleasure in his eyes as he spoke.

3

Towards the end of the meal, Miss Steele, who at half-past twelve had already admitted to being "tiddly", gave a toast.

"Well, here's to Mrs. Payne," she said, though Mrs. Payne was not in the room. "And here's Christmas wishes to all."

The company assented shyly and murmuringly, and there was a clinking of glasses.

"And here's to next Christmas," Miss Steele went on. "A real Christmas of Peace, we hope."

"Yes," said Mrs. Barratt. "Of peace."

"Yes," said Vicki, in a rather strange tone. "Of peace—and understanding."

Miss Roach pricked up her ears. What was this? She did not like that tone in Vicki's voice, nor that little pause before "—and understanding."

What, pray, did she mean to imply? That when peace came understanding would return between the German nation and her enemies? That it was only through lack of this "understanding" that the present war was being prosecuted? That Nazi Germany was, therefore, as much "in the right" as her opponents? That Nazi Germany was, in fact, *more* "in the right" than her opponents, because her opponents had so foolishly misunderstood her?

Miss Roach hoped that she had not meant to imply this. Vicki had recently made more than one slightly ambiguous remark of this sort. This one seemed, really, hardly ambiguous. But Miss Roach hoped that she was wrong.

If she was not wrong, and any more remarks of this sort were made, there was going to be trouble—Miss Roach would be forced to do something. She had put up with a lot from this woman, swallowed, very patiently, the increasing liberties she had chosen to take. But if she was now going to start either slyly to suggest, or to come out into the open with, the opinion that concentration-camp Nazi Germany was of all countries the one deserving sympathy and support in the present situation—this was going to be too much, and Miss Roach would be forced to do something. She did not know what she would do, but she would do something.

CHAPTER TWENTY-ONE

I

You would have thought they'd stop. You would have thought that after their big Christmas meal they would call it a day. But they didn't. It was carried on all through Boxing Day. And on the evening of Boxing Day the Lieutenant came to see her in her room!

After that Christmas lunch there had been a brief period of calm, for the Lieutenant had vanished. But he was back again at a quarter to six, with another bottle of whisky, in the Lounge. At least Miss Roach afterwards heard that he had brought a bottle of whisky—she herself was up in her bedroom when he arrived. She had heard noises from below, and, roughly realising what was happening and might happen, had decided to dodge it by going out for a long walk. On the way downstairs, passing the Lounge, she had heard all the noises of a Lieutenant entertaining others with a bottle of whisky.

She took care not to return until five minutes after dinner-time, and on entering the dining-room she found (what she had hoped to find) that the Lieutenant and Vicki had gone out to dinner.

Mr. Thwaites, having evidently been wise enough to refuse any invitation to join the others, or perhaps having not been asked, was at his table and noisy. He had clearly been taking something from the bottle upstairs, but was (if Mr. Thwaites could ever be said to be exactly this) in possession of his senses. Mrs. Barratt's son had gone, and so had Mr. Prest.

The next day, Boxing Day, the Lieutenant was round again at half-past eleven, not with gin-and-orange as on the previous morning, but with another bottle of whisky. This was going too far. He might have again got away with the gin-and-orange, but at the sight of the bottle of whisky both Mrs. Barratt and Miss Steele were plainly shocked, and made early excuses to leave the room.

Mr. Thwaites again accepted the whisky, and grew noisier and noisier, and more and more excited.

Christmas morning was to a certain extent repeated. Miss Roach had another appointment with the Poulton boy at the River Sun, and there they were again joined, and looked at a good deal from a distance, by Vicki and the Lieutenant, and Mr. Thwaites, who had on this occasion accompanied them....

Mr. Thwaites was noisier than ever at lunch, and the lunch as a whole was probably the noisiest ever experienced in the dining-room of the Rosamund Tea Rooms. For the Lieutenant had decided to join them, and, sitting at the vanished Mr. Prest's table, and in a semi-intoxicated state, he shouted across the room at the Thwaites table all through the meal.

After lunch there was an ugly episode in the Lounge, for the Lieutenant, now rather more fully than semi-intoxicated, persisted in demanding that Miss Steele should have a drink of whisky, and Miss Roach had to intervene.

"No," Miss Roach had to say. "She doesn't want it. Don't you see? She doesn't want it!"

"It's all right," said Miss Steele. "I'm going. It's all right. I'll go." And she went.

"You know, you can't turn her out like that," said Miss

Roach. "If you want to drink, why don't you go somewhere else?"

"All right," said the Lieutenant. "Let's go somewhere else. Let's go to your room."

"You can come to mine if you like," said Vicki.

"No," said Mr. Thwaites. "Come to mine." And he looked at Vicki. "What? Will you come to my room? What?"

"All right, we'll go to yours," said the Lieutenant, and they went.

"That's right," she heard Mr. Thwaites saying as they went. "You come to my room. What! You come to my room. What! . . ."

At that moment she foresaw that there was shortly going to arrive some sort of climax in Mr. Thwaites' behaviour. Like an over-excited and pleasure-surfeited child at the end of its birthday, the man had an unnatural brightness of eye, an air of boldness, inconsequence and hysteria, which was going to lead to some sort of disaster. The child, she was certain, was going either to break its toy or commit some outrage, and be taken by physical force screaming to bed.

When they had gone she went and knocked on Miss Steele's door, and told her that the coast was clear for her return. Miss Steele gratefully returned to the Lounge.

"I think they're going a little too far, don't you?" she said. "I know Christmas is Christmas, and nobody likes a little fun more than me, but I think they're going a little too far."

Miss Roach agreed. She talked peacefully to Miss Steele for about twenty minutes, and then went up to her room to try to do some work.

The door of Mr. Thwaites' room was half open as she passed it, and electric light was burning inside, for it was a dark afternoon.

She could not see what the Lieutenant was doing, for he was out of sight. But she saw Mr. Thwaites and Vicki, who were on the edge of the bed. Mr. Thwaites was trying to kiss Vicki on the mouth, and one of Vicki's legs was up in the air.

Miss Steele had been right. Christmas was Christmas, but they were going a little too far.

A pretty scene, in a pretty boarding-house, in a pretty Christmas, of a pretty war.

2

The Lieutenant knocked at her door at half-past six.

She had refrained from going down to tea, and, having become more or less immersed in her work, had not realised it was so late. She had been aware, from noises floating up to her from below, that the Lieutenant was still in the house, and it had struck her as possible that he might come up.

"Hullo," he said. "Can I come in?"

As far as she could judge he was almost completely sober again. This man's inconsequence was such that you could not even rely upon him to remain drunk!

"Yes. Come in," she said.

So thoroughly had the evil and madness of Christmas permeated herself and the atmosphere that it never even crossed her mind that there was any impropriety of any sort in inviting a man into her bedroom for a talk.

"Are you coming downstairs?" he said, sitting on her bed. "We thought we'd go out and have a drink."

"No—I don't think I will," she said. "I've got some work to do, and I think you'd better leave me out of it."

"Come and sit down here," he said, and held out his hand. "I want to have a talk with you."

"Yes?" she said, and took his hand, and sat down beside him. "What is it?"

"What in hell's the matter with you?" he said. "Have I done something wrong, or something?"

"No," she said. "What should you have done wrong?"

"Then what's the matter?" he said. "Why won't you come out? Why aren't you playing any more?"

"There's nothing the matter. I just don't want to come out, that's all. I've got some work to do."

"But *why*? What's the *reason*? You used to come out."

"There's no reason. I just don't want to."

"But there must be a reason. Come on. What is it?"

"No. There's nothing. There's really nothing."

"Oh, come on," he said, and tried to kiss her.

"No," she said, and turned her head away.

"But what *is* it?"

"Nothing."

There was a pause.

"Is it anything to do with *her*?" said the Lieutenant.

"Who?"

"You know who I mean."

"Vicki?"

"Yes."

"No, of course it's not. Why should it be?"

"Sure?"

"Yes. Of course I'm sure."

This, of course, was a complete untruth, but what on earth could she say?

"Absolutely sure?" he said.

Miss Roach decided to come out with it.

"I suppose she's been telling you," she said, "that I'm jealous, or something like that."

"Oh—what does it matter what people say?"

"Oh—so she *has* been saying that?"

"Oh—what does it matter? You know you're the one I love, don't you?"

"Am I?"

"You know that," said the Lieutenant, and tried to kiss her again.

"No," she said, and again turned her head away.

"I thought you liked me at one time," said the Lieutenant.

"I *do* like you," said Miss Roach. "What are you going on about?"

(Oh, what a *muddle* all this was, thought Miss Roach. What were they both *talking* about?)

"I thought you were serious," said the Lieutenant.

"I thought *you* were serious," said Miss Roach.

"Well, so I am," said the Lieutenant. "Aren't I?"

"Are you?"

"Well, don't I *seem* to be? What's the *matter*? That's all I want to know."

"Nothing."

"Let's go out together, and leave her out of it."

"Is she downstairs now?" asked Miss Roach.

"Yes. But that doesn't matter. Let's go out together alone."

"No," said Miss Roach. "I don't want to."

"Why?"

"I don't know."

And this was true. At first she didn't know. Then she realised why this was. Her pride would not allow her to put herself into competition with such a woman. Presumably, it was now within her power to go out with the Lieutenant alone and to win him back. But nothing could make her do it. It was beneath her even to score off that woman.

And how was the poor Lieutenant to understand this? What a muddle, what a *muddle*!

"Don't you like me any more?"

"Yes. Of course I like you. I like you very much."

"Then let's go out together."

"No. I don't want to."

"Aw—come on," said the Lieutenant, and tried more emphatically to kiss her.

"No. You must leave me alone," said Miss Roach. "I want to be left alone, that's all."

"Aw, come on!"

"No. Leave me alone. Please leave me alone. Really!"

"Aw, I don't understand you. You've got me beat. It seems to me you're acting all feminine."

"I'm sorry," she said. "I've no doubt I am. But I want to be left alone. Go on. Leave me. I want you to leave me. Will you leave me? Please."

There was a pause in which the Lieutenant looked at her.

Then, "Aw, hell," he said, and with a look of anger such as she had never seen on his face before, he rose and left the room.

3

And so that was that! There, through the door and out of her life, it all went—the Lieutenant, his Laundry, his inconsequence, his habit of drinking too much, his failings, his niceness, his kissings in the dark, her little "romance" and renewed interest in life because of him, all.

The trouble was that she liked the man, would, indeed, if he had approached the matter in a proper and serious spirit, probably have been willing to marry him. He was stupid over certain matters, of course, and he drank too much: but who could blame a man in such circumstances—so far from his own home, and in the shadow of such peril as awaited him when the second front began—for drinking too much? The drinking probably accounted for his inconsequence, and back home, in Wilkes Barre or whatever it was, he was no doubt a normal and excellent citizen.

If the conversation which had just taken place had taken a different turn, might the situation have been retrieved? No. Nothing would have altered her decision not to go out that night. Her hatred of that woman exceeded in power any fondness she might have or develop towards the Lieutenant. To have allowed herself to become her "rival", to have put herself in the position of competing with her, of gaining here or losing there (and in view of the Lieutenant's inconsequence she might well lose anything she gained at a moment's notice!)—this would be to violate the holiest of inner sanctuaries of pride and dignity, and was quite beyond her. It had to be as it was.

And, of course, it would never be possible to explain this to the simple-minded Lieutenant, who would no doubt, to the end of his days, think that she had behaved childishly, pettishly, in a feminine and ridiculous way. He would probably, indeed, accept the solution, which had obviously already been suggested to him by Vicki, that she was consumed with jealousy and hatred—the jealousy and hatred of the prim "English Miss", the prude, the soured spinster! Well—let him think it—she didn't really care enough about him to mind.

Why had life treated her thus, and how had fate contrived to land her in this grotesque, fantastically, wickedly false position? It was, in a manner, a sort of accident, one of those tricks which life just plays. The evil mind of the German woman was not wholly responsible for what had happened. The trouble had begun on that first night when the three of them had gone out together, and that had been a pure accident. Vicki's name had somehow cropped up on the telephone and somehow she had been invited, without the conscious volition of either the Lieutenant or herself. What would have happened if her name had not cropped up and she had not been invited? Might the whole course of events not have been different?

Impossible to say. Impossible, also, to do anything about it now. The Lieutenant had gone, and the door was closed.

4

The Lieutenant and Vicki were absent from the house and dinner that night, and Mr. Thwaites was quieter.

But there was still the gleam in his eye of the child who was going to break his toy, and Miss Roach was more than ever conscious of the imminence of climax and storm.

She went to bed early that night, and managed to get to sleep by ten o'clock.

At half-past ten she was awakened by Sheila, and had to go down in her dressing-gown to the telephone.

She imagined she was to answer a Lieutenant again in drink, but this was not so. The call was from Guildford, and the news was that her aunt was seriously ill. This news was conveyed by a Mrs. Spender, the friend with whom her aunt had been staying ever since she had left Thames Lockdon.

Miss Roach asked if she should go to Guildford at once, but Mrs. Spender thought this unnecessary. She should, however, hold herself in readiness, and Mrs. Spender would phone her again tomorrow.

Among other things, then, she was probably going to lose the only living relation of whom she was fond and with whom she kept in touch. In this manner the season of goodwill came, for Miss Roach, to an end.

CHAPTER TWENTY-TWO

I

BUT the climax did not actually occur until a few days later, when it was least foreseen, and on a Sunday night, and in the dining-room. And it was not at all the sort of climax which Miss Roach had anticipated.

On the Saturday night Miss Roach had returned at a late hour from Guildford, where she had found her aunt unconscious and almost certainly about to die within a week. Over-tired, she had spent a practically sleepless night.

Before the storm occurred there was as little atmosphere of storm as there could possibly have been—as there could possibly have been, that is to say, in a room in which Mr. Thwaites, Vicki Kugelmann, and Miss Roach were sitting together.

The gale of Christmas had blown itself out: the Lieutenant, as was his habit, had vanished completely: deathly dullness and boredom gripped the house, whose guests looked at the end of the year, and the beginning of the next, with misery and stupefaction.

At Mr. Prest's table there was a newcomer, a small, thin, dried-up old lady called Mrs. Crewe. Mrs. Crewe's presence added to the reigning stupefaction.

Mr. Thwaites had spoken little throughout the meal, and, of course, while he remained silent, no one else had spoken.

It happened at the end of the meal, a minute or so before they were due to rise. If they had risen a minute or so earlier it would almost certainly never have happened at all.

Miss Roach never remembered exactly how it was led into. Mr. Thwaites, who had been listening in to the news before dinner, was discussing the war and post-war problems.

"Yes," said Mr. Thwaites, summing up. "A complicated world we live in, my masters."

Whenever Mr. Thwaites alluded thus to the world in general terms, calling it "funny" or "strange" or "wicked", he always said "My masters" afterwards.

"Yes," said Vicki, and that curious tone was in her voice again. "A very complicated world. . . . A very complicated situation altogether."

Miss Roach knew exactly what she was getting at. This was "Yes, Peace—and understanding" all over again. Her suggestion behind the stress she laid upon the complication of the situation was as clear as day. She meant that the world was in a state of complication owing to misunderstanding generally, and of Nazi Germany in particular.

Now Miss Roach was not going to stand for this. She had made up her mind she was not going to stand for this. She could stand, and had stood, practically everything from this woman, but somehow this was the one thing she did not mean to stand.

She hesitated, and then spoke in a calm, off-hand, and quite good-natured way.

"Oh," she said. "I don't know that it's so complicated."

"What do you mean?" said Mr. Thwaites, sharply, and with the old bullying look, "'It's not so complicated'?"

"Oh," said Miss Roach. "I just don't think it's so complicated, that's all."

"I know. You said that," said Mr. Thwaites. "But I want to know why."

There was a pause.

"Go on," said Mr. Thwaites. "Why?"

"Oh," said Miss Roach. "I just think it's quite simple, that's all. It's a simple conflict between all that's decent and all that's evil—and it's *simple*, that's all. . . ."

There was another pause, and then Vicki made the remark which, blowing up the ammunition dump, disclosed the amount of ammunition stored away.

"Simple, perhaps," she said, ruminatingly, "to people with simple minds. . . ."

"No," said Miss Roach. "Only complicated, actually, to people with simple minds—or people with distorted minds."

"Perhaps," said Vicki, "we had better not talk international politics."

"No, perhaps we'd better not," said Mr. Thwaites, looking at Miss Roach as if to say that Miss Roach had better not, anyway.

It was the two-against-one business that got Miss Roach. If it had not been for that she might still have kept her temper, which now she lost completely.

"And were you suggesting," she said, looking at Vicki, "that I'm a person with a simple mind?"

"I think, perhaps," said Vicki, "that we'd better not talk about international politics."

"That's not the point—" began Miss Roach, but Mr. Thwaites cut in.

"No, I think we'd better not," he said, glaring at her threateningly.

"Yes, but that's not the point—" began Miss Roach, and this time Miss Steele cut in, in a last moment bid to avert total calamity.

"No," she said, "it's never wise to talk about politics—is it? I quite agree with Miss Roach, as a matter of fact—but it's never wise to talk about them."

"No," said Vicki, "we had better leave politics to those who are qualified to talk about them."

There was another fearful pause.

"Are you suggesting by that," said Miss Roach, "that *I'm* not qualified to talk about politics?"

"Really," said Vicki, appealing to Mr. Thwaites, with a little smile, "she is in quite A Pet—no?"

"Or are you suggesting," said Miss Roach, "that *you* are more qualified than I?"

"Possibly," said Vicki. "I have travelled a little about the world, you know."

"I think it'd be better if we went upstairs, don't you?" said Mrs. Barratt, but nobody answered her, and nobody showed any sign of going upstairs.

"And does that mean," said Miss Roach, "that *I* have *not* travelled about the world?"

"Really," said Vicki, "I do not know about your travels. All I know is that you are not altogether—what shall we say?—cosmopolitan in outlook? No?"

"I think we'd better go upstairs," said Mrs. Barratt.

"Yes, I think we had," said Miss Steele. "Shall we?"

"And does being cosmopolitan in outlook," said Miss Roach, "mean that you think things are so complicated that you support the Nazis in all the murder and filth and torture they've been spreading over Europe, and still are?"

Miss Roach knew that she would regret what she was doing, that she should really stop. But she could not do so. That use of the word "cosmopolitan", with its cunning reversion to the "English Miss" theme, had goaded her beyond recall. She was also amazed by her own courage. The reason for this was the fact that the argument was at root impersonal. If this had been a quarrel over the Lieutenant, she might have been suspected, or suspected herself, of self-interest. But it was not: it was an argument about the guilt of Nazi Germany. And she just wasn't going to let the woman get away with it!

"Really," said Vicki, again appealing to Mr. Thwaites, "she is very rhetorical—is she not?"

"Very," said Mr. Thwaites. "And there's no need to bring nationalities into it."

"I'm not talking about nationalities," said Miss Roach. "I'm talking about Nazis."

"And there's no need," said Mr. Thwaites, "to insult a German woman in her own—" Mr. Thwaites stopped himself just in time. He had, in his confusion of mind, been going to say "in her own country". But this, although it sounded so good on the surface, wouldn't do. In her own country was exactly where the German woman was not, and Mr. Thwaites had the wit to see this before finishing his sentence.

"I'm not insulting anyone," said Miss Roach. "I'm just not going to have remarks made like this when people are dying all around us for what they think's right."

Miss Roach realised that this was rhetorically and logically a little feeble, but she could do no better.

"Do not mind her," said Vicki, and looked at Miss Roach. "She is really quite A Pet. She is really quite A dear!"

"If you go on calling me a *pet*," said Miss Roach, "and if you go on calling me a *dear*—there's going to be trouble!"

"I think we'd better go upstairs," said Mrs. Barratt, and rose. Mr. Thwaites rose too.

"Don't bother about her," he said, putting his napkin into his ring. "They always say hell knows no fury like a woman scorned."

"What do you mean by that, Mr. Thwaites?"

"Oh, nothing," said Mr. Thwaites, and began to move towards the door.

"No," said Miss Roach, who had also risen. "Will you please tell me what you mean? What woman has been scorned?"

"Never mind," said Mr. Thwaites. "I know what's been going on. I've got eyes in my head."

"Yes?" said Miss Roach, and to prevent Mr. Thwaites leaving, she put her hand on his arm. "And what has been going on? Will you tell me, please?"

"All right, let a fellow go upstairs, will you?" said Mr. Thwaites, and pushing her hand away, he left the room and began to climb the stairs. Miss Roach followed him out.

"*Will you please tell me what you mean, Mr. Thwaites?*"

"All right," said Mr. Thwaites, climbing the stairs. "Don't you bother. It's not the first time a woman's been cut out. It's not the first time a woman's had her nose put out of joint by another. It's not the first quarrel about a man!"

"*Will you tell me what you're talking about, Mr. Thwaites?*" said Miss Roach, following him up the stairs. "What woman has been cut out by what other woman? What man are you talking about?"

Mr. Thwaites had now reached the landing.

"Oh—a certain gentleman in uniform," said Mr. Thwaites. "You haven't got to pretend you don't know."

Miss Roach had now also reached the landing, which was well lit (Mrs. Payne having recently permitted the reintroduction of electricity on this floor), and they were facing each other.

"Do not mind her!" cried Vicki, from below. "She is quite A pet! She does not bother me!"

"I think we'd better stop all this—don't you!" cried Miss Steele, also from below.

"*Will you tell me what man you mean, Mr. Thwaites?*" said Miss Roach.

"Oh, don't let's bother about the man," said Mr. Thwaites, with his hands in his trouser pockets. "If you didn't bother about men so much you'd be a lot better, wouldn't you? That's your trouble. You've got the men on the brain, my worthy spinster dame, haven't you?"

"Mr. Thwaites. Will you explain yourself, please?"

"And just take one tip of mine, will you?"

"Yes. What tip, pray?"

"Leave 'em alone at a certain age, will you? Let 'em be over eighteen. If you must go after 'em, let 'em be over age. People see what's going on, you know. Leave 'em alone until after a certain age!"

There was a silence. For a moment Miss Roach did not realise what he was talking about. Then, with the sudden realisation that he was alluding to the Poulton boy, Miss Roach lost control. With the realisation of his implication, with the memory of her walks with the Poulton boy, of their innocence and simplicity, of the glad, sad, maternal feelings which she had felt towards the boy as he had unfolded his ambitions, with the idea of gossip of such a kind having arisen in regard to such a relationship, Miss Roach lost control. The filth of the suggestion seemed like filth reeling round in her own head and blinding her.

"How *dare* you say that!" she heard herself saying in a black mist, and she pushed out her hand, violently, half to strike Mr. Thwaites, half to throw the filthy suggestion out of her way.

After that she did not quite know what happened. Mr. Thwaites, with his hands in his pockets, staggered backwards. Having his hands in his pockets he was unable to balance himself properly, and the next moment he had fallen down and was sitting up against the wall.

Miss Roach looked at him, and he looked at Miss Roach.

She felt Vicki brushing past her.

"Are you all right, Mr. Thwaites?" Vicki was saying. "Are you hurt?"

"She Pushed me!" said Mr. Thwaites. "She Pushed me!"

"Are you hurt?" said Vicki, but all Mr. Thwaites would reply was "She Pushed me."

Mrs. Payne had now arrived on the scene.

"What's all this about?" said Mrs. Payne. "Are you hurt, Mr. Thwaites?"

"She Pushed me," said Mr. Thwaites, now exchanging his original tone of horror and surprise for a tone of incredulous awe.

"Yes," said Miss Roach. "And I'll Push you again if you say things like that!"

Mr. Thwaites was now on his feet again, supported each side by Mrs. Payne and Vicki, and gazing at Miss Roach.

"So you Pushed me, did you?" he said. "You'll pay for that, Dame Roach!"

"Yes. And I'll Push you again!" said Miss Roach. "And you needn't pretend you're hurt!"

"Well, let's go into the Lounge, shall we?" said Mrs. Payne. "I think that would be best."

Still allowing himself to be supported by Mrs. Payne and Vicki, Mr. Thwaites moved slowly into the Lounge.

"She Pushed me" Miss Roach heard him saying, in the same awed tones, when he had got inside. "She Pushed me." And these were actually the last words she ever heard Mr. Thwaites use.

She stood still for a moment, then rushed up to her room, and before long was weeping passionately on her bed.

CHAPTER TWENTY-THREE

I

WELL, it was all over now, it was all over now!... Following her failing torch, in the blackness of the street, in the desperation of her unhappiness, there was a gleam of consolation in the thought that it was, at any rate, all over.

She had no idea where she was going, and it all at once occurred to her that it was Sunday night.

As soon as she had recovered from her tears, her one ambition had been to get outside. Wiping her eyes at the mirror, she had heard a knock on her door, and Miss Steele had put her face into the room.

"Don't you worry, my dear," Miss Steele had said, with infinite knowingness. "It'll all come out in the Wash." And Miss Steele had then instantly disappeared.

What this had meant exactly it was impossible to say—it was one of those conventional phrases of consolation elusive of precise interpretation—but it meant that she had someone on her side, someone not against her, at any rate.

It was all over now. Even if Mrs. Payne did not actually expel her, she would have to go.

She should have kept her temper, of course. Losing that, she had lost her dignity, and they somehow still had scored, put her in the wrong, more or less maintained her in the grotesquely false position into which they had intrigued her.

This would be all over Thames Lockdon in the morning, she imagined. And what stories would be told, with all of them against her!

She shouldn't have pushed Mr. Thwaites, of course. She should not have allowed herself to use physical violence. Besides, the weak-minded old man was not really responsible for what he said or did. He had only been repeating, in his anger, tactlessness, and confusion of mind, what that woman had been putting into his head. It carried her signature. No one else could have thought up that business about the Poulton boy. She remembered, now, the look Vicki had given herself and the Poulton boy as they had left the tea-shop that day. She remembered the glances she had cast across at them when they were in the River Sun. She must have thought it up, and then told it to Mr. Thwaites in one of their long private talks at the Rosamund Tea Rooms. Beyond hinting, she would probably not have tried it out on the Lieutenant. Foolish as he was, he would not have given credence to propaganda of that sort, or even have countenanced its utterance. Though you never knew—you never knew anything about anybody. . . .

Where on earth was she going? She couldn't go back, but she couldn't go on walking round. What about a drink at the River Sun? No—not there—with the chance of meeting the Lieutenant—but what about a drink?

She remembered a bar in a small house by the river where in her early Thames Lockdon days she had once had a drink with Mrs. Poulton. By the light of her torch, which was now giving practically no light at all, she found her way round there, and boldly opened the door.

She regretted this the moment she had done it, as the bar was stewing with men and smoke and American G.I.s, and she couldn't see another woman in the whole crowd.

She saw, however, standing by himself at the far end of the bar, Mr. Prest, and Mr. Prest at once saw her, smiled, waved, and came over to her.

"Hullo!" he said. "What are you doing here? Come over out of the crowd and have a drink."

When he had ordered her drink, "But what are *you* doing here?" she said. "You weren't in to dinner."

"No," he said. "I'm just down for the night to collect the last of my luggage. I'm staying at the Stag."

The Stag was Thames Lockdon's pound-a-day-or-thirty-shillings hotel. In addition to being back at "work", whatever that meant, had Mr. Prest come into money?

"Well," said Miss Roach for something to say, "you ought to have come in to see us."

"Oh—I don't know," said Mr. Prest. "I've got a feeling it's a good idea to dodge meals round there whenever you can. Haven't you?" And he looked at her with a smile.

This was undoubtedly a new Mr. Prest.

"Why, yes," she said, smiling back, and encouraged by his smile. "But you missed something tonight."

"Did I? What?"

"We had a row," said Miss Roach. "Or at least I did. I'm afraid I lost my temper."

"Ah," said Mr. Prest. "I thought there was a row coming. I've thought that for a long while."

"Have you?" said Miss Roach, looking at him, puzzled by his wisdom. "Well, it certainly came tonight."

"Good for you," said Mr. Prest. "And how are they all? How's the venerable Mr. Thwaites?"

"Oh—he's all right. He's the chief one I had the row with."

"That's better still," said Mr. Prest. "He's a funny one, all right."

"Yes. He's a funny one."

"And how are the others? Is the American still about—the Lieutenant—I never knew his name?"

"No, I haven't seen him for some days," said Miss Roach, and then something made her add, "He can be a bit of a funny one too."

"Funny!" said Mr. Prest. "I should just say he can!"

"Why—do you know a lot about him?"

"Oh—only what you see and hear in the town."

"Why—has he a reputation?"

"Reputation!" said Mr. Prest.

"What for?" asked Miss Roach.

"Oh—only drink and girls," said Mr. Prest. "Girls mostly."

"Girls?" said Miss Roach, swallowing. . . .

"I should say. Lockdon, Maidenhead, Reading, and all around everywhere," said Mr. Prest. "But it isn't the amount of them that matters so much. The trouble is he asks them all to marry him."

"Really?" said Miss Roach.

"With the consequence that complications ensue," said Mr. Prest. "You don't know what goes on in this town unless you go round the pubs, the way I do."

"So he asks them all to marry him, does he?"

"Yes. He's got a kink that way, it seems. . . . Well, I suppose he's entitled to a good time while it lasts."

"Yes. I suppose he has. . . ." So here, at last, was the explanation of the Lieutenant's absences! She had to think about this afterwards! Not now! Now she must change the subject.

"So you're leaving us for good, Mr. Prest?" she asked.

"Yes. I don't expect I'll be back, so long as I'm in work. Now the young ones are away, the old 'uns are getting back a bit."

She looked at him to see if she might be bold enough, and was so.

"What kind of work is it you're doing, then, Mr. Prest," she said, "just now?"

"Oh, the old game. Wicked Uncle this time," said Mr. Prest and grinned shyly.

Seeing her slightly bewildered look, Mr. Prest went on.

"Babes in the Woods," he said. "Down at the Royal, Wimbledon. If you're coming to London, would you like to come and see us?"

"Why, yes," she said. "I'd love to."

"Can you manage Wednesday afternoon?"

"Why, yes, I think so."

"Well, if you can, that's fine." Mr. Prest fished in his breast pocket. "Here's two seats. I was going to give them to a pal down here but he can't use 'em. There you are. Is that a date?"

"Why, thank you. That'll be lovely. Thank you *very* much," said Miss Roach.

"Have another drink?" said Mr. Prest, a little later.

"No, I don't think I'd better. I think I'd really better be going," said Miss Roach, and Mr. Prest, hailed at that moment by a friend, did not urge her to stay. She was glad of this, because she wanted to get out and think.

"Well, see you Wednesday," said Mr. Prest, as she left him amidst the noise, and "Yes!" said Miss Roach, and "Come round and see me afterwards!" said Mr. Prest, and "Yes! Thank you! Goodbye!" said Miss Roach, and she was out again in the blackness.

So it was really all over now!

So that was the sort of man the Lieutenant was. So this was the final touch to her "romance". She had known well enough already that it was at an end, but now it appeared that there had never been any "romance" at all. What she had always suspected—the shop-girls—everything—was true. And the shop-girls, no doubt, were offered marriage and taken to the same seat by the river!

And she had allowed herself to be flattered by his offer, even if she had never seriously thought of accepting it. And she had, if she faced facts, at moments even thought seriously of accepting it, if only as a means of escape from certain spinsterhood and her present mode of existence. And she had, if she faced facts, at moments not altogether disliked his kisses in the dark. And she had even taken a certain pride in the fact that she had "her" American in the town.

Instead of this she had never had any offer, for if it was offered to all it was no offer, and she had never had "her" American, and she had been simply made a fool of, deprived of any sort of dignity, in a typical set-up of war-time wildness and folly which comprised Vicki Kugelmann and the hostile shop-girls in the town.

"*Old Roach.*" "*Old Cockroach.*" Driven out on to the streets, and walking about in the blackness, as she had done that night, months ago, before all this had begun. "*Old Cockroach.*" That was her. That was how they had started with her, and that was how it would always be. She might have known this—she might have known better than to have suspected the possibility of any brighter destiny.

If she hadn't cried herself out already, she could go back and cry. But she had cried herself out. It was all over now—even tears.

CHAPTER TWENTY-FOUR

I

But it was not all over.

That extraordinary next day began in an extraordinary way.

Miss Roach, going downstairs to have breakfast, and passing Mr. Thwaites' door, heard the sound of groaning within.

At least she was almost certain she heard this: she did not stay to listen.

As she went on down the stairs it struck her either that Mr. Thwaites, unknown to her previously, practised Yogi breathing exercises in his room, or that he was in pain. But she could not associate pain with so healthy and virile a man.

Also the absurd idea occurred to her that Mr. Thwaites somehow knew that she was passing his room, and was groaning for her benefit: that he was pretending he had just that moment been pushed over and was groaning with pain, shamming "hurt."

2

Only because, late the night before, she had had a little talk with Mrs. Payne, was she now going down to the dining-room for breakfast: she had not originally intended to have another meal in the dining-room of the Rosamund Tea Rooms.

Late the night before she had had to go downstairs in her dressing-gown for another telephone conversation about her aunt with Mrs. Spender. At the end of this Mrs. Payne had come into the room.

"Oh," she said. "I'm very sorry about tonight, Mrs. Payne. I suppose I'll have to go away from here as soon as I can."

"Oh no," said Mrs. Payne. "I hope not. I hope *you* won't be going."

"Well," said Miss Roach, "I really think it would be for the best. I'm very sorry for what happened."

"Oh no," said Mrs. Payne. "I'm sure you were very much provoked. It's not you who I want to go. It's another person I want to go. In fact, I'm going to ask them to leave."

"Oh, really?" said Miss Roach, and wondered whether Mrs. Payne was alluding to Mr. Thwaites or Vicki.

"Yes," said Mrs. Payne. "I didn't like certain things that took place on Boxing Day. I didn't like it at all."

So Mrs. Payne had also had glimpses through open doors! Miss Roach now felt almost sure that Vicki was the one who was going to be asked to go. In boarding-house and landlady psychology it was always the woman to whom was attached the initiation and guilt of scandals of this sort.

"Well," she said, "I really don't feel I can have any more meals in that room."

"Oh—that's all right," said Mrs. Payne. "We'll put you at a separate table. That'll be all right."

And there the matter had been left.

3

It was very awkward, going to that separate table.

"Good morning, Mrs. Barratt," she said, and smiled at her, and Mrs. Barratt said "Good morning" and smiled back. Vicki, fortunately (and she had reckoned on this when deciding to brazen it out), had her back to her.

"Good morning, Miss Steele," she said, and Miss Steele said "Good morning" and smiled back with a wink which suggested again that all things would ultimately come out in the Wash.

Miss Roach's separate table was in the window, near to the table of the newcomer, Mrs. Crewe.

Miss Roach, without speaking, smiled at Mrs. Crewe, who smiled back in what seemed to Miss Roach a rather uneasy way.

As a complete newcomer, the situation was, of course, very

difficult for Mrs. Crewe, who, presumably, took what had happened last night as the normal standard of behaviour at the Rosamund Tea Rooms, and who, no doubt, thought that Miss Roach would at any moment take her up on the matter of international politics, insult her, drive her up the stairs and push her over.

Miss Roach sat down, and Sheila served her.

Although she had consented to being put at a separate table last night, Miss Roach now doubted the wisdom of this decision. Did it not look as though she had disgraced herself and been put in a corner? If Mrs. Payne was on her side, ought not Vicki to have been put in the corner? It was all very involved.

It was a grey day, and a hideous spiritual heaviness lay all over the room. A storm was supposed, in the ordinary way, to clear the air. But so far from this having happened, the atmosphere, in a new way, was more stiflingly oppressive than ever before.

For the first time it now occurred to Miss Roach that Mr. Thwaites was not in the room. How silly of her!—how could he be in the room if he was groaning or doing Yogi exercises upstairs? But what was the matter? Why was he not down? She had never known him not to be first in his place before.

Miss Steele voiced her thoughts.

"Where's Mr. Thwaites this morning?" she asked. "It's not like him not to be down."

"I don't know," said Mrs. Barratt. "No—it's certainly not like him."

Then Vicki spoke.

"He is ill, I think," said Vicki quietly. "Quite badly ill."

And something in Vicki's voice told Miss Roach that this remark had been addressed to her—or uttered so that she in particular might hear.

What was this? What new trick was the woman up to?

Were she and Mr. Thwaites going to try and throw Mr. Thwaites' illness, if he had one, on to her?

Were they going to try and pull an injured spine, or something of that sort, out of the bag?

They were capable of anything.

4

After breakfast Miss Roach had some shopping to do.

Going up to her bedroom to dress, and passing Mr. Thwaites' door, she heard the same sound of groaning.

Coming downstairs again, five or six minutes later, she heard nothing. Relieved, she went out into the town.

Returning three-quarters of an hour later, and passing Mr. Thwaites' door, she again heard Mr. Thwaites groaning, this time more loudly, and, it seemed to her, in genuine physical anguish.

She went up to her room, walked about it, and then went downstairs to try and find Mrs. Payne.

But there was no sign of Mrs. Payne. There was no sign of anybody. She seemed to be alone in the house with a groaning Mr. Thwaites. . . .

Well—it was not her business. She was sorry for Mr. Thwaites, if he was ill and in pain, but it was not her business.

All the same, she was conscious of a silly sort of fear, and felt that she must get out of the house. Get out and stay out.

She went for a long walk, which calmed, without removing, that funny feeling of fear, and she had lunch at a restaurant in the town.

Then she went for another walk, and returned to the Rosamund Tea Rooms at about a quarter past three.

CHAPTER TWENTY-FIVE

I

SHE had not set foot in the house before she realised that panic was reigning within its walls—had been so reigning for a considerable time.

Mrs. Payne, rushing down the stairs, hardly looked at her as she dashed into her room. She heard Mrs. Payne using the telephone.

She climbed the stairs, and the groaning met her as she rose. "Oh! . . . Oh! . . . Oh! . . ."

Mr. Thwaites' door was closed, and she listened outside.

"Oh! . . . Oh! . . . Oh! . . ." she heard, and, beneath this noise, the sound of two strange men talking in quiet and level tones. Only doctors, and frightened doctors at that, would be talking in just that quiet and level way.

Was Mr. Thwaites going to die? And had she killed him?

She rushed down to Mrs. Payne's room. Mrs. Payne had just finished her telephone call.

"What's the matter, Mrs. Payne?" she said. "Is he ill?"

"Yes. He's very bad, I'm afraid," said Mrs. Payne. "He's got to have an operation. They're sending an ambulance."

"But what *is* it?" asked Miss Roach passionately. "What's the *matter*?"

"It's peritonitis, they think," said Mrs. Payne. "And he's got to go to Reading at once and have an operation."

"Oh!" said Miss Roach. "Then it's not anything else?"

"How do you mean?" said Mrs. Payne.

Impossible to explain to Mrs. Payne what she had really meant! She had meant, of course, that since it was peritonitis, something to do with his stomach, it was nothing to do with his fall, nothing to do with herself. She saw Mrs. Payne looking at her in a puzzled way.

"How awful!" she said, but her voice throbbed with relief. "Is there anything I can do?"

"No. I don't see there's anything, thank you very much," said Mrs. Payne. "It's so sudden, isn't it? It was just the same with my brother. It comes out of the blue. It looks pretty bad to me."

Had Mrs. Payne's never-before-heard-of brother died of this complaint? Miss Roach did not like to ask. Was Mr. Thwaites going to die? It looked as though Mrs. Payne thought that he was.

"Well, let me know if there's anything I can do," said Miss Roach as she left the room, and Mrs. Payne said that she would.

That groaning, as she went up the stairs! Was the man completely lacking in fortitude, or did those groans express the genuine agony they seemed to? Of course, he had a noisy, nasal, resounding enough voice always, and he was hardly the sort of man to make light of his own illness. All the same, she somehow believed in those groans. Why didn't they give him morphia or something?

2

When the ambulance came, at four o'clock, Miss Roach was in the hall.

She was in her out-door clothes, for it had not occurred to her to remove them, and she had spent the intervening period walking about her room and going out on to the landing and listening.

Mr. Thwaites' door was opened, and the groaning came out into the open and down the stairs.

Mrs. Payne and Sheila were there, but no one else was present.

Even whiter of face than she had anticipated (and she had certainly anticipated a white face), in the white blankets of the stretcher, Mr. Thwaites groaned.

"*Oh! . . . Oh! . . . Oh! . . .*" he groaned, and, as the stretcher paused in the doorway, he caught her eye, and looked at her, and groaned at her.

"Oughtn't someone to go with him?" she said to Mrs. Payne, and "Yes!" said Mrs. Payne. "Go on! You go with him. Can you manage it? Go on. You go with him!"

"All right," said Miss Roach. "I'll go."

And so it came about that the ex-schoolmistress took her place with the boarding-house bully in the ambulance going to Reading.

3

The ambulance moved slowly through the darkening town and she sat on the seat opposite and looked at him. She would have held his hand, but his hands were beneath the blankets.

He looked at her, in the electric light of the interior, and groaned, and went on looking at her.

There was no reproach in his look, no dislike—only a look of intense mystification at what was happening to him, and of concentration on the pain inside him. It was a far-away look and an inward look at one and the same time. If his eyes were saying anything to Miss Roach they were asking her to offer some explanation.

When they got out into the country they began to move faster, and she talked a little to the attendant, who explained that for some medical reason or other morphia could not be given in cases of this sort. . . .

At one time, Mr. Thwaites, still groaning, tried to sit up and look out of the window, as if to find out where they were going, as if it was his business to see where they were going. Then she took his hand.

"It's all right, Mr. Thwaites," she said. "We'll soon be there now. It won't be long. You'll soon be out of pain."

And he let her hold his hand, looking into her eyes, and still groaning. But in a more peaceful and resigned way, she thought, or liked to think.

At the hospital casualty entrance Mr. Thwaites was snatched away from her in the blackness, and she was put into a waiting-room—much like a railway waiting-room—in which a feeble electric light illuminated chairs and a meaningless table.

Half an hour later she was walking along vast ether-smelling corridors, and was taken into a ward, palatially large (how well she knew this smell of ether in these palaces of pain!), in the middle of which, behind screens, Mr. Thwaites was groaning. "*Oh! . . . Oh! . . . Oh! . . .*"

He did not look at her any more, but only groaned at the ceiling.

There was really nothing to do. The sister, who was, thank God, "nice", told her that he would soon be going into the theatre, and that there was no point in staying.

She touched his hand again, saying, "Well, goodbye, Mr. Thwaites. You're going to the theatre soon. You'll soon be out of pain," but, groaning at the ceiling, he did not look at her, or even seem to hear her.

She left, blundered about in the blackness of Reading to the station, caught a lucky train, and, wondering whether Mr. Thwaites was about to die, was taken homewards.

4

Mr. Thwaites was to die.

After Miss Roach left him Mr. Thwaites was not taken immediately to the theatre, for there was a hitch in the arrangements owing to shortage of staff and other war-time conditions—the war, of course, having taken fully as much interest in hospitals as it had in shops and in all other places and things.

In the long wait Mr. Thwaites' groans grew louder and louder, so much so that a patient the other side of the ward, a coarse man, and also dying, cried out, "Oh, shut up over there, will you! Shut up!" The coarse, dying man, who had been dozing off, had the impression that it was the middle of the night and that Mr. Thwaites had no right to make such a noise at such a time. Such unhappy miscalculations and incidents are not uncommon in public wards.

But, whether Mr. Thwaites heard this or not, he did not shut up. And in his groaning there could be heard something of the same thing that Miss Roach had in the ambulance observed in his eyes—intense mystification at what was happening to him, along with intense concentration upon the pain inside him. As a man who had hardly ever had a day's illness in his life, a man without knowledge of pain, a man whose hobby in life had, in fact, been nothing other than that of giving pain to others, his groans seemed to ring with a kind of querying, querulous, and amazed sense of affront.

At last they came and took him away to the theatre, and the coarse man opposite cried out, "Jolly good thing too!"

5

After the operation he was brought back to the ward and did not fully recover consciousness until about seven in the morning. Then, in a state of delirium, all he wanted was a cup of tea.

Though Mr. Thwaites was in a bad way, at this time he was not in a bad enough way for him to be given what he wanted, and he was unable to get a cup of tea.

He wanted nothing but a cup of tea, and he imagined that he was on a railway station trying to get it. He said he had a train to catch, and argued over the buffet counter, bluffing at certain times, pleading at others.

Then he saw that it was because he could not pay for his tea that they would not give it to him, and he begged the nurses who came near him to give him his purse. So persistent was he that at last they got his purse from his clothes and let him play with it.

"Yea? Verily? Tea?" he said to the nurses, as they tried to soothe him. "Yea? Verily? Verily? Tea?"

And the young nurses replied "Yea, Verily", and giggled and winked at each other over the dying man, as young nurses will in public wards of hospitals.

By eleven o'clock that morning it was realised by those in charge that he had no chance of living. He was therefore given what he wanted, and made more "comfortable" in the charming hospital phrase—"uncomfortable" being, presumably, the word with which the hospital would have described the prolonged groaning torment which had preceded this happier state.

As Mr. Thwaites sank he went on murmuring "Yea. Verily ..." and he mentioned Miss Roach. "Dame Roach?" he said, in a hopeful tone, "Dame Roach?" And then, as if at last satisfied, "Dame Roach!" These, actually, were his last words.

At four o'clock in the afternoon the familiar stertorous breathing from behind the screens resounded through the listening ward (in which tea was being served) and reached an apparently never-to-be-reached climax with appalling abruptness. Mr. Thwaites was dead.

Thus suddenly—having been given less than forty-eight hours' notice of any sort, and in the bloom of his carefree and powerful dotage—this cruel, harsh, stupid, inconsiderate, unthinking man, this lifelong nagger and ragger of servants and old women, this confused yet confusing bully and braggart in small places, died. The boarding-house tempest had blown itself out, all at once magically subsided.

CHAPTER TWENTY-SIX

I

"YES. *I thought very soon after his fall that something bad was on the way.*"

And Miss Roach, instead of rising from her separate table in the dining-room and going over and confronting Miss Kugelmann, had elected quietly to leave the room, go upstairs for her hat and coat, and take yet another walk in the blackness!

It had been a bewildering day, concerned with death in a double way for Miss Roach, and Mrs. Payne's telephone had been much used.

At first the hospital had said that Mr. Thwaites was doing as well as could be expected: then at midday they were less hopeful, and at five in the evening the Rosamund Tea Rooms was informed of his death.

Just before dinner Miss Roach was called to the telephone to talk about her aunt with Mrs. Spender. In the course of this conversation Mrs. Spender informed Miss Roach that on her aunt's death she would benefit by the will roughly to the extent of five hundred pounds. Miss Roach had always known that her aunt was going to leave her "something", but this amazed her.

"Five hundred pounds!" she exclaimed, and Mrs. Payne, who was in the room, must have heard this, for when Miss Roach had finished telephoning she said humorously, "Is somebody giving you five hundred pounds?" and Miss Roach had to reply, "Yes. So it seems!"

She had hardly had time to think about the possible effects, if any, of this sum of money on her future life (and anyway her aunt had not yet died and she didn't want her to die) when the gong for dinner was hit.

When they were all seated, all wondered who was going to begin it. Normally such a thing would have been left to Mr. Thwaites himself, but the circumstances prevented precisely this, and at last Miss Steele undertook the task.

"Well," she said. "It's very terrible about Mr. Thwaites, isn't it?"

"Yes," said Miss Roach. "Terrible." And Mrs. Barratt said "Yes. Appalling." And Vicki said "Yes. Terrible. Absolutely terrible."

"I mean it was so sudden, wasn't it?" said Miss Steele.

"Yes," said Mrs. Barratt. "So appallingly sudden. I never had any idea there was anything really serious until I heard he'd been taken away in the ambulance. Did any of you?"

"Oh yes," said Vicki. "I had an idea, as a matter of fact."

"Really?" said Mrs. Barratt, and then Vicki had said it.

"Yes," she had said. "I thought very soon after his fall that something bad was on the way."

And then Miss Roach, instead of obeying her initial impulse and rising and confronting Miss Kugelmann, had quietly left the room, gone upstairs for her hat and coat, and gone out for yet another walk in the blackness.

2

"*Yes. I thought very soon after his fall that something bad was on the way.*"

She must keep calm! She must compose herself! She had managed to leave the room in a calm manner, and now she must remain calm.

Perhaps the woman had not meant it. Perhaps she had meant that, coincidentally with his fall, merely coincidentally, she had observed something amiss in Mr. Thwaites. Perhaps Vicki was entirely innocent of the faintest innuendo. Perhaps she, Miss Roach, had the wicked, distorted mind.

Nonsense! Of course she had meant it! "Very soon after his fall." The very tone, the grave, unctuous tone in which she had uttered the words, proved that she meant it. That tone took it unctuously and serenely for granted that the fall had caused the illness, which had caused the death. And the fall, of course, had been caused by the Push. And Miss Roach, already an "English Miss", a prude, a spinster consumed with jealousy, a sex-ridden maker of advances to boys in their teens, was now a murderess!

Oh dear God, she had thought it was all over, but here it was, all over again. She had thought this woman had done her worst, that Mr. Thwaites had done his worst, that the climax of Mr.

Thwaites' death was the extra, gratuitous, and final climax, but instead of that, here it all was, back again.

If she hadn't meant it, why had she mentioned the fall at all? Anyone must have known that she was sorry for pushing the old man over just before his death, and only hell-inspired spite could have caused her to refer to it. What hell-inspired spite was it, that dwelt in this woman?

But worst of all, much worst of all—was there any dim conceivable truth or half-truth or quarter-truth in the allegation? Was it absolutely impossible for the fall to have been in some obscure way connected with or to have started the illness? What was peritonitis, anyway? Was she to be haunted by the fear, until her dying day, that she, in the one moment of real fury she had ever allowed herself in her life, had caused a death? That was what Vicki had put into her head—had meant to put into her head—and how was she ever going to get it out?

No, no! she must not give way. She must keep her promise to herself to keep calm. She was in a nervous state. It had all been too much for her recently. She was practically unhinged. She was letting the woman drive her mad. Apparently that was what the woman wanted to do, and she was getting away with it.

But how could you keep calm if you had murdered an old man? How could you ever be calm again for the rest of your life?

She found herself by the station. Always, on these black occasions and wanderings, she found herself making for the railway. Was this some subconscious impulse to get away from the town, to take a train anywhere, to return to London?

Where was she going now? Where was she going, in a general way? Now, surely, she could not spend more than one other night under that roof. But where did you go? Where did a murderess go and live, where did she spend her remaining days repenting her murder?

She must pull herself together. This was pure lunacy. Any sane person, knowing what was going on in her head and regarding her objectively, would see that she was out of her mind.

Well, if she was a lunatic, there was one lunatic thing she could do. She could do it now, if she had enough courage. She decided she had.

3

Just before his dinner that evening, Dr. Mackie, who lived in a pleasant Georgian house half-way up the hill the other side of Thames Lockdon bridge, was in his consulting-room and heard the bell ring.

The doctor—a thin, tall, spectacled man who looked like a schoolmaster, and behaved like an amiable one—was at the moment immersed in papers and figures in connection with his income tax. These were complex, and at the moment the doctor was a fatigued, harassed man. The sound of the bell, therefore, caused him apprehension.

Half a minute later his silly fat new maid, whom he now despaired of training, came into the room without knocking and said there was a lady to see him.

"Oh. Really?" he said, rising and speaking in a low voice. "Who is it, do you know?"

"No, I don't know," said his silly fat new maid.

"Well, will you go and ask who it is?"

"Yes, sir," she said, and went out.

The doctor realised that he was almost certainly for it, just before dinner, and he walked unhappily up and down the room. He heard some mumbling going on outside in the hall, and then his silly fat new maid returned.

"Please, sir," she said, "she says her name's Miss Roach."

She said this as though Miss Roach was only saying this, and didn't really bear that name. That was typical of her silliness. The name of Miss Roach conveyed nothing to the doctor, but he supposed he would have to see her.

"All right," he said. "Show her in, will you?"

A moment later Miss Roach came in, and he shook hands with her, and smiled, and said, "How do you do?"

He saw a slim woman, nearing or just past forty, with a nice face, and liquid brown, appealing eyes. Although greeting him pleasantly, she seemed to be ill at ease, and he wondered what on earth it was all about and how long it was going to take.

He put her in a chair, and then sat opposite her, and then put on that kindly but defensive look which doctors wear during this familiar consulting-room pause.

"Well—" he said. "Can I—er—?"

"I'm awfully sorry to have disturbed you like this," said Miss Roach. "It's very good of you to see me."

"Not at all," said the doctor. "Just tell me."

"I'm afraid you'll think it's rather silly," said Miss Roach. "But it's just something I'm very anxious to ask you, that's all."

The doctor now suspected that Miss Roach was afraid that she was going to have a baby, and gloomily foresaw a long interview.

"Not at all," he said. "Go ahead."

"Well—it's about Mr. Thwaites. You know—down in Church Street. I think you were called in to him."

"Yes. That's right," said the doctor, now mystified, but preferring Mr. Thwaites to babies.

"Well, I'm afraid you'll think it's awfully silly, but it's just something I want to know."

He wished she wouldn't go on about it being silly, but come out with it.

"Yes. Never mind," he said. "Go ahead."

"Well, it's just this. I just want to know if it could be at all possible—conceivably possible—if he had had a fall—and he *did* have a fall the night before he was taken ill—I can't go into the details, it's all really so silly—I live in the same house, you see. . . ."

"Did he have a bad fall?" asked the doctor, out of mere curiosity.

"Oh no. Nothing bad. In fact, he was walking about and perfectly normal after it. Well, the only point is—the only thing I want to ask you is—could it be in any way possible that his illness could be connected with it—could there be any possible connection between the two?"

The doctor looked at Miss Roach, thinking quickly. Thank God, he had a simple truthful answer and might get her out of the room in two minutes. But he just had to make sure that Miss Roach didn't *want* the fall to be connected with Mr. Thwaites' illness. No, surely such a thing would be ludicrous—out of the question. No psychological complication could bring about such a desire.

"Well," he said, having decided this, "I can give you a perfectly simple and straightforward answer."

"Yes?" said Miss Roach, her liquid, limpid eyes looking into his. "What?"

"Not the faintest connection," he said. "No connection of any sort."

And, seeing the look of exquisite relief which came into those liquid, limpid eyes, he knew he was on safe ground, and went ahead.

"Not the *remotest*, *faintest*," he said. "You can get *that* out of your mind."

"Oh, thank God," said Miss Roach. "That's all I wanted to know."

There was a moment in which the doctor thought that Miss Roach was going to cry.

"Yes," he said, "you can set your mind at rest about that. I'm afraid poor Mr. Thwaites had it coming to him, as they say."

"Oh, thank heavens," said Miss Roach.

"As a matter of fact," said the doctor, "I'd been attending him for indigestion, and there were all the symptoms there. It just happened suddenly like that, as you know it does."

"Oh, thank you," said Miss Roach. "Thank you very much."

"Not at all," said the doctor, putting forth a getting-up atmosphere. "Is there anything else you want to know?"

Miss Roach rose.

"No. Nothing else. I just had to ask you, that's all. I'm afraid you'll think me very silly."

"Well, that idea *is* silly!" admitted the doctor humorously, and rose also. "But I know what ideas people get about these things."

"Oh, thank you," said Miss Roach, going to the door. "I can't thank you enough."

He took her out into the hall to the front door, reflecting that actually he could hardly thank her enough for going so quickly and not being a nuisance.

"Will you let me have a bill, or will you tell me what I owe you, or what?" said Miss Roach.

"No. No bill," said the doctor. "I'm only too glad."

"Well, that's terribly kind of you," said Miss Roach, and "Not at all," said the doctor, and "Thank you *again*," said Miss Roach as they shook hands, and "It's pretty dark, I'm afraid," said the doctor, and "It's all right, I've got a torch. And thank you *so* much. Good night!" said Miss Roach, and she had gone.

Returning to his consulting-room, the doctor reflected for a few moments on the oddity of the interview which had just taken place. He was glad to have been able to tell the truth, and he was conscious of having done it tactfully and well.

It struck him that it was conceivably arguable by medical men that a fall might be put down as some sort of secondary cause, but it hadn't struck him at the time, and of course he would never have told the miserable woman that. He returned to his income-tax problems, and forgot about her permanently.

He did not know that the miserable woman was at that moment almost prancing down the hill in the blackness with divine, divine happiness in her heart—with that divine serenity of happiness which only relief, as opposed to mere joy or pleasure, can bring, and which exceeds any joy or pleasure known to human beings.

And the miserable woman had decided in her divine happiness to pack her clothes that night and go back to London tomorrow. She didn't know where she'd get in, but she'd get in somewhere —a police station or workhouse, if necessary.

CHAPTER TWENTY-SEVEN

I

ODDLY enough, that feeling of divine and serene happiness was, in a quiet and modified way, still with her next morning. Indeed it persisted, really, throughout the entire day.

She had told Mrs. Payne the night before of her intention of leaving, and now, this morning, she rose earlier than usual, and was down before breakfast in Mrs. Payne's room telephoning her employer, Mr. Lindsell, at his London flat. She was a little afraid of annoying him by phoning so early, but she knew that it was his habit to rise at seven.

He was surprised to hear her at this time of day, but cordial in his tone, and after an exchange of greetings, asked her facetiously what he could do for her.

"Well," she said, "there *is* something you can do, as a matter of fact, if you can manage it. I've got to leave this place down here suddenly, you see. In fact, I've got to clear out today."

"Oh yes?" said Mr. Lindsell. "Any trouble?"

She had told Mr. Lindsell, when she had seen him just before Christmas, that she was not too happy where she was, and she saw that he was now going to be pleasantly understanding, as he always was. He was a nice man.

"Yes," she said, glad of Mrs. Payne's absence from the room, and looking at the door to see that it was properly closed.

"Quite a lot. It's all very absurd, but I've really had a very bad time."

"Oh dear," said the nice Mr. Lindsell.

"Well, the point is," said Miss Roach, "that I've got to get in somewhere in London, and I'm wondering if you can help me."

"Oh dear," said Mr. Lindsell. "That's a bit difficult nowadays, isn't it?"

"Yes, I know, but I don't mind where I go. I mean I don't mind what it costs. Surely one can get in at a really expensive hotel, can't one? I mean a really expensive place."

"M'm. I see what you mean," said Mr. Lindsell. "M'm. . . . Now let me think. . . . You mean a *really* expensive place?"

"Yes. It doesn't matter if it costs the earth. I need only stay a night or two, and then I can find somewhere else."

"Yes. I see. Do you mean a sort of place like Claridge's? Because I've got some pull there, and I think I could get you in."

For a moment Miss Roach wavered. Claridge's! The resort of princes! But, because of her serene mood, she felt she could even cope with Claridge's.

"Yes," she said. "That'd do, excellently. Do you think you might manage it?"

"Well, I'll have a try," said Mr. Lindsell, and a few moments later, having said that he would ring her back when he had tried, he rang off.

Claridge's! From the Rosamund Tea Rooms to Claridge's! Miss Roach's soul smiled to itself.

2

Miss Roach's soul was still smiling to itself when she entered the dining-room for breakfast, and she was still filled with that curious residue of the divine happiness which had fallen upon her last night. It was because of this, and because of a remark made by Miss Steele, that she was able to revenge herself upon Vicki.

She went to her separate table, and was aware that Miss Steele was looking over at her more than she usually did. At last Miss Steele spoke.

"You're looking very pleased with yourself this morning," she said, smiling amiably.

"Yes," said Miss Roach. "I'm feeling in very good form."

"Is it true that you're a great heiress now?" said Miss Steele. "Is it true that you've come into an enormous sum of money?"

Mrs. Payne had evidently been gossiping, and this was the crucial moment. Normally Miss Roach would have told the truth—would not have equivocated in the smallest way. Normally she would have said that she had not as yet, strictly speaking, come into any money, and that five hundred pounds was not the enormous amount of money which Miss Steele's tone was suggesting she had come into. But today, because of that residue of serenity and happiness, she did otherwise. She condescended, even, to be mischievous. She glanced over at Vicki, who was silently putting food in her mouth.

"Yes," she said, "it's pretty good. It's quite enough for me, at any rate."

And the room was filled with a picture, not of five hundred, but of five thousand pounds.

"Well, I'm sure you deserve it," said Miss Steele, "if anybody ever did. And so you're leaving us today?"

"Yes. That's right. I'm going back to town."

"Where are you staying?" asked Miss Steele. "Have you got somewhere nice to go?"

Miss Roach again glanced over at the eating, silent Vicki, and again equivocated.

"Well, it's very hard to find anywhere," said Miss Roach, "so I'm staying at Claridge's just for the time being."

"Claridge's!" said Miss Steele. "I say! You really are an heiress, aren't you?"

Miss Roach got the impression that Miss Steele, instead of really speaking to her, was, like herself, really speaking to Vicki.

"Well, it's all extremely nice," she said.

"Extremely," said Miss Steele. "I said everything would come out in the Wash, didn't I?"

"Yes. You did. Indeed."

The heiress about to put up at Claridge's looked over at the silent German woman, and wondered whether she should punish her further. She decided that she was in the mood to do so, and that she would.

"But what's making me really cheerful," she said, "is that I saw the doctor last night—Mr. Thwaites' doctor . . ."

"Oh yes?"

"You know, I was afraid there might be some sort of connection between that push I gave him and his illness. But he told me there's absolutely no connection—no conceivable connection of any sort."

"Of course there wasn't," said Miss Steele, almost angrily, and now definitely glancing at Vicki. "It'd be absurd to think of such a thing. . . . But I'm glad the doctor told you."

And Miss Roach looked at Vicki as well.

And seeing her at that moment, glumly and silently eating (she had always been a filthy eater, by the way, but that had been a mere detail), and having nothing to say, and not being an heiress who was going to stay at Claridge's, but an alien under sentence of expulsion from the boarding-house in which she was now obviously disliked by all—seeing her thus, Miss Roach felt that she had somehow obtained her revenge at last.

Miss Roach, a modest woman, had modest notions of revenge. She was at that moment, and ever afterwards, completely satisfied.

CHAPTER TWENTY-EIGHT

I

SHE aimed to catch the eleven-twenty-five to London, and before this time she was twice called into Mrs. Payne's room to answer the telephone. The first call was from Mr.

Lindsell, who told her that he had managed to get her in at Claridge's, and the second was from the Lieutenant, who asked her to spend the evening with him. She explained that she would not be able to do this as she was going to London, and he said that this was a pity, as he was being moved away from Thames Lockdon in two days' time, more than a hundred and fifty miles away, and for good, and that it would have been nice if they could have met before he went. She agreed politely that it would have been nice, but did not see what could be done. He then said that he would have to come and see her when he had some leave in London, and that he would "write" to her.

As a final piece of perfect inconsequence he was ringing off without making any enquiry as to where he could write to her in London, and she pointed this out, telling him that she could always be got care of Reeves and Lindsell. She was entirely certain, however, that she would never get any letter from the Lieutenant, and that she would not ever see him again.

She permitted herself a little further malicious pleasure in the thought that Vicki as well as herself would not ever be seeing the Lieutenant again. Quite conceivably the Lieutenant had also suggested to Vicki that she should marry him: she would be the sort of person to take such a suggestion at its face value: and her not ever seeing him again would make her decidedly despondent. Somehow, everything seemed to be going against that woman now.

At ten past eleven, when she was already thinking about the arrival of the taxi to take her to the station, she was thrown into a sudden panic by finding, in her bag, two seats for a performance that very afternoon at the Theatre Royal, Wimbledon. In all the excitement of the last few days she had completely forgotten about Mr. Prest! She did some quick thinking, and then realised that it was all right, she could manage it. In fact, it would do her a lot of good to go to the theatre that afternoon: nothing could be nicer.

She said goodbye to Miss Steele, and to Mrs. Payne, and Mrs.

Barratt was looked for, but could not be found. Then she said goodbye to Sheila, and tipped her, and Sheila carried her suitcase for her into the taxi. She was only taking one suitcase with her: the rest of her things were going to be sent on.

It was only when she was sitting in the train, and the train had started, that it dawned upon her that there was not really any need for her to fly from the Rosamund Tea Rooms and return to London. Mr. Thwaites was dead, Vicki had been told to leave, and it would have been more than easy to endure the company of the sometimes somewhat foolish Miss Steele and the lethargic Mrs. Barratt. And yet here she was, and there was no going back now!

Such were the psychological accidents, errors, and complications which governed a person's movements and destiny.

2

On arrival at Paddington she put her suitcase into the cloakroom and then telephoned Mr. Lindsell again on a matter concerning a manuscript which she thought might be urgent, and which she had forgotten to mention over the telephone in the morning. The matter was not urgent, and Mr. Lindsell, in a cheerful mood, possibly induced by sherry, asked her how she was doing, and suggested that she should have a drink with him at Claridge's at six-thirty, as he was going to be about the Brook Street part of the world at that time. She accepted eagerly, and felt that this was heaven, to have someone, when she first arrived, who knew the ropes in the big, frightening hotel.

She had a help-yourself lunch at a crowded Lyons, and then made her way to Wimbledon partly by bus and partly by District Train.

Mr. Prest had told her to remember that it wasn't the Wimbledon Theatre, but the Theatre Royal, Wimbledon, and this she had to find.

She arrived a quarter of an hour before the curtain went up.

The medium-sized theatre was packed with people and excited children, and she took her seat, which was about nine rows back and on the side. In view of the crowded house she felt guilty because the seat at her side was being wasted, but there was nothing to be done about it.

Before the curtain went up, the children were going half mad, and appalling expectancy reigned when the house-lights at last went down.

Then, on a darkened stage with a front cloth, in an awful green light, an awful green monster appeared, with awful green sparkling eyelashes and long green sparkling finger-nails. And this character announced its intention to do every kind of damage in every possible way to everybody concerned. Then, in a dazzling silver light on the other side of the stage, a fairy appeared with a sparkling silver wand, and she declared, in tones at once defiant yet serene and confident, that none of this damage would be done. One would now have to see which was right. The children seemed rather bored with this, but Miss Roach was excited and interested.

Then the lights went up on a complete stage set, and there was a great deal of singing and gaiety, on the part of a lot of people, and then Mr. Prest appeared as a wicked but absurd uncle, quite absurdly and preposterously dressed in green.

Piercing yells of pleasure and screams of laughter greeted all that Mr. Prest said and did, and Miss Roach saw at once that he was going to be the hit of the show.

Mr. Prest! How could you believe that this was Mr. Prest? . . . And yet here he was! Here he was, painted, preposterously dressed! Here he was, with a whole house of children screaming at him, here he was answering them back, winking at them—dancing, singing, falling, getting into difficulties with his trousers, exultantly triumphing!

Somehow his triumph seemed to be Miss Roach's triumph as well, and her heart was lifted up with pleasure. She had never realised that children could make such a noise—she had, really, forgotten there were such things as children—and here was Mr. Prest of the Rosamund Tea Rooms, who had invited her to see the show, thus gloriously reminding her of what she should not have forgotten!

The "common" Mr. Prest. . . . Yes, indeed "common"—very much "commoner" here than at the Rosamund Tea Rooms—at moments vulgar perhaps—and yet, with these children, how very much the reverse of "common", how shining, transfigured, and ennobled!

Oh yes, Mr. Prest, sitting at that table alone, had turned out to be the dark horse, all right!

Looking at him, she had a strong desire to cry, and she roughly guessed what was actually the truth about this Archie Prest—guessed that the elderly comedian, owing to the war and the shortage of actors, had at last managed to get a job in this somewhat out-of-the-way theatre, and was pulling it off tremendously in spite of his age and long retirement, astonishing everyone, even himself.

After the interval there was no sign of any abatement in the excitement of the small mad people, the children, and towards the end a sort of frenzy and agony of laughter and hysterics came upon them.

In the short scene before the finale Mr. Prest, who had already made them sing (first of all in rivalry from all sides of the house, and then in stupendous unison), came forward and took them into his confidence.

He explained that he was going to play all manner of tricks upon the other comedian, and that he desired the children to maintain, when he appealed to them, that he had done none of these things.

The children assented to this quietly, it seemed almost reluctantly, and then Mr. Prest began. He came up behind the other comedian, and banged his hat down over his eyes. Then he came forward to the children and said:

"*I* didn't do it, children, did I?"

And then it was seen that the children were on the side of Mr. Prest.

"*NO!*" they cried.

Mr. Prest, pursuing this cruel conspiracy, now tripped the other comedian up.

"*I* didn't do it, children, did I?" asked Mr. Prest.

"*NO—O—O!*" was the answer, as if such a suggestion, concerning this second assault, was pure wickedness, whereas there might have been some doubt about the first one.

And thereafter it was "*I* didn't do it, children, did I?" "*NO—O—O!*", and "I didn't *do* it, children, did I?" "*NO—O—O!*"

And as Mr. Prest continued to seek and obtain repudiation of his guilt in a wild crescendo of yells, Miss Roach looked at the children—laughing, writhing, clapping, all at once standing up and looking at the stage with silent and ferocious intensity, all at once sitting down and appealing to their parents with their eyes to understand the superb piquancy of the situation, and rubbing their hands and bouncing about, and crying "*NO—O—O!*" . . . "*NO—O—O!*" . . . "*NO—O—O!*" . . .

In the middle of this a quiet, spectacled, stoutish man in a dark-blue suit came quietly up to her seat at the side and asked her if she was Miss Roach. She said yes, that was right, and then he explained that Mr. Prest had asked him to come round and ask her to go behind, and to escort her there. Would she like to go now, or did she want to wait till the end? Not knowing what she was wanted to say, she said she would go now, and the man made a sign to her to follow him.

He took her through the Exit curtains near the orchestra, and then up a few stairs and through a door marked Private, and then up some stone stairs, and through a huge door made of iron and on to the stage. She had never before been to the back of a theatre, and she was impressed by an enormous air of tension and quiet amidst noise.

"*NO—O—O!*" she heard the children crying, but it was

altogether a different sort of sound from here. And she heard great bumping sounds coming from the stage, and Mr. Prest's voice. And she stood in the dim light, peering, along with the man in the dark-blue suit, through a small space, at Mr. Prest, who was only visible when he came forward to the front of the stage. And she was aware of the near presence of painted and powdered chorus-girls waiting to go on for the finale—madly painted, they seemed from here, and exuding a sort of crude, oppressive glamour and vitality and fleshiness which added to the general mystery and novelty of the atmosphere. . . .

Then Mr. Prest for the last time asked, "I didn't do it, children—did I?" and the children yelled for the last time "*NO—O—O!*" and the next moment Mr. Prest was rushing off the stage, and, having seen her, coming up to her.

Mr. Prest was madly painted too; and sweat was pouring down all over his elderly, pugilistic face.

He was so excited that he did not so much as greet her properly.

"Aren't they *grand*?" he said, looking into her eyes and taking her by the arms. "Aren't they *lovely*? Isn't it grand to hear 'em? Aren't they lovely kids?"

And looking into Mr. Prest's excited eyes Miss Roach believed that she positively discerned tears of joy and triumph. It might, of course, have been the sweat which seemed momentarily to blind him—but she believed that it was otherwise. And, if these were indeed tears, she fancied that they arose from something else besides mere joy and triumph. There was an extraordinary look of purification about the man—a suggestion of reciprocal purification—as if he had just at that moment with his humour purified the excited children, and they, all as one, had purified him.

And, observing the purification of Mr. Prest, Miss Roach herself felt purified. She would have been surprised, a few months ago, if someone had told her that she was one day going to be purified by Mr. Prest—that that forlorn, silent man in the corner, that morose wearer of plus-fours, that slinker to his room, that stroller to the station, that idler and hanger-about in bars, had within him the love of small children and the gift of public purification!

3

"How are you, my dear?" said Mr. Prest, pulling himself together. "I've got to rush and change now. Charlie'll look after you, and then we'll have some tea." He fled.

She would have been surprised also to learn, a few months back, that Mr. Prest would one day be calling her "my dear". Charlie, apparently, was the quiet man in the dark-blue suit.

With Charlie, who talked to her, expatiating quietly on the remarkable success of her friend Mr. Prest in this pantomime, she had glimpses of the finale, and then was taken through another iron door and along passages to Mr. Prest's dressing-room.

Mr. Prest returning to this, she went outside while he changed, and then was called in, and watched him taking off his make-up with cream. This he did with tremendous between-the-matinée-and-evening-show haste and vigour, and talked to her the while.

"Well, how are you, darling?" he asked. "And how are all the folks down at home?"

("Darling"!)

"Oh," she said, "I've left there—I got fed up. I came up today."

"My God," said Mr. Prest. "So did I! And are you staying in London? Where are you staying?"

For some absurd reason she could not tell a man like Mr. Prest that she was staying at Claridge's—it would sound too silly!

"I'm not absolutely sure at the moment," she said. "But they're fixing it up for me. I'll know this evening." She changed the subject. "I thought you were absolutely wonderful this afternoon, Mr. Prest."

"Oh, I don't know..." said Mr. Prest, suddenly shy. "Those kids are wonderful. They just do it for you."

People kept on knocking at the door and coming in and going out, and Mr. Prest's dresser came and went busily.

After a while there entered a tall, middle-aged woman, in whom Miss Roach, on being introduced, recognised the glittering fairy who had defied the monster with such serenity and assurance. She evidently knew Mr. Prest well, and for a little while they talked about matters which Miss Roach did not understand.

"You were doing pretty well for yourself this afternoon, Archie," the middle-aged woman then said, "if I may say so."

"Yes," said Mr. Prest. "It was going over big, wasn't it? Those kids are grand. They've never been better."

"Yes, he was wonderful, wasn't he?" said Miss Roach, and the middle-aged woman, while assenting to this view, looked with sardonic affection at Mr. Prest.

Then Mr. Prest and the middle-aged woman became in their talk a little more vulgar than Miss Roach was used too, and then, when Mr. Prest was dressed, they were joined by a plump, pretty chorus-girl in plain clothes, and all of them went out to the stage door and into the blackness of the world at war.

Mr. Prest took Miss Roach's arm, the two women went ahead, and a minute later all had arrived safely at a crowded tea-and-coffee bar in which there were marble-topped tables all along the wall. In spite of the crowd there was a table kept in the corner for Mr. Prest, who was evidently, for the time being, a public character in this part of the world.

They were given tea, and horrible sausages on nice chips, and slices of bread and margarine. Mr. Prest talked mostly to the proprietor, and other acquaintances who accosted him, and Miss Roach talked cordially about coupons, and points, and rationing with the middle-aged fairy and the plump, pretty chorus-girl.

If they could only see me at the Rosamund Tea Rooms now, thought Miss Roach, if they could only see me!

Soon enough they had to race back to the theatre for the

evening show, and they raced Miss Roach back with them. Just inside the stage door the two women said goodbye to her and flew away, and Mr. Prest asked if she could find her way all right in the dark. She said that she could do this easily, and thanked him eagerly for the afternoon.

"Not a bit of it, darling," said Mr. Prest. "And look us up some time. Let's know where you are."

"Oh yes, I will," said Miss Roach, with the same eagerness, but with a feeling that it was not likely that she would ever see Mr. Prest again. "And thank you *so* much. Goodbye!"

"Goodbye, dear," said Mr. Prest, and, as he shook her hand, she had a final look at the coarse, battered, pugilistic face of the low comedian—the purifying and purified being—and went in to the darkness again, astonished and haunted by the mystery of all things under the sun—or rather under the black-out.

CHAPTER TWENTY-NINE

I

HAVING to collect her suitcase at Paddington, she was only just able to reach Claridge's by six-thirty, and this only because she had managed to get a taxi at the station.

On her arrival at the famous hotel a porter with a torch opened the door of the taxi, and her luggage was somewhat alarmingly snatched away from her in the darkness. As she was fumbling in her bag to pay the fare she heard, with relief, Mr. Lindsell's voice at her side.

"I thought it was you," he said.

Having Mr. Lindsell with her, the business of entering Claridge's, so far from being the ordeal which she had been dreading during the last half-hour, was an adventure and delight.

She was taken to a bright reception room where she was registered under the polite surveillance of a young man in a frock-coat who knew Mr. Lindsell, and the whole atmosphere and suggestion was that there was nothing fantastic or absurd about Miss Roach staying at Claridge's at all.

Then Mr. Lindsell said that she was to have a drink before she did anything else, and she was taken into the big bright main lounge.

They found a table in a corner, and Mr. Lindsell, persuading her to take whisky, ordered two large ones. Before long she was talking volubly with Mr. Lindsell and looking around her with a feeling of having already settled down.

She did not recognise anyone approximating to her notion of princes. Instead she saw one or two old ladies very much of the type of Miss Steele or Mrs. Barratt (only with an air of being bored to distraction in much greater luxury, space, and comfort), and there were many men in uniforms, English and American.

These uniforms reminded her that she was back in the centre of things, the world and the war. She was glad to be back, in spite of the danger of bombs. You had to square up to the war. The horror and despondence of the Rosamund Tea Rooms resided in just the fact that it was not squaring up to it. The Rosamund Tea Rooms was hidden away in the country, dodging the war, in its petty boarding-house lassitude almost insensible of it, more absorbed in the local library. And this was not a war to be taken in a local-library way.

2

Mr. Lindsell persuaded her to have two large whiskies, and took three himself. Then, getting excited by a discussion with her in regard to technical publishing matters, he decided to have dinner with her, and took her into the restaurant. Here they had wine.

That was a happy, excited meal she had with her scanty-haired, harassed-looking, hard-working, nice employer. Afterwards he insisted upon having a final brandy in the lounge (where she herself took coffee), and then he saw that it was nearly nine, and said that he had to fly away.

He did not say where he had to fly away to, and she was pretty certain that it was a woman—that our dear old friend "love" was at the back of it. "Love", like drink, under the influence of the war, was exerting a new sort of pressure everywhere, affecting people it would not have affected before, and in an entirely fresh way.

She escorted him into the black-out, where a horrible war-argument and panic was going on about taxis, and Mr. Lindsell, after having repeatedly and in a panic admonished her to go in and not bother, at last got a place in a taxi with five other people.

"Goodbye!" he yelled. "See you tomorrow. Goodbye!" And she yelled back "Goodbye!" and went in.

3

And, in spite of the taxi-panic, still that feeling of happiness, and of serenity, and of purification, persisted in her soul. Because of this feeling she decided that before going to bed she would go by herself into the lounge and have a final drink. She was too happy and serene to mind the people, or to bother about being alone in it.

She decided to have a whisky, and here, needless to say, the war got in a little good-night crack at her—the whisky was Off. This did not disturb her, and she ordered a large pink gin instead.

An orchestra was now playing in the lounge, and, sitting having that last drink, almost heedless of what was going on around her, something else was added to Miss Roach's frame of mind. In addition to her sense of serenity and purification there came a sort of clarification of mind, in which she could see in their correct proportions all the things which had occurred to her in the last few months.

She saw Mr. Thwaites in his right proportions. Why had she ever let him anger and torment her? The trouble with that man was that he had never stepped beyond the mental age of eleven or twelve, nature having arrested him, and preserved him, at a certain ugly phase—the phase of the loquacious little braggart at school so often met with at that age. If he had grown up, he would have grown out of it.

She saw the Lieutenant in his right proportions. Not strong of mind, easily affected by drink, in a foreign land, agitated by a mood of sexual excitation, in fear of the future and over-anxious to live to the full while he could, the poor man had gone about in drink making love to the girls and asking them to marry him. He had probably blindly imitated all that marriage-offering business from some soldier friend: he was, really, too good-natured and scrupulous, too lacking in initiative, to have thought of it himself. Oddly enough, she believed that the Lieutenant probably liked her better than all the others, and she could probably have had the Laundry if she had really tried. Anyway, if he was not killed, he would almost certainly one day settle down with a wife and his Laundry and be sensible again.

She saw Vicki in her right proportions. A wretched woman that—more wretched than evil. Sex-obsessed, of course (but weren't we all?), and savagely egoistic. And, in her sex-obsession, vain. And, in her vanity, cruel. And, with that dreadful maladroitness of manner, speech, and soul, a fiend from hell to live with, if you had incurred her dislike. No—on second thoughts Vicki was possibly as evil as she was wretched. It was hard to say.

She probably wasn't really the concentration-camp, stadium-yelling, rich, fruity, German Nazi which Miss Roach had at times thought her (and yet she also very possibly was!), and Miss Roach now found it easy to forgive her.

But how she (Miss Roach) had gone on about it all, and how fearfully she had suffered! Those nights at Thames Lockdon, arriving in the blackness. . . . Those dinners, in the pin-dropping silences around Mr. Thwaites. . . . The rumbling of the lift behind the screen. . . . The bedroom with the red chequered curtains and the counterpane which slithered off. . . . Coffee in the Lounge. . . . The arrival of the German, the comb in the bedroom, the patience-playing with Mr. Thwaites. . . . The English Miss, Miss Prim, Miss Prude. . . . "Really, you are rather A dear." . . . The walk against the wind in the sunset, the walks in the dark! . . . The breakfasts, lunches, teas, dinners. . . . The Push! . . . The weird interview with the doctor. . . .

Well, well, she supposed that was all part of boarding-house life, that something of the same sort was going on in places of that sort all over the country—all over the world. It was just that she was not cut out for boarding-house life.

And here she was at Claridge's—from the Rosamund Tea Rooms to Claridge's—and now she must go to bed.

4

Leaving the crowd, and exchanging the cheerful sound of the orchestra for the sudden seriousness and silence of the luxuriously mirrored lift with its blue-uniformed attendant, Miss Roach felt her mood of exhilaration and clarification slipping away from her, and she realised that she was very tired.

She had not seen her room, into which Mr. Lindsell had arranged to have her bag sent up, and, in spite of the instructions of the lift-man, for a long while she could not find it, wandering about dimly lit, hushed, and thickly carpeted corridors for three or four minutes.

She was somewhat dismayed, on entering, to observe that it was a double room, but there was her suitcase (looking very forlorn, on a sort of trestle), and so there was no mistake, and there was nothing to be done about it.

Presumably a double room was all they had, but what was going to happen if her aunt didn't die and she didn't get that five hundred pounds she didn't know, for although she had four ice.

Fri, May 1, 2020
Standard
Jim
oldie_stuff

s Classics) [Paperback] [2007] Hamilton, Patrick; Lodge,

then click the "seller profile" link for this order to get

ping label. Please have your order ID ready.

back for the seller please visit www.amazon.com/feedback. To
seller's name under the appropriate product. Then, in the

Order ID: 113-2446165-8347452

Thank you for buying from oldie_stuff on Amazon Marketpla

Shipping Address:	Order Date:
Jim Stewart	Shipping Service:
11 GARDEN ST	Buyer Name:
CAMBRIDGE, MA 02138-3605	Seller Name:

Quantity	Product Details
1	**The Slaves of Solitude (New York Review Boo** **David** **SKU:** 7372 **ASIN:** 1590172205 **Condition:** New **Listing ID:** 0829U9I253M **Order Item ID:** 08316380647106

Returning your item:
Go to "Your Account" on Amazon.com, click "Your Orders" a
information about the return and refund policies that appl
Visit https://www.amazon.com/returns to print a return sh

Thanks for buying on Amazon Marketplace. To provide fe
contact the seller, go to Your Orders in Your Account. Click
"Further Information" section, click "Contact the Seller."

----

hundred odd pounds of her own saved in the bank, that was for old age and illness, and she was not the sort of person to go in for double rooms at places like Claridge's.

The luxury of the room itself also dismayed her for the same reason, and when she found that a door led off to a private bathroom only one half of her was delighted while the other half was intimidated.

She found the room too hot, and turned off the heat, and opened the windows as well as she could without causing offence to the black-out authorities, and began to unpack.

Well, this was something better than her bedroom at Mrs. Payne's! Or was it? Was she really able to adjust herself to such a change in a single night? Wouldn't she, for a bedroom simply as a bedroom, rather have Mrs. Payne's? Was this really her line of country?

Why was she always complaining about everything she got?

"*Waiter. Chambermaid. Valet*" she saw printed under some buttons to press by the side of her bed. She was horrified by the idea of ringing any of them, and hoped that she might spend the night, and escape from this hotel next morning, unmolested by waiter, chambermaid, or valet. . . .

She must have a Private bath. She must have one tonight, and another tomorrow morning, and linger in both of them. She must privately bathe some of the money back.

As she went into the bathroom, and tried to find out how to work all its wonderful gadgets (which she was not clever enough to do readily), it struck her that it would be funny if the sirens suddenly went and the blitz came back to London the night she returned to it. That would be just her luck, and no doubt it had to come back some time. Or was she getting morbid again?

Then Miss Roach, knowing nothing of the future, knowing nothing of the February blitz shortly to descend on London, knowing nothing of flying bombs, knowing nothing of rockets, of Normandy, of Arnhem, of the Ardennes bulge, of Berlin, of the Atom Bomb, knowing nothing and caring very little, got into her bath and lingered in it a long while.

Then she got out and dried herself, and then put on her nightgown, and cleaned her teeth last thing, and then went back into the double room, in which the presence of the other bed made her feel that she was sleeping with the unhappy ghost of herself.

Then Miss Roach—this slave of her task-master, solitude—had to choose which bed she was going to sleep in, and chose the one nearest the window, and then got into bed and stared at the ceiling, and then decided that they were heavenlily comfortable beds anyway and that was all that mattered, and it was lovely and quiet and that was all that mattered, too. And then she decided that she felt like sleeping, and would probably have a good night and so everything was all right, in fact very nice. And then she realised that it would be a bad thing if she didn't have a good night as she had to be up early in the morning looking for somewhere to live, and then, of course, she had to go to the office, because Mr. Lindsell had said "See you tomorrow" when he had left her, not realising that she had to look for somewhere to live. And then she thought she might phone Mr. Lindsell, and ask if she need not go, and then she thought that this might offend him after all his kindness, and then she was sure it wouldn't because he was a nice man, and then this thing, and then that matter, and then this thing again, until at last she put out the light, and turned over, and adjusted the pillow, and hopefully composed her mind for sleep—God help us, God help all of us, every one, all of us.

THE END

Dec 10 2007

TITLES IN SERIES

J.R. ACKERLEY Hindoo Holiday
J.R. ACKERLEY My Dog Tulip
J.R. ACKERLEY My Father and Myself
HENRY ADAMS The Jeffersonian Transformation
CÉLESTE ALBARET Monsieur Proust
DANTE ALIGHIERI The Inferno
DANTE ALIGHIERI The New Life
WILLIAM ATTAWAY Blood on the Forge
ERICH AUERBACH Dante: Poet of the Secular World
W.H. AUDEN (EDITOR) The Living Thoughts of Kierkegaard
W.H. AUDEN W. H. Auden's Book of Light Verse
DOROTHY BAKER Cassandra at the Wedding
J.A. BAKER The Peregrine
HONORÉ DE BALZAC The Unknown Masterpiece *and* Gambara
MAX BEERBOHM Seven Men
ALEXANDER BERKMAN Prison Memoirs of an Anarchist
GEORGES BERNANOS Mouchette
ADOLFO BIOY CASARES Asleep in the Sun
ADOLFO BIOY CASARES The Invention of Morel
CAROLINE BLACKWOOD Corrigan
CAROLINE BLACKWOOD Great Granny Webster
MALCOLM BRALY On the Yard
JOHN HORNE BURNS The Gallery
ROBERT BURTON The Anatomy of Melancholy
CAMARA LAYE The Radiance of the King
GIROLAMO CARDANO The Book of My Life
J.L. CARR A Month in the Country
ANNE CARSON Grief Lessons: Four Plays by Euripides
JOYCE CARY Herself Surprised (First Trilogy, Vol. 1)
JOYCE CARY To Be a Pilgrim (First Trilogy, Vol. 2)
JOYCE CARY The Horse's Mouth (First Trilogy, Vol. 3)
BLAISE CENDRARS Moravagine
EILEEN CHANG Love in a Fallen City
UPAMANYU CHATTERJEE English, August: An Indian Story
NIRAD C. CHAUDHURI The Autobiography of an Unknown Indian
ANTON CHEKHOV Peasants and Other Stories
RICHARD COBB Paris and Elsewhere
COLETTE The Pure and the Impure
JOHN COLLIER Fancies and Goodnights
IVY COMPTON-BURNETT A House and Its Head
IVY COMPTON-BURNETT Manservant and Maidservant
BARBARA COMYNS The Vet's Daughter
EVAN S. CONNELL The Diary of a Rapist
JULIO CORTÁZAR The Winners
HAROLD CRUSE The Crisis of the Negro Intellectual
ASTOLPHE DE CUSTINE Letters from Russia
LORENZO DA PONTE Memoirs

ELIZABETH DAVID A Book of Mediterranean Food
ELIZABETH DAVID Summer Cooking
MARIA DERMOÛT The Ten Thousand Things
ARTHUR CONAN DOYLE Exploits and Adventures of Brigadier Gerard
CHARLES DUFF A Handbook on Hanging
J.G. FARRELL Troubles
J.G. FARRELL The Siege of Krishnapur
J.G. FARRELL The Singapore Grip
KENNETH FEARING The Big Clock
KENNETH FEARING Clark Gifford's Body
M.I. FINLEY The World of Odysseus
EDWIN FRANK (EDITOR) Unknown Masterpieces
MAVIS GALLANT Paris Stories
MAVIS GALLANT Varieties of Exile
JEAN GENET Prisoner of Love
P. V. GLOB The Bog People: Iron-Age Man Preserved
EDMOND AND JULES DE GONCOURT Pages from the Goncourt Journals
EDWARD GOREY (EDITOR) The Haunted Looking Glass
VASILY GROSSMAN Life and Fate
OAKLEY HALL Warlock
PATRICK HAMILTON The Slaves of Solitude
PETER HANDKE A Sorrow Beyond Dreams
ELIZABETH HARDWICK Seduction and Betrayal
ELIZABETH HARDWICK Sleepless Nights
L.P. HARTLEY Eustace and Hilda: A Trilogy
L.P. HARTLEY The Go-Between
NATHANIEL HAWTHORNE Twenty Days with Julian & Little Bunny by Papa
JANET HOBHOUSE The Furies
HUGO VON HOFMANNSTHAL The Lord Chandos Letter
JAMES HOGG The Private Memoirs and Confessions of a Justified Sinner
RICHARD HOLMES Shelley: The Pursuit
ALISTAIR HORNE A Savage War of Peace: Algeria 1954–1962
WILLIAM DEAN HOWELLS Indian Summer
RICHARD HUGHES A High Wind in Jamaica
RICHARD HUGHES The Fox in the Attic (The Human Predicament, Vol. 1)
RICHARD HUGHES The Wooden Shepherdess (The Human Predicament, Vol. 2)
HENRY JAMES The Ivory Tower
HENRY JAMES The New York Stories of Henry James
HENRY JAMES The Other House
HENRY JAMES The Outcry
RANDALL JARRELL (EDITOR) Randall Jarrell's Book of Stories
DAVID JONES In Parenthesis
ERNST JÜNGER The Glass Bees
HELEN KELLER The World I Live In
YASHAR KEMAL Memed, My Hawk
YASHAR KEMAL They Burn the Thistles
MURRAY KEMPTON Part of Our Time: Some Ruins and Monuments of the Thirties
DAVID KIDD Peking Story

ROBERT KIRK The Secret Commonwealth of Elves, Fauns, and Fairies
ARUN KOLATKAR Jejuri
TÉTÉ-MICHEL KPOMASSIE An African in Greenland
PATRICK LEIGH FERMOR Between the Woods and the Water
PATRICK LEIGH FERMOR Mani: Travels in the Southern Peloponnese
PATRICK LEIGH FERMOR Roumeli: Travels in Northern Greece
PATRICK LEIGH FERMOR A Time of Gifts
D.B. WYNDHAM LEWIS AND CHARLES LEE (EDITORS) The Stuffed Owl: An Anthology of Bad Verse
GEORG CHRISTOPH LICHTENBERG The Waste Books
H.P. LOVECRAFT AND OTHERS The Colour Out of Space
ROSE MACAULAY The Towers of Trebizond
JANET MALCOLM In the Freud Archives
OSIP MANDELSTAM The Selected Poems of Osip Mandelstam
JAMES McCOURT Mawrdew Czgowchwz
HENRI MICHAUX Miserable Miracle
JESSICA MITFORD Hons and Rebels
NANCY MITFORD Madame de Pompadour
ALBERTO MORAVIA Boredom
ALBERTO MORAVIA Contempt
JAN MORRIS Conundrum
ÁLVARO MUTIS The Adventures and Misadventures of Maqroll
L.H. MYERS The Root and the Flower
DARCY O'BRIEN A Way of Life, Like Any Other
YURI OLESHA Envy
IONA AND PETER OPIE The Lore and Language of Schoolchildren
BORIS PASTERNAK, MARINA TSVETAYEVA, AND RAINER MARIA RILKE Letters: Summer 1926
CESARE PAVESE The Moon and the Bonfires
CESARE PAVESE The Selected Works of Cesare Pavese
LUIGI PIRANDELLO The Late Mattia Pascal
ANDREI PLATONOV The Fierce and Beautiful World
J.F. POWERS Morte d'Urban
J.F. POWERS The Stories of J. F. Powers
J.F. POWERS Wheat That Springeth Green
RAYMOND QUENEAU We Always Treat Women Too Well
RAYMOND QUENEAU Witch Grass
RAYMOND RADIGUET Count d'Orgel's Ball
JEAN RENOIR Renoir, My Father
FR. ROLFE Hadrian the Seventh
WILLIAM ROUGHEAD Classic Crimes
CONSTANCE ROURKE American Humor: A Study of the National Character
GERSHOM SCHOLEM Walter Benjamin: The Story of a Friendship
DANIEL PAUL SCHREBER Memoirs of My Nervous Illness
JAMES SCHUYLER Alfred and Guinevere
JAMES SCHUYLER What's for Dinner?
LEONARDO SCIASCIA The Day of the Owl
LEONARDO SCIASCIA Equal Danger

LEONARDO SCIASCIA The Moro Affair
LEONARDO SCIASCIA To Each His Own
LEONARDO SCIASCIA The Wine-Dark Sea
VICTOR SEGALEN René Leys
VICTOR SERGE The Case of Comrade Tulayev
SHCHEDRIN The Golovlyov Family
GEORGES SIMENON Dirty Snow
GEORGES SIMENON The Man Who Watched Trains Go By
GEORGES SIMENON Monsieur Monde Vanishes
GEORGES SIMENON Red Lights
GEORGES SIMENON The Strangers in the House
GEORGES SIMENON Three Bedrooms in Manhattan
GEORGES SIMENON Tropic Moon
CHARLES SIMIC Dime-Store Alchemy: The Art of Joseph Cornell
MAY SINCLAIR Mary Olivier: A Life
TESS SLESINGER The Unpossessed: A Novel of the Thirties
CHRISTINA STEAD Letty Fox: Her Luck
STENDHAL The Life of Henry Brulard
ITALO SVEVO As a Man Grows Older
HARVEY SWADOS Nights in the Gardens of Brooklyn
A.J.A. SYMONS The Quest for Corvo
EDWARD JOHN TRELAWNY Records of Shelley, Byron, and the Author
LIONEL TRILLING The Middle of the Journey
IVAN TURGENEV Virgin Soil
JULES VALLÈS The Child
MARK VAN DOREN Shakespeare
EDWARD LEWIS WALLANT The Tenants of Moonbloom
ROBERT WALSER Jakob von Gunten
ROBERT WALSER Selected Stories
SYLVIA TOWNSEND WARNER Lolly Willowes
SYLVIA TOWNSEND WARNER Mr. Fortune's Maggot *and* The Salutation
ALEKSANDER WAT My Century
C.V. WEDGWOOD The Thirty Years War
SIMONE WEIL AND RACHEL BESPALOFF War and the Iliad
GLENWAY WESCOTT Apartment in Athens
GLENWAY WESCOTT The Pilgrim Hawk
REBECCA WEST The Fountain Overflows
PATRICK WHITE Riders in the Chariot
JOHN WILLIAMS Butcher's Crossing
JOHN WILLIAMS Stoner
ANGUS WILSON Anglo-Saxon Attitudes
EDMUND WILSON Memoirs of Hecate County
EDMUND WILSON To the Finland Station
RUDOLF AND MARGARET WITKOWER Born Under Saturn
GEOFFREY WOLFF Black Sun
STEFAN ZWEIG Beware of Pity
STEFAN ZWEIG Chess Story